Levels of Truth

Levels of Truth

Reece Brett

Black Lyon Publishing, LLC

LEVELS OF TRUTH
Copyright © 2017 by REECE BRETT

Our books may be ordered through your local bookstore or by
visiting the publisher:

www.BlackLyonPublishing.com

Black Lyon Publishing, LLC
PO Box 567
Baker City, OR 97814

This is a work of fiction. All of the characters, names, events,
organizations and conversations in this novel are either the products
of the author's vivid imagination or are used in a fictitious way for the
purposes of this story.

ISBN-10:   1-934912-82-4
ISBN-13:   978-1-934912-82-9
Library of Congress Control Number: 2017914791

Published and printed in the United States of America.

Black Lyon Contemporary Romance

To my husband and lover: The touch of your hands, the passion of your kiss and the feel of your arms around me are my inspiration and delight.

To our children who support me from afar.

To Kerry McQuisten and Black Lyon Publishing for their encouragement, guidance and their dedication to their writers.

To my Beta readers, Carol, Karin and Rochelle, who add strength to my characters and a more colorful world for my readers.

To Barb, for your insight.

To Susan P for sharing a "pink granite" inspirational point.

To Dr. B and staff for "time to work."

To my friends in NJRW and Writing Community at Bogart's who are encouraging, wise and fun!

CHAPTER ONE

"Home."

Caroline turned off the ignition and studied the house from the safety of her car. Until her mother's attorney handed her the photos, she hadn't even known this place in New Jersey existed. The structure appeared older than the photographs now scattered across the passenger seat.

The rental car door squeaked as she exited. She wrapped her arms around the fence post. Home, the place she was born. No emotional tug or a remote connection to the place. Nothing.

What did she expect? Bells and whistles? The nagging burn in her stomach returned. It had never mattered she was adopted. To her, Grant and Annabelle were her parents. When Grant died, her relationship with Annabelle melded into a close bond. But if they had been that close, why had Annabelle lied about coming here?

She was born here, but what was Annabelle's connection? She pushed in the center of her abdomen. The burn intensified. What else about her mother's past had she missed? Until she inherited this house, none of these questions mattered. She kicked the gate and returned to the car.

After unpacking at the B&B, she'd call the realtor handling the place. She'd see the inside, put it up for sale and go home to Seattle. End of story.

She tapped her nails along the railing. She couldn't check in for another two hours. Her index finger clicked on the metal. How long had it been since she had endless time with on deadlines, no to-do lists and no demanding surgeons needing materials right now? A stack of to-be-read books still awaited her at home. She should have brought a few with her.

She locked her car and headed downtown. Her assistant, who booked her reservations, had shown her a map and babbled about an arts district and quaint shops. Maybe she could learn to like that.

The Readers' Haven Book Shoppe sign stated, "Open at 10," but the door was ajar. Hearing a low groan from inside, Caroline pushed open the door. A noticeably pregnant woman sprawled on the floor beside a bookshelf.

"Are you okay? Did you fall?" Caroline knelt beside her.

"Just awkward," a soft voice answered. "I'm glad the agency was able to reach you, Gloria." She stacked the books rapidly as she chattered. "I won't be able to give you the week's orientation." She attempted to stand. Caroline wrapped her arm around her and helped her rise. "I'm starting labor early."

"Did you call 911? Can I get you anyone?"

The woman nodded. "My husband is on the way. I contacted the doctor. The baby is due in three weeks. I thought I would have two weeks for orientation, but the baby is on its way. Gloria ... I ..." She paused mid-sentence. The woman's hand rested on Caroline's arm. She tilted her head. "You're not Gloria."

"I'm Caroline. I don't know what you are talking about. How can I find this Gloria?"

The woman squeezed Caroline's arm and a Cheshire cat-like smile emerged. "You aren't Gloria, but you'll help and I need you." Again, the woman pushed her hand on her extended belly and sucked in her breath. She inhaled deeply, then she added, "But you are the help I really need."

"Excuse me?" She knew women in labor often acted strangely, but this woman's ranting was bizarre.

"Ryan will be here soon. I quite obviously need to go the hospital as soon as possible. I can't just leave. Gloria was temporary help, but you'll be just great." She patted the top of Caroline's arm. "I need you to take over. Ryan will contact you tonight or tomorrow morning."

"You want me to take over? A bookstore?"

"Do you read? Work with books?"

"I'm senior medical researcher for hospitals in Seattle."

A knowing smile and a smug nod came first, then she said, "That's it. I knew you were the right one."

A young man with long brown curls held firm with a rubber band rushed through the door, talking as he did. "The car is ready I have your bag, all the phone numbers. Just talked with the doctor. If your water broke and the contractions are regular, we need to meet him at the hospital." He nodded at Caroline. "Good thing the agency reached Gloria."

"Not Gloria," Caroline and the woman stated simultaneously.

He blinked, looked from one woman to the other. "But you'll stay. I'll call later. I'll help any way I can from the phone and will stop after the baby i-s born."

"I just walked in off the street. I heard your wife's groans and came in."

The woman held her belly and her lips became a thin line.

"She needs to leave. You can't have a perfect stranger take over your shop."

The man took his wife's hand. "I've learned never to doubt my wife's wisdom of others. Her touch is remarkable. If she thinks it's okay, it is."

In between deep breaths, the woman added, "I can trust you. Will you stay?"

Caroline nodded. "You need to get to a hospital. I'll stay until you find Gloria or someone to take over."

"There are written notes next to the cash register." She paused at the door. "By the way, I'm Larkin Henderson. Serendipitous of you to stop today, Caroline. You'll do fine."

A car door slammed. The car sped away. Caroline leaned against the marble counter. What had she gotten herself into? In forty-eight hours, she took three days off work, flew across the country, settled in a town where she knew no one to chase a ghost of her past. Now she agreed to run a store for two people she met minutes before. Had she dropped through some rabbit hole and ended up in a make believe land?

Clusters of chairs invited one to sit and browse. Nice layout. A coffee bar with cups, several selections also were inviting. Coffee. Good idea. She fingered the spines of familiar titles: *Beekeeper's Ball, Four Friends, One Man's Music* on the shelves.

Behind the counter as Larkin promised were several detailed sheets were stapled next to an antique cash register. No computer was hidden behind the shelf. She'd been seventeen the last time she'd used a cash register.

The instructions were broken down in categories and covered any emergency. What kind of person did temps send these days? She unearthed minute facts, details and statistics for world-renowned surgeons who saved people's lives with that information. *I can do this, for God's sake.*

She poured a mug of coffee, added her half and half and sat in the big cushioned wicker chair near the window. Although the shop was on a side street, the front bay window offered a good view of the main street of the town. Good location. She could observe many from town and maybe meet many if they were readers, but would any of them be relatives? Would she learn any answers while here? More pressing problems now. She scanned the directions.

A bell announced her first customer. A light-haired male with a well-trimmed beard entered talking, "Larkin, I came to pick up the book, Meg ..." Seeing Caroline instead, he smiled, which added warmth to the room. His green eyes lit up with that smile and reminded Caroline of an Irish Spring soap commercial.

"You must be Gloria. I just stopped to pick up a book."

"I'm not Gloria." *This could be a long day.*

That stopped him midway to the marble counter. He turned and plopped down in a wicker chair across from her. "Then, who are you?"

"Caroline from Seattle."

"Long way from home. What brings you to South Jersey?"

"Business transaction I must take care of," she said. "A little rest and relaxation."

"And you took on Readers' Haven Book Shoppe as rest and relaxation?" He rested his ankle on his right knee. "And she touched your hand and wanted you here."

Caroline shook her head. This was a strange place. "Does she do that often? And do people accept her instant character judgment?"

His smile appeared again and Caroline decided she could

stay here all day watching it.

"We've learned to listen—she's never wrong. I'm David Montgomery." He stretched out his hand. The warmth evident in his eyes extended to the clasp of his hands. "Welcome to Lakeside."

He leaned back in the chair. Sleeves of his steel blue shirt rolled up revealed muscular tanned arms, which one might assume belonged to a construction worker. But that image didn't go with the pressed khakis and shiny shoes. His green eyes flickered over her reading more than she was comfortable revealing.

"You said something about a book." She rose and moved to the safety of the counter and away from the warmth and intensity of the man.

"A book order." He followed her. He perched on a counter stool and studied the line of books on the shelf behind her. "There." He reached for the book as she did, their hands touched. His body was inches from her and a heat enveloped her body. She backed closer to the register. A flush still burned her cheeks. Too early for hot flashes but the climate in the bookstore turned up a notch.

He studied the label on the book's spine and avoided her gaze. "You shouldn't have too much trouble taking care of the store. People come in, some for books, but just as many for coffee and to talk." He tapped the top of the counter. "Everyone will help you." At the door, he paused again. "Especially if they know you were chosen by Larkin's touch."

Caroline felt the coldness of his leaving. His warmth, his smile with devilish green eyes had filled the room. He could make it worth looking for books every day. *Careful, woman. No time for an enticing male.* The mission was to learn about that house.

She heard the group of women before they arrived. She refilled the water and the coffee pot was filling as they walked in the door.

"Is Larkin in the hospital? Are you the temp?" asked the lead woman. Others came in and sat in the chairs around the coffeepot. One pushed a woman in a wheelchair. Others maneuvered chairs to create a circle.

"I agreed to help today."

"We're the Readers' Haven Book Group. Who are you? Did Larkin have her baby yet?"

Before Caroline could answer, a gum-chomping teen arrived, opened a box of cinnamon buns, took out a plate beneath the coffee serving area, arranged the buns, and walked to the door. She acknowledged Caroline's existence with a nod. No one in the woman's group noted anything peculiar, but dropped money in a waiting mug, and helped themselves to coffee and cinnamon buns.

This certainly isn't Seattle and not a Starbucks. No one asked prices, nor pulled out debit cards. She'd have to see what Larkin had written about this.

"Come," said the lead woman. "Pull up a chair. We're regulars here and friendly, curious and we don't bite." Most of the women nodded and smiled. The circle moved back a little to fit in another chair.

Caroline perched on a stool on the outside of the group. "May I get you anything?"

That produced a laugh. "We're here so often we know where everything is and help ourselves."

"We are also helpful to you if you need us." The white-haired woman confined in the wheelchair spoke up. "I'm Meg Ottinger. The gabby, curious one." Meg rolled her eyes. "That's Irene. She's a true spokesperson—but she speaks at length. The cinnamon buns are good to start your day. May I get you one?"

"No, I can ..." Before she could arise, Meg wheeled to the coffee bar, placed a bun on a plate. "Butter?" After Caroline's nod, she placed two pats of butter and a plastic knife. When she handed Caroline her breakfast, their eyes and their hands met. Caroline felt an instant connection to this woman.

She pulled her stool closer to Meg. "I'm Caroline. I'm in Lakeside ... I came for personal business and landed in an adventure. When I walked in this morning, Larkin was in labor."

"Did she have the baby?" several asked simultaneously.

"Not that I know of, although Ryan said he would inform me when the baby arrived." She finished a bite of her bun, giving her time to formulate her words. "Larkin needed help and I'm here for the day."

"She touched you and decided," Irene proclaimed. Several nodded as if they were Irene's chorus. "You're not from here. Not the right accent."

"Seattle."

Meg tilted her head. She studied Caroline's features. "We're glad to meet you. You took Larkin's proclamation calmly and she trusted you to stay."

"I think I was more concerned she would deliver in front of me. I guess I had nothing better to do today."

"Are you here for a while?" Meg asked before Irene could add more.

"I told the owners I'd watch the store today."

"But you'll stay if they need you." Meg squeezed Caroline's fingers. Both were startled. It was as though warmth bolted their fingers together at a mere touch.

Irene shuffled in her large brown purse and handed Caroline a list. "Our numbers. If you need help, call us. We owe Larkin so much in our lives."

"I'm sure I'll only be here today, but if I need anything, I'll be sure to call." Caroline folded the paper. "Thank you for offering."

Meg turned her chair toward Caroline. "I hope you'll stay. I think you will find what you need here."

The words circled Caroline's head for the rest of the day. Although she hadn't said anything to anyone about her real purpose, Meg had been perceptive about her search. She liked her. Irene was a bit bossy, but the group of women was interesting. Annabelle would have loved to converse with them.

Shaking off her musings, she rinsed all the leftover mugs, locked the money in the safe as instructed and scribbled notes for whomever took over the next day. By five, her feet hurt, her temples throbbed, and she was glad the store closed soon.

Her day was busy. She helped a mother find her son's required reading book, located "oh-that-book-the-one-with-the-funny-cover" for two different people and located "just need something good to read" for another customer.

Customers appreciated what she did and didn't rant and rave and demand the way doctors did.

The chime on the door signaled yet another person. The light-haired man from the morning waited in the doorway. David. He brought white wine and bags of food. "I'm presumptuous, but I hadn't eaten and you aren't from the area." The whiff of food produced a rumble deep within, which was loud enough to elicit a laugh. His eyes danced and an impish grin appeared as though by magic.

He glanced around the store. "How was the day? Could you use some food? "

Two minutes ago, she wouldn't have thought of dinner, but the aromas sparked her hunger. "If I drink any wine, I may fall asleep in one of these chairs for the night, but the food smells delicious. I'm so glad you thought about dinner," Caroline admitted.

Ryan arrived in a rush, paused at the door. "Glad I caught you, was afraid you had bailed ..." He stopped at the bags of food.

David said, "I brought enough for an army. I wasn't sure what anyone would eat. Sit. Have you eaten today? Did the baby arrive?"

"No food since yesterday." He flopped into the closest rattan chair. "Dylan Joseph arrived at noon."

David clapped him on the shoulders. "Congrats, Daddy!"

"Clients ... customers have been asking questions all day. I'll have to fill in everyone."

Ryan's wane smile accented his tiredness. "You will be here tomorrow? That's good. We didn't scare you away."

David opened boxes and handed out paper plates. "Eat. Then fill us in."

Ryan dug in the Lo Mein. "Dylan is 8 pounds, 22 inches. He has his mother's eyes." He bit into a spring roll. "Thank you for sharing dinner." He turned to Caroline. "You're still here and breathing normally."

"The Readers' Haven Reading Group arrives in the morning and they talk. Trust and honesty make people pay exactly for cinnamon buns. *Hunger Games* is assigned reading this year. Little Marianne wanted some book. I think that summarizes my day."

Ryan placed his chopsticks on the edge of his plate. "Thank you." He touched Caroline's hand. "I know this must seem bizarre to you. I've learned to trust Larkin's instincts. We really need you."

"The touch. I heard about that ... several times." Caroline said. Her body was tired, but Meg's words, 'I think you will find what you need here' rang in her ears.

Ryan fiddled with the noodles. "I know you aren't from the temp agency and didn't plan for this." He studied the chopsticks. "This store has been her baby up to now. She wouldn't leave it to just anyone. Could you stay a little longer? Larkin is obsessed with Dylan and learning what to do. But she's worried about the store and is adamant I get you to stay. Please."

Caroline rearranged opened containers from smallest to tallest. Surgeons rarely thanked you for doing your job. They barked orders, grabbed papers, or demanded more work, but rarely thanked you for helping them. She had comp time she hadn't used. Jean could email problems at work. They could talk.

She nodded to Ryan. "I could stay through next week. That should give you time to locate Gloria or her replacement."

Ryan stretched back in his chair and closed his eyes. A long sigh escaped from deep within. "I have a son. And Larkin will be okay." His eyes opened. He looked at Caroline directly. "Thank you."

"Do you dare drink wine?" Caroline reached for the bottle David had opened while Ryan talked. "Or would water be better?" She moved to the small refrigerator behind the counter. "Give me more details about this baby. I'll be expected to fill in everyone. Everyone ..." She rolled her eyes. "You have a loyal clientele here." She pulled her cell phone and typed baby's name and vitals.

Caroline felt David's gaze upon her as she produced water for Ryan and jotted notes for tomorrow. She was in way over her head in so many ways. Dinner from a man she met this morning. That man caused a little flutter in her heart every time he looked in her direction. When was the last time that happened? *And* the craziest notion—she had just agreed to take on a bookstore for a week. Whew, was there something in the water here? She never acted this way in Seattle.

Ryan handed her a card. "This has my number. If you have questions, call. I'll keep you posted on Larkin and the baby." He paused at the door. "Thank you."

David handed her a paper plate. "You okay? This isn't too much?"

She dumped rice on her plate and took a spring roll from a package. "No, this is fine. I dealt with angry surgeons, anxious doctors, crazy hospital personnel. All want information yesterday." She dipped her spring roll in duck sauce. "Here, clients need help finding books and are very appreciative when you find them."

"I delivered the book today before I came here. It's 'The Book' for the next book club discussion. She was very appreciative." David wiped his fingers on a napkin.

One of the women in that group was his mother? All were too old to be girlfriends.

"I liked today. Helping a five-year-old decide on a book was a new experience." She chuckled. "I had a big cleanup job from sticky fingers and piles of books."

"I'm glad you agreed to stay." Their hands touched over spring rolls and the warmth of his fingers lingered. "I think you will help Larkin and be a good addition here."

Okay. Way over your head. Her heart raced and she got a ditzy grin every time those green eyes focused on her. Luckily, she had only committed to a week. Before she ever got to know more about this man she would be back in Seattle. She moved her hand.

"Thank you for dinner and the support." She smiled but didn't focus on his face. "I need to grab a few things before I leave. I think after today and the wine, I'll be asleep."

Why was she babbling? He said nothing about any time or commitment past dinner. She watched his retreating figure through the window. Of course, if he did come back, he would make her time here more interesting.

She pulled pages of directions and locked up. The evening was still light and the air warm for May. She took the long way back to the B&B and headed down Sassafras. The house with its green shutters looked as though it had a face. She tapped her finger on the iron fence. She'd been in this small town with a tacit creativity and already she personified the house. *Get a grip. You want to feel a tug to this house, to this town.*

She was just here to learn about her past and get answers about the house.

It wasn't rocket science. As a researcher, she'd focused on minute details medical personnel needed in seconds. A few clicks on a mouse and she'd find all the relatives she'd need. Then once in the house, all the questions about Annabelle would be answered. Done. Then go home. She drove to Homey Hearth Bed and Breakfast, which looked as though it had been pulled from *Victoria Magazine*. With her computer bag and her carryon weighing down her shoulders, she trailed her large dark green suitcase across a brick pathway to the entrance.

A woman with grey-tinged hair hurried from behind the reception desk to grab her bag. "You must be Caroline. I'm glad to see you. We expected you earlier."

She dropped her bags and plastered on her practiced smile. "I was ... delayed."

The gum chewing teen from this morning slipped in, grabbed her bags and bounced them down the hall.

"I'm Stephanie Cambridge. We talked on the phone. So sorry for the loss of your mother. I'll miss seeing her."

Although it had been a year since Annabelle died, she still felt the stab of longing twist in her chest. They had been close, sharing conversations and treasured moments of their lives. "Thank you. I found the name of this B&B among her papers."

"I enjoyed the yearly visits with your mom."

The knot twisted tighter.

"It's good to finally meet you. Are you keeping Greystone House and continuing Annabelle's excursions?"

"I'm selling the house." Caroline regretted her curtness. She plastered the courteous smile, the one she reserved for an intern or doctor's receptionist. Her gut churned. *This woman chatted with Annabelle and I had no idea my mother was in New Jersey.* "Annabelle must have loved the house."

"It's funny Annabelle never brought you here with her all

those years."

"Yeah." Caroline fidgeted with the handle on her bag. *Funny, Annabelle never told me about the house. Funny, she never mentioned any connection to New Jersey.*

"Oh." She reached for materials in small postal boxes behind the desk. "Kevin McLaughlin, the realtor, dropped this off." She handed her a thin brass key. "The renters leave today and you may go in." She pushed an envelope across the desk. "This is from your mother."

Caroline turned the key over in her hand. It was unlike the modern jagged keys to her townhouse—this one was a key from another era.

"Your room is down the hall where Nicole disappeared. If you need anything, let me know."

Her room was cozy and charming. A large poster bed dominated one room. The attached sitting room had a small desk large enough for her laptop. She unpacked, placed directions on the desk. She paused with the brown envelope with Annabelle's handwriting, then stuffed it in the back of the drawer. Not now.

Although she had picked up two books to browse before bed, she dozed in her chair before she opened either. Her cell phone ring interrupted.

"You're asleep. It's only nine o'clock."

As Caroline recounted the day's happenings, Tina alternately squealed, laughed and fired questions. She had the most questions about David.

"Why don't you take a real vacation and take off more than another week. You have worked for Andoer Research for over seven years. You haven't taken vacation days or comp days. You deserve to take a week or two."

"I did take a vacation with Griscom to Italy." She sat up straighter.

"A vacation with Griscom couldn't have been relaxing or fun. I bet he told you what art pieces to look at and what impressed him. And he pointed the whole time. Griscom was a scumbag and a mistake."

Caroline winced at Tina's accurate assessment and flopped back on the pillows. "Okay, Griscom was not model boyfriend material and the vacation ..." Tina always cut to the chase. Her boldness, fearlessness had attracted Caroline to join her on the playground. As an adult, Tina was her sounding board.

"You've been restless, wanted change," Tina said. "Here it is. This is a gift. Stay. See what you discover about dreamy David. About your family. I heard Jersey has great beaches and Philadelphia, NYC and even DC are close. Take time for you."

Caroline kicked her shoes off onto the floor. Helping someone else today had felt good. "I have time to stay, but there's no real reason. Once I get in the house, I'll get answers."

"You're quiet. Did you find out anything? "

"No, I ended up with a job for a week. Nothing else happened the way I planned."

CHAPTER TWO

Caroline survived Saturday at Readers' Haven. Part of the book group appeared mainly to have coffee, a cinnamon roll and chat. Children tucked in beanbag chairs in their own section discovered new books. The postmaster loved mysteries and she learned two mothers thought it was okay to drop off their three children while they had a manicure every Saturday.

Stephanie stopped in with a bag of supplies and a bill. "I heard you took over the bookstore. Are you staying until Larkin returns?"

"Just temporary." She took the bill from Stephanie. "I'll call Ryan about this and see how to get you the payment."

Stephanie shrugged. She moved to the coffee table and straightened the sugars and artificial sweeteners. "I'm not concerned. So you are not staying long? You renting or selling your mother's house?"

"Selling." She attached a sticky note to the paper and wrote a note to Ryan. "Maybe rent it as my mother did." Where did that idea come from?

"Your mother never had any trouble filling it."

"Did she visit it often or only when she rented it?"

Stephanie stopped wiping out containers on the coffee table and faced Caroline. She frowned. "Almost yearly."

"She didn't talk much about her visits." Caroline doodled on the yellow square before her. She needed clues about her mother's visits, but she also didn't want to raise questions about her lack of knowledge about her mother's doings. "This was her getaway place. What did she usually do?"

"Walked every morning early. Around six AM. Usually to

Morningstar Cemetery."

"Cemetery? Why?"

"Maybe she liked the peace and quiet there." Stephanie pulled out cans of coffee from her bag. "Every morning, she walked there, then took a book to Buck Park."

Caroline let this sink in. Her mother never got up before nine. A walk at six AM? She couldn't get Annabelle to go on walks with her even mid-morning.

"She travelled to Philly or New York City. She also wandered back streets and found items." She checked the containers of decaf and regular coffee then added more. "Then she always rented a U-Haul to go home."

Caroline continued, "Every vacation we ever went on, we ended up having to rent a U-Haul to take back Annabelle's finds. A doily, a lamp, but then an oak sideboard, a maple dresser … Whatever she found interesting."

"She found treasure in other people's junk. She had a real eye for antiques. Helped me furnish the inn to attract more customers. Helpful." Stephanie tapped down the coffee and sealed the lids. "Sounds like you and your mom were close."

Caroline nodded. "My father died when I was young. It usually was just the two of us." She moved around the counter.

"Funny she never brought you here, too."

Caroline avoided the obvious interest. She straightened magazines on the long table. "Annabelle talked about someone … a woman she spent time with, but I can't remember her name." She forced a smile. "You know how you always tune out your parent's voice."

Stephanie frowned and scratched her neck. "I never saw her with one person. Just her antiques and a good book."

That was Annabelle. When she wasn't finding the treasure buried under a dull finish or presenting a piece of vintage jewelry in the best presentation, Annabelle was buried in a book. She returned to the safety of the counter. "I'll make sure Ryan knows about the bill today."

"So you aren't staying long?" Stephanie packed her supplies back in her paper bag with handles. "You're leaving soon."

"Yes, I agreed to a week to give them time to get a long-term worker."

Stephanie nodded and headed to the door. "And you are selling. I probably won't see you again. I'm sure you won't have trouble selling that house." She shut the door behind her.

She watched her hustle down the path to town. Stephanie knew details about Annabelle and was upset by her death, but she seemed to want Caroline to leave. *Odd. Wonder what I did to rub her the wrong way.*

She texted Ryan, cleaned up the children's area, and locked the door. Instead of following Stephanie's path to the bed and breakfast, she detoured down Sassafras Street and stood before her house. Tomorrow she'd be in. Had Annabelle decorated this? Or was it a mismatch of styles as each renter left furniture behind?

That night, she had a fitful sleep. Her dreams had been troubled with glimpses of Annabelle, her father, a musty basement and falling bookshelves filled with paperbacks. What if her house were in deplorable condition inside and she couldn't sell it?

In the morning, she packed a large coffee, a breakfast sandwich, and marched to the house just after sunrise. She flipped the key in her palm. The house had survived wars, droughts and whatever other tragedies New Jersey, nature and mankind had thrown at it. It looked secure and inviting. That didn't explain the growing knot in her stomach.

She unlocked the door, turned the knob and the door opened with a resounding screech. WD-40 needed here. The foyer took her breath away. A doorway opened to a formal, old-fashioned parlor. She placed her key and bag on the marble-top table near the front door.

The three-step wooden stairway led to a landing and then a steep flight up followed. She recognized the three-seated bench, which lined the short wall of the family room. She and Annabelle had picked it out at a sale in Tacoma.

Although Caroline could identify period pieces and knew value of many antiques on sight, she did not have the knowledge Annabelle had. She could have gone through this house and labeled what was original, what and when it had been modified. Her mother's choices of antiques matched the time period of the house, yet were inviting and cozy.

A hall rambled to her left. She opened a door and gasped. A huge library. She spun in the middle of it. One end was a bay window. Large cushions beckoned.

A reader's paradise. The floor to ceiling bookshelves on either side of the fireplace was crowded with books. Curling up in the window seat with the warmth of the sun on your back was the perfect reader's spot.

She dropped into the window seat and settled against the cushions. If she could only transport this to Seattle.

She shut her eyes. Mementos of Annabelle dominated the house. Caroline knew she was brought home to Seattle as an infant and had grown up within the comfort of Annabelle's and Grant's love. Occasionally, Annabelle brought up the adoption, but where and when she was born had never bothered her until this damn house. Now that it was too late to ask anyone, she wanted answers.

If I were born here, who are my natural parents? She glanced upward. *Why keep the house a secret and then give it to me after your death? Annabelle, you have a week to give me a clue, then I'm selling and going to Seattle.*

Who am I really?

CHAPTER THREE

The next day she joined the reading club's rousing discussion of Fitzgerald's *Great Gatsby*. She always hated the characters in that book and as she discussed it this time, she realized how Griscom reminded her of Daisy's husband.

The afternoon quieted to nothing—no reading group, no small children wanting to hear stories. Caroline straightened and dusted shelves. When Gloria was found and ensconced as the temporary manager, a clean bookstore would help.

She wandered through the stacks. What readers chose to discard and what to save interested her. A used bookstore was the give and take of varied interests. A large white spine book protruded from the top shelf. As Caroline reached to straighten it, it fell at her feet. The title, *The Adoptee's Chase,* glared at her. She jumped. What irony that book would be out-of-place.

She carried it to the round table in front of the windows and leafed through the table of contents. This would get her started and send her in the right direction. She could use her own researcher skills to find her family. That's one of the reasons for flying here—find out her past. She skipped to the to-do information begun in chapter one. "Jot down all the information you already know or think you know about your adoptive parents and your adoption."

She pulled her tablet from her bag beneath the counter. She wrote Annabelle's name on one column, Grant's name at the top on the other column. She scribbled notes beneath each name.

Annabelle and Grant married after their junior year in college. Annabelle's birthday was June twenty-first and

Grant's October eighth. The birthdate listed on her amended birth certificate was March fifteenth. The only other details she remembered were from bits and pieces of conversation. They all flew together when she was an infant, but she wasn't sure if that was a family trip or after her adoption.

Annabelle never had more children because of complications during her pregnancy and an accident. She tapped her fingers on the edge of her tablet. What other tidbit? She knew Grant liked and often sang the song—off-key, *Sweet Caroline.* Her middle name was Kelly. She had asked her mother about that but couldn't remember the outcome. Annabelle's head had disappeared inside a cabinet she had been refinishing and that answer was lost. Caroline had her amended birth certificate. Not much on the list. Certainly wouldn't fill a spreadsheet.

She poured a coffee and set up her computer near the window. The store was unusually quiet. She could look a little until someone came in. She searched accessibility of hospital and adoption records. Damn, New Jersey had closed records. She searched Vital Statistics. She scanned through pages of names, dates. An hour later, she stretched the kink out of her neck. She made fresh coffee.

She researched minute facts—*think*. She sipped her fresh coffee and again tapped in dates. Bingo. A baby girl. Lakeside, New Jersey born March twelfth. A hit. Not her date, but sometimes amended birth dates were different. Baby Jennifer Ann Feratti was born to Gram and Anna Feratti on March twelfth. No other baby girls were born anywhere near her birthdate. That had to be it.

I'm Jennifer Feratti. She slumped in the chair and looked out the window. Jennifer. She didn't feel like a Jennifer. She sucked in her upper lip. Jennifer. She closed her eyes. Jennifer. That was easy. She'd found out her parents' names. She'd seen her house. She knew her birth name. That's that. She closed the computer. Done.

No elation. No ta-da moment. Just a name. She licked her lips to void the flat taste. She wished Annabelle were here to talk with—or more important—Grant to wrap her in one of those big hugs she remembered.

She knew the facts. Now she could go home.

She retrieved her feather duster and ran it down the shelves between the romance and thrillers.

"Caroline?" A baby's muffled cry echoed Larkin's voice.

Caroline peered around the shelves. Larkin, Ryan and a small bundle waited near the chairs. Larkin unwrapped the infant's blanket.

"Meet Dylan," said Ryan.

He was a still-pink infant, in the stage Griscom always referred to as indistinguishable slugs.

Ryan cradled him and eased him into Caroline's arms. "Dylan, this is your mother's new best friend—she saved your mother."

Caroline touched his soft cheek. She couldn't remember the last time she held one. No one in their crowd ever brought babies to outings.

Larkin perused the store. "How are you surviving? Anyone make you want to race back home? Are you sorry you walked in here?"

"No, I've actually enjoyed myself." Caroline sat in the rocker near the book stacks. Caroline filled in tales of Irene's new grandson, the book group discussion of *Great Gatsby*, four-year-old Sherrill's discovery of *Green Eggs and Ham* and her own learning of the trust and honesty system with coffee orders. Larkin alternately nodded and clapped her hands and chuckled with Caroline's tales.

Larkin rubbed her hands together. "Would you stay longer? I have no idea what hours you keep or why you're here … I know you're a medical researcher somewhere. You fit in here." Larkin touched her baby's head. "I didn't expect to feel this way. I can't leave Dylan now."

She sucked in the bottom corner of her lip. This wasn't a career—just a temporary reprieve. She should put the house up for sale and return to her life in Seattle, but the lives of people here, like Meg, tugged on her heart. She still had vacation days and comp time.

She directed her questions to Ryan. "How long? I'm on a leave—I could stay longer. I haven't finished my business here." She was hedging. She had to sell the house. She knew her name and birth parents but hadn't looked for the real person. Nor did she know Annabelle's connection. "It will take you time to find a permanent replacement for someone to run the store for you. I could stay longer." She handed the baby back to Larkin.

"How long could you stay?" Ryan tapped his fingertips on the chair. "We could compensate you for your time."

Again, Larkin touched Caroline. "You are part of this — us — Dylan's life. Odd you showed up when you did." Larkin paused. "Could you stay for a month?"

Caroline studied the magazines on the circular table. The pull to stay was unrealistic. "I don't know. I need to think about this. I'll call you tomorrow."

Larkin released a deep sigh and hugged Dylan close to her chest. "Thank you. This store is important. I have a feeling…" She shrugged. "I think you'll be glad you stayed."

Ryan stood. "Larkin is torn. Any way you can help is appreciated. We'll talk later." He helped Larkin to her feet and wrapped his arm around her as they ambled to the car.

Caroline watched as they left. Great couple — if Griscom had been half as attentive as Ryan appeared to be … Griscom was out of the picture and —

A month. She'd have to call Griscom and inform him herself she was taking time off if she stayed. She slammed the door. She didn't relish that. She wrinkled her nose. Maybe that's why she liked it here. She didn't have to see him every day.

When she'd started at Andoer she'd been so impressed by his knowledge, his contacts — and she'd been so flattered he'd been interested in her. He'd moved into her condo and taken over her life.

She emptied the coffee grounds into the trash. She did have new friends here and knew more about the women's lives in the book club than she did about her fellow employees at Andoer. She had worked with them for seven years. When she returned to Seattle, she would accompany Tina on more adventures. Do more than work. She checked the room.

All neat and ready for tomorrow.

It was a warm evening. She stopped at her bench near the river. It was still light — a murky light. River meandered slowly before her.

"I can't resist this spot either." David walked down the path toward her. "Private thoughts or can I disturb you?"

She slid over on the bench. "It's a beautiful night. I needed a walk to clear my head. Join me."

David sat beside her. "Something else is going on? You're frowning. Can I help?"

"Larkin and Ryan want me to stay — to help out longer."

"Willing to move here?"

Her heart skipped a beat. "Oh no, no." Staying here, that hadn't been a thought … until David said that. "I had agreed to a week and a half. They want me a month. I'm not sure about staying any longer."

"Are you leaving family during your time here?"

"No family. My mother died a year and a half ago." As soon as the words slipped out, she realized he was fishing for information. "No husbands waiting. No fiancées, lovers or anyone who eagerly awaits my return. I can stay here without disturbing a family."

His wide grin pleased her.

As if motivated by the same internal signal, they meandered down the pathway near the water.

"Nothing to make you race back?"

She shook her head. "I'm on leave from my current job. They can learn to get along without me." Where had that come from?

"What is your career of the moment?" He matched her stride.

"I have been a senior research director for Andoer Medical Research. We investigate for surgeons and doctors," She plucked a tall weed from the grasses beside the trail as they walked through a wooded pathway. "Exciting, stimulating work when you find the odd tidbit that will really help a doctor solve a medical problem." She picked the leaves from the weed.

"But you're not interested now?"

She ran her fingers the length of the weed's stem. "Many changes occurred in the last year." She plucked the second frond. "It's just not as fulfilling as it has been." She ran her fingers along the tips of the weeds and flowers next to the path.

"And that's a new thought. You hesitated."

Caroline nodded. Talking to anyone other than Tina was equally a new sensation.

"What would you like to do now? Research for a different company? Not research?"

"I don't know. Working here … The changes have me rethinking." Her life spun to a different dimension when she arrived in Lakeside. None of these thoughts ever occurred at home. "It's … my plans … my path has always been clear. I knew what happened next, where all the pieces of life fit."

She flung the weed into the river. "Now my life is as though someone threw the puzzle pieces on the floor—all jumbled."

"Maybe coming here was …" He paused. "Serendipitous. Time you need to think."

Returning to Seattle, listening to Griscom's droning voice had the same appeal as dragging a metal fork across your teeth. "I have more leave time if I need it. I'll stay the month until Larkin and Ryan find a replacement."

"I'm glad." He took her hand between his palms.

Feeling his closeness, she wholeheartedly agreed. More time to get to know this man with enticing green eyes. An interesting man.

"South Jersey has beaches, Lucy the Elephant, Pine Barrens, rivers to explore. I'll gladly show you the best of Jersey for the weeks you are here." He rubbed his thumb across the back of her hand.

"Lucy the Elephant?"

He chuckled. "Not in competition with the Space Needle. It's an oddity tourist attraction near the Jersey Shore." He held her gaze. "Ever kayak?"

"I watched the kayaks since I've arrived. I never really had the time. Griscom had an ostentatious boat used to impress clients. I didn't enjoy that."

David pointed to the water moving below. "That river connects to the lake. We could take kayaks on the river."

Caroline squealed and hopped on one foot. "Really?" She had watched others in small boats in Seattle. Never kayaked. Of course, she had never run a bookstore either. "I would really like to try that."

She was rewarded with his marvelous grin and dancing green eyes.

She paused at the end of the walkway. "We haven't talked about you. What do you do? Staying with your job?"

He leaned against the wooden slats along the walkway. "Principal. Elementary school."

Caroline masked her reaction. In education? No fast track. She, Griscom and several of their friends mocked teachers and educators. No pushing to get ahead. Do-gooders.

"Does it surprise you that I'm a principal?"

"Not sure what being an elementary school principal involves. I work in a cutthroat business world where competition and long hours' rule. What do principals do?"

Her question produced a deep-throated laugh. "I work with students, teachers, parents ... all the problems are my concern. I keep things running smoothly so teachers can teach. It's a safe, inviting environment for the kids."

"Whatever made you get into education?" All the people she knew perceived teachers as shirkers who made very little money so they could have summers off.

"Originally, it gave me time to do what I really loved and earn a living. My mother was an elementary teacher and ... others also influenced that decision."

Caroline noted the pause and wondered about what "others." She rubbed the smoothness of the railing and waited for him to continue. "You asked me about lovers, fiancées ... married. Anyone in your life?"

A wane, soft smile crossed his face then disappeared. He avoided eye contact. "Not now."

No further explanations were forthcoming and a brooding silence enveloped them. Caroline wasn't sure what to say or add. The conversation stopped. She had invaded his space. He wasn't sharing any more. She turned to head back up the path. "I would like to kayak before I go home."

He touched her arm. "I would love to share the area with you." His voice was inviting. "I own three kayaks."

"I like this river. The peace, the slow movement, the trees and birds. I have watched kayakers here. Do you kayak right here?" She turned back to the water. This was her favorite spot in Lakeside. She had no favorites in Seattle, as least not this peaceful. David moved next to her—his nearness created a tingle. Being with him would make time here worthwhile. She wanted to know more about him.

"We can put in nearby. Show you the city from the water." He tapped the railing with his palm. "No moose, no salmon here."

"Salmon … oh salmon, Seattle. I have no expectations. I have never been on a river like this."

He squeezed her shoulder. "If you like rivers, we could kayak a different river every week of the summer." That smile, which attracted her the first time she saw him, melted her a little right then.

"The end of the summer? That's three months!"

"A man can hope."

This was turning into a vacation, not a duty. She liked the people she met … certainly liked this man beside her. The month looked better and better.

"So if you have agreed to kayak with me, you are staying … for a while?"

She nodded. For a while. Tina's words rang in her ears. "I do have sufficient leave time. I could stay, but not long. I have things here to finish. I don't know how long they will take. But I do need to return home."

"If you want to look for a job, I have contacts here. I could offer."

She shook her head. "My life has had recent abrupt changes. The trip here will help me decide what I want to return to. Working here—" She searched for the right words. "—has been fulfilling." She shrugged. "That surprised me."

"Maybe it's time for a change and going away just highlighted that for you. What are you looking for here?"

"I need to settle a real estate inheritance. One I recently found out about."

David said nothing. She wasn't ready to share that part of her past yet.

David's hand slid down her arm and he again clasped her hand. "I have a choir practice to attend. I'm glad I ran into you today." He didn't let go of her hand, but studied the intertwining of their fingers. "I'll stop by the book shop to set up dates ... for our kayaking."

Caroline watched the river after David left. She had been restless and wanted change and she got it—different job, new people, and David. Her life was one she didn't recognize. It was as though she stepped into someone else's shoes.

CHAPTER FOUR

Caroline sipped her coffee on the porch of Greystone. She liked this morning tradition—soaking in the peace of the early sun, listening to the birds chatter, and attempting to identify the ones who populated the feeders. A book she'd borrowed from the store helped. If anyone in Seattle knew she was a bird watcher, no one would have believed it. Her life there had been so much bustle—onto the next event, next item on her to-do list. Taking a few moments for her before work was new territory.

She walked through the garden with her second cup of coffee. Roses with multiple pink blooms bent the limbs to the ground. Another bush had bright red tiny flowers as if someone shrunk the perfect rose. She'd picked up bits about roses from Andover office chatter. They were difficult to grow, great big fresh flowers bloomed in June. Jean, her assistant, brought in cut fragrant flowers. This was early May, why were her flowers blooming now?

She got scissors and a small plastic bag from inside the house. If she took in samples, maybe she could match them in a book in the store. A beautiful rose garden would add to the sale of a house.

She arrived forty-five minutes before Readers' Haven opened to prepare for the day. The coziness of the shop welcomed her. Putting away the materials from the day before, scanning the shelves for stray paperbacks and touching the spines of the old volumes helped her focus before her customers arrived. Books had always been a comfort to her—an escape from the ordinary din or her controlled tense existence.

Early summer sun warmed her cheeks. She flipped through pages and pages of pink, red or multi-colored roses. She shut the book then closed her eyes. She had no idea what she had in the garden, let alone what to do with them. Nothing matched the leaves she had in the plastic bags next to her.

She stretched. Meg wheeled down the street toward the shop. Caroline opened the door and waited, "Good. Someone to keep me company."

Meg called as she drew closer. "What, no Irene? I could call her for you." She pulled up to the door. "I'm sure she could keep you busy."

Caroline moved aside for her. "No thanks. I'm glad to see just you."

"I'm wasting time waiting for Abby to finish grocery shopping then she is driving me home. I could always use a good cup of coffee, a good book or—" She patted Caroline's hand. "Time with a good friend."

Meg's attachment to her as a friend pleased her. It would be great to be included in her circle of friends. "Time in a book shop is never wasted. Would you like tea or coffee? What do you like in it?"

"A hot tea today. I can fix it." She slid to the coffee setup and paused at the table. "Roses. Who pulled these books out?" She ran her fingers across the covers.

"I have roses on my property. I don't want to kill them."

Meg flipped through the pages. "What kind do you have?

"I don't know enough to tell you. I don't have much luck with plants. Even the ones I had inside died … from neglect." Caroline studied the pages. She pointed to the colorful pictures in the book Meg held. She produced the leaves from the plastic bag on the table. "These are the leaves."

"Gardening is relaxing and rewarding." Meg touched the roses on the pages. "I miss the work, clipping the roses, digging in the earth and feeling it with my fingers. The blooms reward you when you do a good job." She pointed to a photograph. "These are good for color and fill in. The leaves are from miniature roses." She shut the book. "If you didn't garden, what did you do to relax?"

"I worked. My job involved long hours. I often worked

weekends."

"What did you do with your friends?"

"Work took much time. Friends were ..." Her lifestyle seemed like a movie set. Preparing for Griscom's parties, not interacting with anyone who came to the condo, just chatting and moving to the next one.

Meg's frowning face prompted her to add, "Tina, my closest friend, and I attend art galleries exhibits and go to movies and concerts."

"Good for Tina. You spend too much time working. Any family activities?"

"My mother dragged me to yard sales every Saturday and to every auction until I became smart enough to stay away."

Her mother's elaborate negotiations to get Caroline to trail her mother up and down aisles of junk had become a game between them. She ran her palm across the book cover.

"You and your mother close?" Meg moved her wheelchair back. "Does your father go antiquing?"

"My mother died a year and a half ago." Caroline said. "We were close."

Meg squeezed her hand. "I'm sorry to hear that."

Silence overtook the room. The pang of loss clutched Caroline's heart. Talking with Meg was like a motherly hug.

"Maybe gardening will be a new escape while you're here. Learn a hobby you can take back with you."

"I have little time for ..." Her job equaled her life. She had devoted little time for anything or anyone else. "Maybe I'll do something, add something in my life and take time to garden."

"Time for family? Married?"

She shook her head.

"No time for that either? No one in your life? What do you do with that life of yours?" Meg maneuvered her wheelchair to the coffee table. "How important is this job of yours that you have to devote all your time to it?"

Caroline sank to the chair. "Important to doctors and surgeons, but ..." She struggled to find the right words. "I don't know if it really helps others." She pinched her nose. "I help doctors or surgeons find information. I suppose, that in turn aids their patients."

"You never see those patients nor learn if you really assisted them?" Meg's spoon poised over her cup.

Caroline shook her head. Had she imagined people she was helping as she did the research? She convinced herself she was caring for individuals, but she had no proof. Maybe that's why she liked the book shop. She saw the smiles when a person's book order came in and she interacted with real people who had faces and names and histories.

"I like the atmosphere here. I can talk with others and help them discover—something very simple—a book that person might like."

"Reading helps escape from the cruelties of life, helps us see the humanity—the best and the worst of the characters in a book. Reading can be helpful in a multiple of ways." Meg paused, her cup midway to her lips. "Heard you are interested in kayaking?" She sipped her tea and peeked at Caroline over the cup. "Kayaking … with David could start something interesting, too."

"Whew, that was a lead in line. Bit of matchmaking going on? I don't live here. This is temporary, Meg."

She put down her cup. "But you are here for now and you should enjoy yourself. You interested?"

Caroline studied the rose photographs in the book in her lap. She searched for the correct response. "David is … " She was about to utter unique, but that sounded so pat. "Someone I would like to spend time with. Kayaking looks fun and would be an adventure."

Meg tapped her finger on the cup. "You're hedging, but I've already talked with him. He wants to try all kinds of new adventures while you are here. And he wants to convince you to stay the summer."

Caroline attempted to hide the grin but was unsuccessful.

"Ahh" was all Meg said.

"I'd be glad to go," she said. "I like talking with him, but I have a life elsewhere."

"A life with no one special. To a job that isn't fulfilling. To a place you have business associates, but no friends." Meg tapped on Caroline's arm. "You should stay as long as possible. You help Larkin, " Her tapping became more persistent. "And help yourself. You're looking for something."

She felt the tug to confide in Meg her real reason for coming to Lakeside. Meg would understand. "Things have changed in my life there. I think a bigger change is brewing, but that doesn't mean I can stay forever."

Meg settled back in her seat. "I'm not sure what brought you here, but it seems to have happened at a good time for many people." She refreshed her tea from the pot and picked up the rose book. "You have access to a great rose food." Meg pointed to the table laden with coffee maker, scones, cinnamon rolls and condiments.

"What food do I have?"

"Coffee grounds. Take home the grounds and spread it around the base of the plant."

"Coffee grounds? If I forget a day, will the plants get a headache?"

Meg's soft laughter filled the room. "I never thought of that, but I know they love the grounds and bloom more and the leaves are greener. I used to baby my roses and was thrilled when the color filled the garden." A deep sigh overwhelmed her body. "I miss digging in the dirt." She flipped to another page. "Some roses take more care."

They chatted about flowers until Abby appeared. Emptiness occupied the room after Meg left.

At the end of the day, Caroline hummed as she dusted the shelves and put away the coffee condiments. She liked many women in the book club, but Meg was special.

She admired her strength and independence. Meg nor the others ever mentioned Meg's accident. Although she admitted to be saddened by not having her garden, she was never overburdened by her injury. She was always fun and upbeat. Maybe there was a subtle way to ask the book club.

She unpacked a book shipment then counted and checked off items in the order.

After finishing the inventory, she sent a text to Ryan and Larkin and prepared to close. She dumped the coffee grounds in a small metal can. Meg's advice better work or she would look silly dumping coffee on the roses.

Strange place, this Lakeside. She chatted with women about interesting topics all generated by their reading. She helped children find the "bestest book." She had read aloud books to small groups of children as well. In her Seattle world, she never saw or dealt with children.

She locked the door. She slung her bag on the way to her house. She dragged her feet. She couldn't put off the inevitable any longer. She had to call Griscom. It was unfair to expect Jean to inform him she was taking a month leave.

Griscom. She pictured his tall stature, his erect posture and that confident air. When she started at Andoer, she had been impressed by that attitude. Griscom had been her boss, then her lover. Their lives glued together. Griscom's motive for doing anything was to get ahead—on the job, in the public eye. They entertained not friends, but the social elite. The silence between them in the evenings alone was her first clue.

Annabelle's first stroke became Caroline's option to move in with her mother. His all-encompassing opinions had been the second rift in the relationship. After a month with Annabelle, she sold her townhouse, forcing Griscom out of her life. His restriction on her clothing, phraseology and appearance finally lifted. They communicated in clipped phrases and tight smiles at work.

Annabelle's death brought so many changes in her life.

She dumped her bag on the counter. She fortified herself with a glass of Malbec wine and dialed his number.

"Are you back? You need to come to work tomorrow. So many calls are backed up. You have to get control of your life and be back where you belong." No hello from Griscom. No questions on how she was doing. Just orders.

"Nice to talk with you, too. Griscom, I'm taking a month's leave of absence."

"You don't dare. It will cost you your job." His face—the one where he screwed up his mouth looking as though he tasted sour milk—came to mind. She could visualize the spit coming out of his mouth. How dare someone contradict his plans? Even the sound of his voice irritated her now.

"Actually, Griscom, I can. I have two weeks accumulated comp time as well as six months' worth of unused vacation and sick time. Also, I'm allowed a week for family business."

"You aren't entitled to just take that at a whim."

"No whim, Griscom. You can look up the contract and contact HR. I already worked it out with them."

Silence. He was probably texting Kate at HR right now. She had talked with her Friday right after she had told her assistant her plans. Both had informed her how many clients were angry with Griscom for his mistakes and inefficiency.

"Griscom, I have every right to take this time off. It's a month. HR will find a temp."

She almost hung up, but Griscom's voice boomed from the cell phone.

"You have six weeks, period, to get whatever is happening to you out of your system. After that, I post your job." He paused, and then quieted. "And you know I can fill it in an instant. Be back in one month." He hung up.

She sat back in the chair and gulped the contents of her wine glass. *Too bad I have no Scotch. What did I ever see in that man?*

CHAPTER FIVE

Wednesday, the shop closed at noon, a tradition in the town left over from when store owners went to the banks on Wednesday. It was a slow day. Many brought in used books for credit. A few searched for new ones. She took inventory, and rearranged shelves.

She tapped her pen on the counter. What would she do this afternoon with her free time? Shopping. If she were to stay for the month, she'd need more food. She jotted a grocery list. Occasionally, she had experimented with cooking in the kitchen, but the condo had not been setup to entertain many and Griscom had hated the mess.

After closing up for the day, she headed to the small grocery store she had passed on her way into town. She had seen no Whole Foods or big name food store. With her list in hand, she pushed the cart inside.

Caroline paused at the fresh fruit and vegetable section.

"You are staying long enough to shop?"

Mary Porter, an avid Harlequin American Romance reader, spoke to her. Caroline withheld the chuckle. She knew people in this town by what they read. No one would have approached her in the grocery at home.

"Yes, just enough to get by for the month."

"There's a farmer's market two blocks from the bookstore, near the waterfront. It's open Thursday through Saturday afternoon. Good fruits and vegetables. When the summer season starts, the finds are incredibly tasty."

Caroline nodded. Good to know. She could walk there after work in the afternoon. Fresh home-grown vegetables tasted better. "What's good around here? What should I look for?"

"Jersey tomatoes can't be beat. Blueberries are locally grown and good for you. Asparagus. Hopefully, you will be here long enough to enjoy them." Mary frowned. She held up one finger. "Corn. Great white corn." She emphasized the white. "Good in June."

Caroline nodded. "Thanks." She filled her cart. As she packed the groceries in the trunk, a bright yellow kayak resting next to the door of a store invited inspection. Varied sizes of paddles rested across some kind of holder. She closed the trunk and walked over. She touched the kayak. Heavy plastic? Would it hold up in the water, over rocks or logs?

"Ah, piqued your interest, didn't I? Which kayak catches your fancy?" The familiar deep voice of David resonated in her right ear. "See all the colors and shapes." He pointed to the dozens lying in the grass near the shop. "You need one to fit you, your body." His voice hesitated as he uttered the last two words.

The air electrified. David's closeness heightened her heart rate. His infectious smile and the intensity of his eyes captured her attention every time. But today, his hands and muscles, noticeable now that he was clad only in a T-shirt, teased her senses as well. His arms showed a strength and endurance. Principals were supposed to be paunchy and puffy from long hours sitting in overstuffed chairs, weren't they?

He was more a compact athlete than a desk jockey. Look away, woman, you are staring at his bode. Say something quick. "It's early afternoon. Aren't you supposed to be at work?"

He covered his forehead with his hand with dramatic flair. "Caught playing hooky."

She frowned. Was he making fun of her?

"I just returned from a three-day conference. I'm 'excused' from work. Which kayak interested you? I might have something to fit your body and we can kayak today."

"So much equipment? Do you need all that?" The area in front of the store was covered with paddles, life-saving equipment and objects she had no names for. The grassy area had at least fifty different kayaks and a multitude of paddles of varied shapes and colors and weights.

David's laugh was low and rumbled deep in his throat. The sound of it delighted her. Even grocery shopping could be awesome in this town.

"Kayaking is a disease," he explained. "You can always find something more to buy. Improved, lighter paddles. Another kayak. PFD." He shrugged. "I have enough to outfit you for kayaking."

She turned back to the paddles along the wall. He knew a great deal about kayaks. It sounded like a fun thing to do.

"Let's go today, and I'll fix dinner for us both afterward."

She picked up the nearest item — a blue-tinted heavy plastic bag — anything to have in her restless hands. Kayaking was tempting, but dinner with David was more of a temptation. She was only here a short time. She couldn't get attached to anyone, but she could have fun. And it had been a long time since simple fun was a pleasure she enjoyed. "Only if I contribute something."

"I'll get steaks to grill. I have tomatoes, fixings for a salad, and can put together a short order blueberry cobbler."

The man had many talents. He obviously didn't believe in ordering out. Dinner sounded even better. "I know just the side dish I want to make."

He nodded. "Give me time to get kayaks and food ready. Want to drive over or want me to come get you?"

"Where are we kayaking? Would it be easier to pick me up on the way or easier for me to drive?"

"Kayaking out my back door for the first time."

"I'll drive then. Give me directions." She wiped her palms along the seams of her capris. "Guess while I'm in New Jersey, I can learn about kayaking, Jersey tomatoes — and discover the state."

"South Jersey. We're the ones with the rivers, wildlife and the shore."

"What should I wear for this adventure?"

His eyes travelled the length of her body and again the heat infused her body with his perusal.

"Comfortable shorts, pants — waterproof if you have them." He studied the windows of the kayak shop in front of them. "If you have flip flops, or waterproof shoes. A jacket or sweater for tonight."

She nodded. "What time?'

"Two PM? I'll write down directions. A GPS complicates the ride." He walked to his Jeep and retrieved pen and paper. He sketched a map as he talked. "You drive east on 49. You'll see a sign for Port Frederick, then a traffic light, go two streets past the light on the right. It's the third house on the right. It's a log cabin. It's easy to see from the street." He paused then added to the paper. "This is my cell phone, in case."

"In case I change my mind?"

He shrugged. "You may decide you only want to watch kayaks. I don't know—just in case you have any questions." He handed her the paper. "Or want to call me in the future."

Caroline folded the paper into squares. Somehow, she had crossed a line here to a new adventure that had nothing to do with kayaks. He appeared as curious about her. Did she make him feel all-antsy and on edge as he did her? Her whole body tingled alive whenever he was present.

She quickly emptied the groceries at home, easily fixed a tortellini salad with fresh vegetables. What to wear? Tina called as Caroline yanked clothes still packed in her suitcase.

"So are you bored out of your mind in the small town?" Tina said.

"No." She paused. "I'm going kayaking this afternoon—and dinner."

Tina squealed so loud Caroline held her phone away from her ear. "It's with that guy... the one you met first day at that store. Okay, fill me in, what do you know about him? What's he look like? Is he hot? Dinner? What kind of dinner ... intimate, low lights. Fill me in."

Caroline paced from the kitchen to her porch and back. "Kayaking and a casual dinner at his house."

"Oh better. His place. Are your prepared?"

"I have a tortellini salad I'm working on now." She popped a cooked tortellini in her mouth to settle the flutters in her stomach.

"No! Prepared to stay over or get closer."

"Tina! First time I have ever been anywhere with him."

Laughter bubbled over. Great! Just like a teenager, she had the jitters and the giggles.

"You're not getting younger and it's been a while. Grab that opportunity. Grab that man. Kiss, pant and whatever. You won't have to look him in the eye in a few months."

Caroline placed her salad dressing next to the bowl. She ran her finger along the edge of the bowl. Tina had a point. She could have an affair—a quickie and move on. No complications.

"You're thinking about it, aren't you? You could have a great time on this hiatus. What do you have to lose?"

"That's not what I'm here for." Caroline stated a little too quickly. "I need to fix the rest of the salad and get ready."

A chuckle was Tina's response. "Call me tomorrow and let me know about your adventure. I want *all* the details."

Caroline fumbled with her clothes. She had the right pants and waterproof shoes—just not here. Maybe that little kayak shop? She still had time. She nestled the salad in a container she found in a drawer.

At the shop, she flipped through the racks. A young man came to her rescue and picked khaki shorts and water sandals. She changed at the store and placed her jeans and shoes in the bag and tucked her jacket on top for the evening.

Once out of town, she passed older houses, a wooded area then she turned right. Between the trees and houses, she glimpsed the blue of water. She turned into his driveway.

A log cabin picturesquely nestled among pines with a body of water rippling behind the building. It was a scene from a postcard—impressive, gorgeous spot—very masculine. On the side close to the water, an open garage revealed a vintage MGB car.

His jeep was parked closer to the water. Several kayaks decorated the ground close to the water. A man of contrasts. Kayaks, Jeep, log cabin—and a sports car that belonged a man who worked with children. David Montgomery was unlike any male Caroline had known.

David appeared in the doorway. He started forward, stopped and stepped back and ushered her in. "There's a room down the hall to your left. Put your clothes and jacket in there." He pointed with his elbow.

The kitchen space was open with an eating area with a long wooden bar and stools was on one end. The living area had comfortable furniture and large stone fireplace. She followed his directions down the hallway past an office stocked with laptop, papers to a small room beyond. A futon chair, a small bureau and a tiny gas fireplace. A quilt decorated the wall.

She leaned against the door and took in the room. A log cabin with a homey touch. Whose touch?

When she returned to the kitchen, David greeted her with, "I love tortellini—great salad."

"This place is phenomenal. How long have you been here? How did you find such a place?"

"About eight years." He sliced tomatoes. An herb-encrusted steak sat on the side. "My friends and I built it." He placed the steaks, salad and tortellini in the refrigerator.

"You built this?" She whirled to take in the varying wood colors and the solid structure.

His smug smile showed his pride with that. "I don't ever want to do it again, but it was a memorable experience." He motioned her to follow him with a nod of his head. She followed him to the deck through large floor-to-ceiling sliding doors.

The sun shone down on the river flowing in his backyard.

"No wonder you own kayaks. You have your own river." She leaned her arms on the upper railing. The river was wider in comparison to the river near the book shop.

David said, "I like the pants—perfect for kayaking. Cameron help you in the kayak shop?"

"Red-haired kid. Tall. Great smile."

David chuckled and nodded. "He's settled a great deal. I knew him as the seventh grader who terrorized the hallways."

Caroline walked down the three steps to the lawn and around the kayaks lying in the grass.

David followed her. "You getting cold feet?"

"What are chances I'm going to be wet?"

"Can always happen, but we're not going into any difficult waters." He tapped a small bright blue kayak with his toe. "This one might be best. It's smaller, more stable." He picked up a vest. "Come on, let's fit this PFD."

"What's a PFD?"

"Personal flotation device replaced the life jacket term." He tugged on straps until cushions of the device closed around her body. He tugged straps and cushions. Each touch prompted goose bumps on the inside of her arms. His touch was gentle and light.

She listened and tried to absorb his directions as he demonstrated paddle techniques and how to move the kayak. Her stomach tied in knots. It looked easy as she watched others on the river; it sounded fun when David suggested it. Now trepidation. *What if I tip? Can I get out or will I be trapped underneath? What made me think I could do this?* She spent days inside a business office. She rode in cars, planes.

"You okay? Ready to go?"

She looked at the river flowing a few feet away. She would never have this opportunity once she left New Jersey.

"I promise you won't get hurt." His hand touched her shoulder. "I'll protect you." His green eyes mesmerized her.

She swayed from one foot to the other. "I'm ready. I said I would try this."

David balanced the kayak as Caroline slipped in. He pushed her into the river and then vaulted in his own. She sat on the water and felt in control.

Caroline jumped as a fish leaped out of the water next to her. David paddled beside her. His paddle silently dipped in. No water dripped down his hand. She wouldn't make a good Native American, she made noise with her paddle and already her hands and legs are wet from drips sliding down the paddle shaft.

David pointed with his paddle to turtles sunning on a log ahead of them. "We'll see baby otters, fish and they come up close. Variety of birds in the trees near the water."

"Do you know the names of the birds you see?" The paddling was easier than she expected. The river was wide enough she moved next to David. He didn't push ahead. She relaxed her grip on the paddle.

"The birds I learned from listening to others. I grew up around here. Some flowers, I know. Learned them more to impress girls."

"You grew up on this property or near here."

"Near here. On the other side of this river. I grew up tramping around through the woods, canoeing on the river."

"You a fisherman and a woodsman?"

He smiled at her labels. "Not much, my father and brothers are avid fishermen and hunters."

"Hunter? As in you kill animals? Do people do that around here?" She couldn't imagine Grant or anyone she knew hunting.

He nodded. "South Jersey has woods, fields, rivers and wildlife. We're not the concrete jungle of North Jersey. Hunting is a family tradition and an annual event around here. I enjoy the tramping around not the sitting waiting for game or waiting for fish."

•

Caroline paddled quietly beside him. This was not part of her world at all. From her body language and her silence, she was analyzing all this, trying to figure out this strange state. Maybe that's what attracted him to her. Since he had walked in the bookstore and met the woman who was not Gloria, he had wanted to explore more, learn more.

He wanted to touch more, too. Because of his position in the public eye, he was careful around women. But with Caroline, he wanted to reach out touch her hair, her skin. He loved to make her laugh. Her laughter rang out and had a musical tone to it. He wanted to pull her into his circle. And he wanted her to stay in Lakeside longer so he could explore more.

"Does your family share your interest in kayaks?"

He paddled ahead around the bend in the river and then moved over to the side until they could paddle next to each other again. "I have a group of friends I kayak with regularly — male and female. My siblings aren't nearby."

She paddled slowly maneuvered easily around a log in the water and kept up with his strokes. She was doing well for a first time kayaker. Cautious, painstakingly exact in paddling — but she seemed comfortable in her boat. She was more intent on glancing around her than paddling faster.

"And your mother?"

Steel gripped his heart as it always did when memories of that day jarred his consciousness. "No." Words came out a bit too sharply. "No, Mother died five years ago." Before he had to answer any more questions about that, he paddled faster and away from her. He slowed a few minutes later. She had nothing to do with that past. He wanted this to be a good experience on the water.

"You okay back there? Arms sore?"

"It's great! It's easier than I imagined. The views—not what I expected either. So close to the water. So much to see."

•

"I'm glad." His kayak next to her heated her up more than the sun. His hand grasped her paddle. He had a strength. She wanted to reach and hold that hand, sure she would find his warmth and strength moved to her. She gripped her own paddle to erase the urge to reach for him. "I understand the addiction."

"Good, I'll promote addiction and bring you to lots of places." He dipped and expertly maneuvered around logs. She followed his example. "A different river each week until you leave."

"You are trying to entice me to stay longer?"

"I can keep you here through fall and we still would have places to kayak." He paused beside her. "Would it work?"

She laughed. "I'm enjoying my time here and kayaking is something I've never done before."

"Get you to stay as long as I can so you don't have to go back to a job you don't like. You aren't involved with anyone there." He turned his kayak and added the line before he moved away. "There's lots I would like to show you here. It gets complicated up ahead. Couple of twists and turns."

Caroline focused on the winding river to avoid running into a bank or an overhanging branch. But his words ran in her ears. Complications in his last retort as well. Maybe Tina was right, he had ulterior motives to this kayak trip. Thinking of what he was willing to show her set tingles down her spine.

Her head spun with questions as her boat and she twisted through a narrow channel of water between the overgrowth.

She did remember David's admonishments about the current jamming the kayak into obstacles. "When you head into a branch or you get jammed into a branch, don't push off with your paddle, you'll tip." She backed up, twisted the boat in the right direction and then tackled the obstructed area again. She liked the challenge and she liked being in charge of the boat. However, by the time they turned a bend and she could see David's log cabin, her muscles ached. It was a beautiful trip on the river, but she'd had a workout.

David pulled the bow of her boat onto the shore as though it were a small stick not a boat with a person her size in it.

He pulled her to her feet as she straddled the kayak. "You kept up, didn't fall in and got yourself out of every jam. Congrats, you're almost a kayaker." He tugged his blue, plastic bag from in back of his seat.

"Almost? When do I become a kayaker? How many hours do I have to log in?"

He hung the blue bag on one arm and draped his other arm across her shoulder. They walked toward the house hip to hip. Caroline liked the closeness of the two. He felt good.

"You have to overturn your kayak, get the water out and get back in and keep paddling." He winked at her.

"Think I'll stay a novice for a while. I'm not anxious to overturn."

He pulled her closer to his frame. "What did you like best?"

She relaxed into the embrace of his arms and matched his strides. "Being that close to the water. I could see so much, the fish swimming, eye level with a turtle." She leaned her head on his arm. "I liked it. Even more than I thought."

David's smile as he studied her warmed her and made the trip even more valuable.

She liked this man more. She added, "I liked the company, too."

He squeezed her shoulders and whispered, "Me, too. " His head rested on hers. "I enjoyed sharing it with you."

He opened the back door for her. They came in through

the cellar. "You can leave the water shoes at the bottom of the stairs." He pulled the back of one shoe off with the toe of his other shoe and then leaned down to extricate the other shoe. "I'm a barefoot man myself." He pattered up the stairs.

When in Rome, she left her shoes and walked barefoot. Something she never would have done around Griscom. She smiled. Something sensuous about bare feet. She usually wore shoes or at least socks. David waited at the top of the stairs.

"You need to change?" When she reached the top, he was so close. Changing seemed to be charged with some other meaning. He opened the door to the small bedroom. "If you'd be more comfortable in drier clothes."

She squeezed between David and the frame as she entered. His hand on her arm caused her to pause. He cupped her chin in his hand. She quivered. She felt like a teenager anticipating a first kiss — except she was a woman. She leaned in and captured his lower lip between her teeth and gently tugged. She flicked her tongue along the edge of his lip.

His arms folded around her until he was pressed the length of his body. He kissed her. The brush of his short whiskers pressed against her upper lip. His lips, those whiskers exhilaratingly sexy. This man was dynamite. She clung to his forearms and savored the taste of him.

He pulled away, but his eyes remained on her face. "I've been wanting to try that since I picked up Meg's book your first day."

"Whew … I didn't expect."

"No, me either, but—" His gaze held promise.

"You certainly know how to throw someone off-guard."

He laughed. "Good, I like that." He moved out of her way. "I think I should probably go grill the steaks before I follow you in that room and help you undress. Too soon." He retreated to the kitchen.

As she pulled off her kayaking shorts, her imagination flipped through scenarios as though she were an animation chart. She wanted him and would have eagerly trailed him in here. Where had that come from? Did Tina's conversation plant that wantonness in her mind? When had she ever kissed someone like that? Especially on the first — was kayaking and dinner a date? She needed to readjust more than her clothes. She yanked on her jeans. She couldn't go out and sit next to him with her body still tingling from his kiss, her body wanting more.

Think of something awful. She needed something to make her a sensible woman not a wanton one. She pictured Griscom in their bed before lovemaking. His kisses never brought out the response that David's just had. Thinking of lovemaking with Griscom dampened her body needs. She never felt consumed by restlessness and desire in anticipation of any physical contact with Griscom.

If David kissed that way and created such a raging passion with one kiss, what would it be like if they explored more? *Down girl. Think of Griscom, cool off.*

She focused Griscom's face and walked back to the kitchen her imagination and libido under control. David had the salads and side dishes laid out on the counter. He had the steaks, a grilling mitt and utensils in his hands.

"What can I do to help?

He nodded to the plates, napkins and silverware he had lined up on the counter. "You could set the table. Would you rather eat in the kitchen or on the deck? Deck has a better view." He opened the deck door with his hip.

A flurry of activity along side of the cabin caught her attention. Deep laughter from David outside near the grill followed. "Wild turkeys. They think they're tough."

"They come right next to your porch?"

"Be careful when you leave. They run out in groups and can be dangerous to cars."

Caroline edged to the window and peeked at the turkeys. One peered back at her. Turkeys that didn't fly away and weren't on a Thanksgiving table. Eye to eye contact with a wild turkey would be another memory of how different their places were.

David joined her carrying a platter of steaks.

Caroline pointed to the turkeys clustered in the yard. "Looks like some of the Seattle commuters who try to stare me down on the freeway."

David laughed. He placed the platter, ushered her to a seat

and sat across from her. "I've only seen Seattle in pictures. Puget Sound, salmon, sailing." He sat down. "But it is a city. How are you surviving in our small city?"

"I miss a Starbucks on every corner." She helped herself to pasta salad and passed it. "I'm discovering new things I enjoy."

"Such as?"

"The book shop. People are welcoming." She ate a bit of salad. "I don't have the headaches I might if I owned it. I like helping readers find books. Lots less pressure than the old job."

They ate in silence. Then she asked. "Were you always a principal?"

"No, worked in Philadelphia for public relations firm." He stabbed a piece of steak.

She tilted her head. "Big shift. What made you go into education?"

He paused, studied a spot through the big windows leading to the outside. "Life changed. I wanted something more meaningful and my life ..." He maneuvered tortellini around his plate. "More meaningful." He looked up. "With little kids, there's always 'hope.'"

She stopped eating. What an extraordinary man. "Meaningful, hope" not the usual phrases she heard from the men around her. "More percentages." "Cost management. "Narrow margins".

He entertained her the rest of the evening with tales of children's look at the world. An unusual man who believed in hope, enjoyed his career, dealt with children yet wasn't married and had no children of his own. Something is not right in his story, something was missing. He dodged or left out the motivations for changes. Of course, she hadn't shared her real reason for being in Lakeside either.

The night passed. She helped clean up. David had music as background throughout the evening. When John Legend's *Slow Dance* began, Caroline squealed. "Oh, one of my favorites. I listen to his music in the car and whenever."

David turned up the volume. "One of my favorites. I sat for hours in the rain to hear him play in Philly."

He walked around the counter and stood close enough she felt warm breath on her cheek. "May I have this dance, my lady?"

With one arm wrapped around her waist and her hand ensconced in his in a classical dance pose, he swung her around the room dodging chairs and tables. Legend's lyrics were sensual, but not as enticing as the strength and the warmth of the man holding her.

She tilted her head and watched the ceiling spin as he whirled her across the floor. John Legend's music had never touched her soul the way it did in this kitchen.

She nestled her head in the hollow of his collarbone. His arms wrapped around her waist. She closed her eyes inhaling the moment. Luckily, Seattle was faraway and she could savor this moment.

•

He pulled her closer until her features melted into his. He knew very little about Miss Caroline Ferraro except that he was attracted to her smile, her laugh. Something about her that inflamed that attraction. The mystery of a woman.

He had given up daydreaming about the future after the loss of Joy. Lately, Caroline's fingers, the delicate motion of her hands as she handled books invaded his thoughts. Those long slender fingers against his bare skin.

The day he met her, he reappeared not even knowing if she liked Chinese food or if she would slam the door in his face. He had just wanted to see her again.

Meg noticed a difference and admitted she felt a strong connection with the stranger who fit so well in the book shop and in the town.

He swirled her out and then back into the tight circle of his arms. She tilted her head back and laughed—a joyous, free laugh. Her eyes sparked. Her face radiated delight.

The song ended and both stood mesmerized by the dance and the closeness.

"I've never done that before … been that spontaneous. Or danced like that." Again, a smile lit up her whole face. Made him want to smile with her. I brought about that smile.

"I … me neither." He held both her hands in his. "This could start a revolution for both of us." His finger danced up the inside of her arms. She shivered. His left hand rubbed her cheek.

She broke his gaze. "I'm not looking for … I—" She looked away. "Depending on how fast I seal the deal on property here, will determine when I return."

"You bought property already?"

"I inherited from a relative." She moved back from his arms. She gazed out the window. "As soon as I sell it or rent it, I go back home to Seattle. I have to leave. Thank you for the kayak and the dinner. What a great adventure."

David remained rooted to the spot. What had happened he wasn't quite sure. He held her in his arms and it felt so right. He wanted to kiss her, wanted …wherever that kiss would lead. She responded to his touch, his kiss and wanted more. And then she moved away.

When she reached the door, he followed her to the car. He held onto her door so she couldn't just drive away. "At least while you are in Lakeside, we could have dinner, see each other."

"As friends, I would like that," She started her car. "Another kayak trip, and I'll cook dinner. I can't make any connections here." She tossed her hair back with her fingers. "I would like to kayak more." Her smile returned. The tension and practiced answers had been replaced by her warm smile.

"We can kayak every weekend. I have some afternoons free. And we can try moonlight kayaking." Moonlight kayaking opened possibilities.

"I had a wonderful time. I'd like to do this again." She reached through the open car window and squeezed his fingers.

Her parting words gave him hope. He stood in the circle of his driveway long after her car disappeared around the bend. His body tingled with energy and life. A long time since he allowed himself to feel so deeply. Maybe if he let himself connect even if it only meant a short time before Caroline returned to Seattle, he could bury Joy once and for all.

•

Caroline wandered through the house when she returned. She couldn't sit, she couldn't read. She needed to return soon. That man's arms had magnetism she never found with anyone else. She needed to get away from that pull before she made a fool of herself. With a touch of his hand and another one of the intense kisses and she would have pulled him into a bedroom.

His kisses ignited a passion she had almost acted on. She never reacted this way to a man. She usually had more control and didn't bend to her animal instincts.

A million thoughts swirled in her mind. She called Tina.

"Wow, unexpected call, anything wrong?" Tina's voice sounded good.

"No-o." How could she explain her restlessness, her questioning, her reasons and reactions? "Just checking in. How's your painting doing? Out of your slump?"

Silence. Then Tina blurted, "I'm not falling for that. You didn't call for that. How's Mr. Hottie? How were the kayak and dinner?"

Caroline heard shuffling as though Tina were moving papers.

"What are you doing home early, no hot passion? Is he interested in someone … or only interested in men?"

She giggled. She missed Tina's wisdom and wisecracks. Caroline curled on a sofa and described her evening with David.

"Why did you leave? Sounds as if he were ready and you certainly were tuned into your body's needs. You could be having hot sex right now."

"I can't get involved right now. I need to find my ancestors, sell the house, return to Seattle."

"So? Doesn't mean you can't have steamy passion while you do those. Sounds like his kisses indicate he might be interested in action. Perfect setup—one most males like—sex, no strings. What better situation for both of you?"

"It's not like I would do that at home—one-night stand

with someone. I didn't with Griscom."

"You're not at home—that's the point. And you need someone to erase that Griscom from your memory. Seduce the man—then let me know how that worked."

"Enough." She needed to get Tina off this subject. A seduction scene already flickered through her mind. Images of David's naked chest already danced inside her head. Time to think of something other than David Montgomery. "How's the house cleaning coming? Unearth any finds, dead bodies, missing china?"

When the economy took a dive, Tina's painting sales had dropped and Tina had to give up her beloved loft. She needed a place to stay. In exchange for rent and a space to spread out and paint, she helped Caroline sorted through Annabelle's antiques and boxes in the overstuffed attic.

"I have need-to-go piles and heaps of things torn, dirty, mismatch. Mounds of you-need-to-decide and piles to donate. Tons of trash—old notes, torn books, unrecognizable items. I've looked up the antique items and tried to price them with information online."

"Thanks for all the help and being willing to tackle that monstrous job."

"Thanks for giving me a place. I'd be homeless, all my paints in a shopping cart. Cleaning up is fair trade."

"Cleaning gives you enough time to paint as well."

"Yes. That is just perfect. I'm sending you a box of clothes."

"Clothes, I can sort through whatever of Annabelle's clothes you dug up …"

Tina squeals of laughter ended whatever thought Caroline had.

"No, *your* clothes. You can't keep wearing the same outfit. Not if you want Mr. Hottie's attention."

"I don't need clothes to …"

"You are so out of practice finding a real man. You need all the help you can get."

Caroline sighed. Tina could be an exasperating friend, but she did need something more suitable. She didn't need power suits and long sleeves in Jersey early summer weather. "I do."

"I can help you out here. I looked up the weather and

the town and already sent you two boxes. I sent you items appropriate for your life ... and Mr. Hottie."

Caroline chuckled. Only Tina. "Okay. Thank you for the clothes. I do need them, I guess. I'll keep you posted about Mr. Hottie. Don't keep your hopes up. I'm only here for a few weeks."

"Remember that and move faster than you usually do. Don't overthink this and make lists—just do it."

With Tina's advice ringing in her ears, she hung up. Just do it. She chuckled and slowly walked upstairs. She should have had this conversation before the evening started.

Then she wouldn't have this disappointed edge. She wasn't like Tina, but David's bare arms and chest could entice to take her friend's advice.

CHAPTER SIX

Refilling bookshelves was a constant. A book dropped from the shelf and as she grabbed it by the open cover and gasped. Annabelle's distinctive scribble lined the top of the page. The book thudded on the floor.

Annabelle had been in Readers' Haven Book Shop and exchanged a book here. Annabelle had been here. Had she talked with Larkin or the book group? A wave of nausea and a dull ache inside her chest overpowered her She gripped the shelf for support. Annabelle never mentioned Lakeside or any person in it. Why hadn't Annabelle told her about this place? The innkeeper said she never saw her with anyone.

What secret was here? She buried the urge to heave the book at the bookcase. At the moment, knocking down every bookcase tempted her. That wouldn't be fair to Larkin. She drew in a deep breath. *Calm yourself.*

"Caroline?" David peered around the shelves. "I ... Caroline." He reached for her. Took the book from her hand. "You okay? Something is bothering you? I'm a good listener."

Her anger still strangled any words forming. How could she explain without listing all the confusion fogging any rational thoughts?

David placed the book on a shelf next to Caroline and held both her hands in his. "Some buried secrets you're not willing to share?"

"No." She released her hand. "I'll be fine."

He frowned. "What is it?"

The ringing of the entrance bell pulled them quickly apart.

Irene arrived with bags of books to exchange. "I'm surprised to see you, David. Thought you would be camped out next to Meg's bedside."

Caroline followed David out from behind the stacks. "Meg is sick?"

Irene swung the two large bags onto the counter. "She has spells where she can't get around. David usually spends every moment there."

Caroline rang up Irene's discount. His hands jammed in his pockets. Everything usually flowed off him.

"David, you want coffee?" If she detained him, she could ask about Meg. Obviously, whatever Irene blurted disturbed him. "Irene, do you want to look for books now, or would you rather wait until later today when the reading group is here?"

Caroline said a silent prayer. Irene liked to flaunt her knowledge of the latest books available and announce the details of the reviews. If she chose her books later, she could show off for the other women.

Irene fell for the bait. "I just needed to get all those out of my car. I'll be back later." Irene waved as she sashayed out the door.

Caroline poured coffee for David. "Is Meg all right? Can I do anything for her?"

David stirred his coffee more times than necessary. He enunciated each word slowly as if measuring each before he spoke. "Occasionally Meg's wheelchair is not enough. She has difficulty getting around so she rests at home until it passes. She doesn't like anyone fussing over her. She's a very private person. I'll tell her you asked about her." He sipped his coffee.

Caroline researched too many medical cases to fall for David's lines. What made Meg incapable of getting out? What was the extent of her injuries? Did the recovery of those injuries come with an addiction to pain pills? They usually came hand in hand. Severe body injuries caused much pain. The treatment caused long-term side-effects. She'd bet good money David was protecting Meg.

"Tell her I miss her and the roses are loving the coffee she suggested."

David chuckled.

"You will let me know if she needs anything." She scribbled

her cell phone number on an index card. "Give her this. She can call me. I have nothing to do when I'm not working. I could get her groceries or whatever."

David flicked the card back and forth in his fingers.

"I'll tell her." He pocketed the card, sipped his coffee. "Nothing to occupy your nonworking hours, huh. I'll have to remedy that."

"I do have some things to do."

"So you telling me you won't go out with me?"

Caroline blushed as though she were a teen. "I have paperwork some nights, but I would love to go out with you."

The heat flushed through her whole body as though she were sixteen again and waiting to talk to a boy at a dance.

Irene returned an hour later with three others from the reading group. She handed Caroline a slip of paper. "The group thinks these might be our choices for July. Could you look up prices for new and used books and let me know if you have any here?"

Caroline typed *Orphan Train, Girls of Mischief Bay, Do or Die, CEO Buys In,* and *All I Ever Wanted.* "I've read the first two; they would be great for discussions." She jotted prices on a card and turned to the women. "How long has Meg been in a wheelchair? After her accident was there any hope she would walk?"

Irene and Abby exchanged glances. Irene turned the paperback over in her hand. "You don't know." The hushed tone was uncharacteristic of Irene.

Abby placed her hand on Irene's arm, stopping her rambling. "Meg likes Caroline. Meg has MS, which makes her wheelchair-bound. It was not an accident."

Caroline gasped. She ducked her head and tried to make sense of all the medical jargon spinning in her head. She paused getting her emotions under control. Multiple Sclerosis. This was not good news.

"MS. Multiple Sclerosis." Caroline watched their faces to assure herself they were discussing the same thing. She had done extensive research for Dr. Stein. Types and symptoms flicked through her mind as though she were flipping through flash cards. "Which type?"

"One of the worst." Irene leaned over the counter as though she were sharing a deep secret. "It's fatal. She's lucky to have survived this long."

"When did Meg have her last relapse?"

"Relapse?" Her face scrunched as if she had offered a sour pickle.

Dr. Stein, the neurologist, had said it was a misunderstood illness. Patients rarely revealed that they were living with the disease because those misinterpretations made life miserable. Caroline rephrased. "Does she get this way often?"

"No," Irene took the card from Caroline. "She has had few times like this. Usually she is out of commission for a short period."

"She has been in a wheelchair for seven years," said Abby. "She has been hospitalized four times."

Caroline nodded and let the information wash over her. "Where is Meg now?"

"She is fatigued and having difficulty moving. She cannot maneuver her wheelchair. She's at home."

"By herself?" Caroline's breath caught in her throat. Meg needed help and these women were so nonchalant and so uninformed.

Irene rubbed her cheeks with her fingers. "David goes there after work. Meg has a visiting nurse who comes in." Irene waved her hand as if waving away a gnat. "During the day— more than once."

"Do you help Meg during the day, too?" Caroline stacked paperbacks on the counter. If she kept Irene in the store, she could find out more. "We only have one copy of each of your choices, but I know we can order new or used for you and have them in a week."

Irene nodded. "We will talk and I'll call you with the order." She paused at the door. "We can't be of much help to Meg. She has a nurse."

Abby glanced at Irene and then the floor. "I call, but she seems tired."

As soon as the women left, Caroline fled to the back stacks to filter this information. Meg had Multiple Sclerosis. She hadn't been injured in an accident. Meg. Time with her promised warmth, conversation and a unique upbeat day. What would Meg need?

She closed her eyes. What Dr. Stein had said? Different types of MS existed. She leaned against the shelf. Meg was seriously ill. Caroline wiped her cheek with her sleeve. Crying wouldn't help anyone.

The vague knowledge she remembered from Dr. Stein wasn't enough. Caroline Googled Multiple Sclerosis and frowned. Certainly not fatal, as the women mistakenly thought, but a dreadful disease. MS attacks the brain, spinal cord and optic nerves.

One's life centered on the good times when you struggled with mobility and sometimes mental alertness, but a person could still have a life. And the bad times, one merely existed. She punched the off button.

Where is Meg in all this? It's such a hard disease to diagnose. Irene and Abby said seven years. She is fine, but it has gotten worse before. From the descriptions of the four types, her guess was Relapsing-Remitting. The patient would have flare-ups followed by recovery periods. *But I don't have the knowledge or understanding of the disease to know.* If what Dr. Stern had said is true. Meg won't discuss it. David said she was very private. Was that a clue to not ask her?

If her friends don't go see her, I will. I can't ease her situation, but I can entertain her or at least sit with her. She chose three books and two audible CDs from the oldies section. If she owned a Kindle or iPad, she could download more later. Meg likes biographies and she often picks up historical fiction.

She closed an hour early, detoured to shops on the Main Street. In a book discussion, Meg mentioned her weakness for chocolate. Next to the framing studio was a gourmet chocolate shop—one that made homemade chocolates and fudge daily. She normally avoided walking past. The smells were much too enticing. She stepped into the shop. Meg was right, one could not avoid chocolate. She grabbed a bite from the sample plate the owner had on the counter. Ah, rich dark chocolate.

She stopped home, dug the pruning shears and clipped two full red roses and a few barely open buds on the pink hybrid rose bush. With her hands full, she marched down the sidewalk.

She hesitated then knocked on the front door. *Did I misread the blooming relationship between them? What if Meg only thought of her as a bookstore friend?*

If Meg was incapacitated, she wouldn't be able to open the door. Caroline pushed the door open a few inches. "Meg, it's Caroline Ferraro, from Readers' Haven. I can leave if you don't want any company right now."

"Come in," a faint voice directed her. "Turn right past the hallway. I'm in the family room."

A formal living room led to a small room off the kitchen. Meg was stretched out on a recliner lost in all the covers and pillows. When Caroline held out the roses, Meg's glow returned to her cheeks.

"Roses! I can smell them from here." Meg stroked the outside of the leaves. "Good healthy roses. Colors are vibrant."

She unwrapped the damp paper towels around the stems. "I'm sorry, but I can't get up. I'm dependent on a visitor. If you look around in the kitchen, vases are on the bottom shelf beneath the sink."

Caroline arranged the flowers and carried them to the small table to Meg's left.

"These roses can thank you for their survival. They love the coffee grounds." She pulled a chair closer to Meg's recliner. "I wasn't sure what you needed."

"Your company is wonderful. Although I can't do much, lying around is boring."

Caroline handed her the books and chocolates. "These are to keep your spirits up." She placed the candy near the roses. "I have another box I'll put on the dining room table for your visitors."

"I don't have too many visitors."

"Do you need to rest?"

"No, no, I'm delighted you took the time to stop."

"Your preferences are biographies I know, but I haven't heard you talk about these copies." She held up each book for Meg's inspection.

"Oh wonderful! What great gifts—you touched all my weaknesses—roses, chocolates and books."

"I thought you might need mental stimulation. You're always active. Chocolates are a cure-all." She winced at her word choice. No cure here.

"Active in my chair?" She pulled at the blanket.

"You never miss a book club meeting. You participate in reading discussions and you always fix your tea or coffee and usually mine." She placed the CDs and earplugs on the table. "For days you might be tired and not up to sitting in the recliner, you can listen to audio books."

"I can't be a proper hostess. I can't offer tea, coffee or treats. You're a guest and I put you to work."

"We're past all that. You helped me during my first weeks with your wisdom, your knowledge of roses and your sense of humor." Caroline waved away her objections. "We're already family. If you can direct me, I'll make us tea or coffee."

Caroline returned to the kitchen. "Talk me through where I find things."

"I'll have tea, thank you. It's in the long cupboard to the left of the microwave. If you would like coffee, it's on the right. The coffeemaker is just below."

"You can look through your books and see if you want them all. I'll get us tea. Any favorite?"

Someone must care of her house even when Meg cannot. Everything was immaculate and ordered. She carried the mugs and pot to the dining room.

As Meg settled into the pillows, her hand trembled as she took the cup Caroline offered. She sunk into her pillows, her eyes half-closed. The animated Meg, who had been glad to see her, had disappeared.

"Does your visiting nurse visit whenever you need her?"

Meg waved her hand dismissing the idea as if it were an errant fly. "Jillian and I have a system we've developed over the years." She sipped her tea. "I don't like constant surveillance. If I need her, I call her, she can be here within ten minutes."

"I came to help, not for you to entertain me. Anything I can do for you while I'm here?"

Meg shook her head. She tapped the books. "Your gifts are so thoughtful. Tell me what's going on at the book shop." She passed the chocolates.

She nodded. "It's all new to me." She nibbled a dark chocolate cream. "Every day is different. Even book group and Irene are ... well, interesting."

Meg smiled. "You help many. The job fits you." She leaned back on the cushions. A deep sigh overtook her body.

Caroline picked up the teacups. "Let me clean these and help you get settled."

"I'd love to talk with you more, but ..."

"You need a rest." She gave her a quick hug. "I'll come back. We can have short conversations"

Meg closed her eyes. "I would really like that."

"Are you okay? Do you need anything?"

Meg held up a shiny disc on a chain around her neck. "Help is just a finger flick away."

"Okay. I'll finish the dishes and will see you later in the week."

Meg was asleep before Caroline could finish cleaning the tea service. She wrote her cell phone number with the note, *Call me if you need anything.*

CHAPTER SEVEN

On Friday, she set aside more books for Meg. She jotted notes from the MS website, ordered brochures to give to reading group. Visiting Meg had been the right thing to do. Something about her had touched her heart. She was a good friend even in that short time. Talking with David might fill in details.

He arrived late afternoon and walked right to the counter. He twirled a book over and over in his hands, and stared on a spot behind her head. What did he need to tell her? Like, *This is a dead-end. You're going back to Seattle. So long.*

"You stopped to see Meg." He gripped the book firmly in one hand. He tapped the spine on his palm.

"I took her gifts to keep her busy," Caroline said.

"She was glad you stopped. Touched that you would think of her." He crossed to the loveseat near the coffee stand and glanced at the dusk closing in. "Said you seemed to know ... understand what she needed." He licked his bottom lip. "Do you know someone with MS?" His words were soft, barely audible.

She moved around the counter. "I only know what I read."

He folded the sleeve on right arm. "She appreciated ... not many understand. You were ..." He rubbed his finger across the fold in his shirt. "A welcome ... needed company."

"I'd like to go back a couple times." She moved to the coffee counter. "Want a coffee or tea? Sit down." Lacing it with liquor might help more.

"Are you closing soon? Want to head to Townline Inn? I can't really drink anything in town and I think I'd like to celebrate Friday with something more than coffee." He stuffed his hands deep in his pockets.

When Caroline paused, David added. "I'll help so we can leave as soon as you finish your work."

She picked pieces of paper, counted her cash, placed it in the safe and finalized accounts while David cleaned the coffee pots.

"I'll drive," she said.

"Thanks. I could use a drink and getting a DUI is definitely not good. My car's right outside."

"Do you go to Meg's house often?"

"As many hours as I can squeeze in. At night, she has a nurse." He settled into the passenger seat. "I'll show you the way. I have no GPS in here."

She pursed her lips to bury the smirk. *Woo-woo!* She was driving a vintage sports car. Wait until she told Tina.

She headed out of town. "I have questions about her. Tonight a good night to ask?"

"If you are driving and I have a shot of Johnny Walker Black, I'll be ready for questions." He studied Caroline for a minute. "You have become a good friend. She talks about you. She wouldn't mind me talking with you."

"I like her. We clicked despite our age difference."

"Meg worries me. I can't do enough. A friend—someone to discuss Meg—is just what I need." He pointed to a side road with no visible street sign.

His words warmed Caroline. Worn by worry, he moved slower. The normal swing to his step was missing. Making him feel better would be a pleasure.

In the car, she followed his directions and pulled into the Townline, a log cabin tucked behind a curve. The bar looked as though it had been plucked from a *Sons of Anarchy* set. She expected to find motorcyclists complete with leather jackets and chains.

Inside were small intimate booths. Musical instruments were already set out on a small parquet floor. A wide age range of customers clustered in groups. College age grouped near the bar and tiny tables nearby. Older couples chatted around larger tables farthest from the music. The inside was quieter and welcoming, which surprised her. The number of people and the varied age range usually meant good food. A distinct aroma of garlic and tomatoes dominated the smells. She followed David to a table for two near large glass doors, which overlooked a garden and a meadow.

He ordered a Johnny Walker and eagerly gulped his first swig then settled back in his seat. "Good seafood here. Clams, crabs, and mussels are caught nearby. Fra Diablo platter if you like to burn the back of your throat while you slurp down clams, and mussels."

"Crabs aren't my usual, but I'll try your recommendations."

He held her hand. "If I entice you with the best Jersey has to offer, will you keep the property and stay?"

Her breathing stopped. Of course, David was joking. He barely knew her. "I'll feast on the best Jersey has to offer in the mean time. Sooner or later, I'll return to Seattle." Right now "later" had a better ring to it. Life in Seattle had no close intimate dinners with David or anyone who had eyes that caused her to forget her train of thought.

"I can wish. I like our time together."

"I'm glad to help you unwind. You seem tense." She sipped her Manhattan to gather distance and avoid being drawn into the appeal of intriguing man with the intense eyes. "This place is unusual and from what you say the food is good, but why so far?"

"Public employees, to whom many entrust their children, can't appear as though they are alcoholics."

"A drink with dinner is a problem?"

"Since you're driving, I may have more than one glass." He toasted her with his mug. "If three people see you out at a restaurant and each sees you with one drink, by the time that tale is told, that's now three drinks."

She laughed. "No one in Seattle knows that much about any one person."

"Lakeside, although a large city, still displays many small town traits."

"What brought you here, as a principal?" She rested her elbow on the table and rubbed her thumb on the back of his hand.

"I grew up here. I moved with my dad to Virginia for a

couple of years. I had ideas during college years, but not practical ones. I planned to go a different direction once." A shadow darkened his face. "Then Meg needed me. I stayed here. Education became my career."

Caroline swirled the ice in her glass. "Can I ask you things about her? Feel free to not answer … whatever she might be uncomfortable about."

"Meg trusts you. She had much to say about you yesterday. Patience is required to carry on a conversation. She fell asleep between sentences, phrases, then picked back up again. Sometimes it's hard for her …" He swallowed his scotch. "And me." He leaned back as the waitress delivered salad plates. "You know about the disease."

"As a researcher you know statistics, facts, not the humanity of it. I don't want to embarrass her. How long has Meg known about her MS?"

"Eight years ago her diagnosis was confirmed. At first, it was minor, yet shocking setbacks. Learning what it was, how to deal with it." He stabbed a tomato. "Within a year, her wheelchair was part of her life. "

"She's determined—not content but certainly seems at ease—confident with herself."

"Meg had tragedies long before MS. There's a toughness, a strength to her being." He toyed with the lettuce on the plate. "There's been more—minor, but frequent problems."

"What happens now?"

"We don't know. One never knows what tomorrow will bring."

Caroline stirred her raspberry vinaigrette dressing around with her fork "We bonded over roses." Sharing the rose book and talking was one of her fondest memories of the bookstore. "I like her. There's something there between us … different from what I've experienced before. How did you become so close? At first, I thought you were her son."

"Meg and my mother were best friends since early childhood. Meg has always been a part of my life especially …" David stopped talking. He stared at his salad as though he had discovered a bug. He flipped the fork onto his plate and turned to Caroline. "Are you close to your parents? "

"Dad died when I was seven. Mom died a year and a half ago."

David nodded. "I'm sorry to hear that. Family loss is tough." He laced his fingers together and rested his hands on top of the table. He focused on his fingers then finally leaned backed in the chair.

The smile plastered on his face wasn't the bone-tingling smile that jump started her heart, but an artificial smile she bet he saved for school occasions. A space opened between them as though he had physically moved to another table. What was he thinking and not telling her?

"Meg would adopt you as substitute parent. She wanted children. She's been through losses. She's a good listener if you are still mourning the loss of parents," he said.

Caroline's stomach churned. She winced at David's word choice. Which parental loss should she grieve? Which mother? The waitress placed a large dish of steamed clams and a bowl of melted butter before them. The smell was so inviting. Any worries about mothers were quickly forgotten.

He flipped two clams onto her plate. "You may pick them up with that little fork or—" He picked one up between his thumb and forefinger and tilted it into his mouth." He licked his lips. "Jersey style. That's how you eat raw clams as well. Try it."

The smell was enticing, she tilted her head back and swallowed a wet, juicy clam. Her instant "mmm" brought out another laugh from David. His eyes flicked across her face as though he had reached out and touched her.

He swallowed another clam and licked his lips. Concentrating on his hands, his lips and swallowing created an unsettling urge. Leaning across the table and capturing that bottom lip and sucking away the clam juice and butter crossed her mind. What would he taste like? Clams were alleged to be the great aphrodisiac, but she'd only had two.

"You like the clams." With his napkin, he reached over and wiped a spot of butter from her chin.

She nodded. "I did." Their gazes held. She couldn't look away. What was he thinking?

"Shh." He pointed outside. Deer grazed a few feet away. He

wrapped his arm around her shoulders. With her head resting on his cheek and her body tight to his, they shared the scene of a doe and two fawns searching the ground right on the other side of the window.

The appearance of three deer, the delectable taste of the clams and the nearness of David ... She snuggled closer. The arrival of the main course interrupted the moment.

"Wait until you taste the flounder with the crab. It makes catching a flounder worth it."

"This is wonderful." The fish melted on her tongue and she could become addicted to the taste of crab. "I don't eat seafood at home and I don't think I've ever eaten crab like this."

"You don't eat seafood and you live in Seattle?"

"Not like this." She nibbled on the crab on her fork. She finished a forkful of the flounder, sipped her drink. "Kayaks and clams, you've introduced me to wonderful elements."

"I have so much more I want to introduce you to."

The intimacy of the words heated her skin.

"Ahh clams are working on you. Please tell me the redness on your cheeks is connection you are feeling between us and not that you are allergic to seafood."

No witty reply tumbled off her tongue. She was so out of practice with attentive men. "Food is wonderful." What a lame comment to add.

David leaned back in his seat. His eyes danced, his slow smile created the magic flutter. "Next we'll try the Mike's crab cakes; they're famous. A moonlight kayak would be exciting. Lots of worlds to explore together."

After this dinner, she the word "explore" embrace new meaning. Meetings with this guy could become addicting. She closed her eyes and tried to imagine her street. She lived in ... somewhere miles away. See, even sitting near him and contemplating what she'd like to be doing fizzled her brain. She lived ... *What was the city's name ... Seattle. He lives in New Jersey. Get your head together.*

"Mr. Montgomery." A boy darted to the table. "Hi!"

"Hello, Cory, you here for dinner, too?"

The drink. Whew, only one glass of his scotch and it was empty. His school caught up with him. A dark-haired woman followed the boy. "Sorry to disturb the two of you."

The woman studied Caroline as if she were a bug in an exhibit. The hair rose on the back of Caroline's neck.

"His dad is playing in the band tonight. We came to hear the first set. Cory saw you and darted to the table before I could grab him." Again Caroline felt the woman's perusal. "Hope we didn't interrupt your dinner." She turned to Caroline. "I'm Miriam Chandler. I've known him since he was three. If you need any stories or information, I can fill you in."

Caroline rose, stretched out her hand. The woman held it, didn't shake it. "I'm Caroline Ferraro. I'm a friend of Meg." Who is this? An old flame? Was she a parent who wouldn't like seeing him in a bar?

"Oh really?" The woman's eyebrows rose, she turned to David. "Meg arranged this?"

David shook his head. "Relax, Miriam, I'm on a date. Go home and don't call my sisters. Go." He waved her away. "Good to see you, Cory, see you Thursday at intramurals." He ruffled the boy's hair.

"She is my sister's best friend and far too curious." He signaled the waiter for another drink.

"You have a sister?" She scooted her chair closer to David.

"Two of them. One is in Maine, the other Chicago, but Miriam will report to them both and will start a chain of phone calls. I have been tormented by sisters and their friends all my life."

"Do they come home?"

"You're safe. Carrieanne has a set of twins and a five-year-old who keep her busy and home-based. Gloria is an intern in Chicago—has no time to breathe. Home is not in her thoughts." He pushed his plate to the center. "Do you have siblings to harass you?"

She shook her head. Not that she knew of. If she found a parent, would she find siblings as well? She had tormented Annabelle about a sister.

"No brothers to support you in your fight against sisters?" She redirected the conversation.

"My brother is in North Carolina. He was my parents' afterthought and came along much too late to help me with

Carrieanne and Gloria."

The waitress dropped off the check and before she could grab it, David said, "My treat of introducing you to another specialty of New Jersey and—" He wrapped his arm around her waist as they headed to the door. "Our first date."

•

Why did I let her drive? Now she drops me off and leaves. I'm not ready for this night to end. I don't want an awkward moment in the car saying goodbye. Come inside to my bed isn't subtle or suave. What kind of men did she date in Seattle?

She hadn't mentioned many except that Gris—what was that odd name. He felt the sexual tension between them. Surely she did. This was easier with women he'd known all your life. He glanced at Caroline' s profile.

The ride home was shorter than he ever remembered. She stopped in front of his cabin.

"Great place, I do like crabs and clams—Jersey style." She gripped the steering wheel.

"You could come in. It's the weekend."

Her answer came slowly. She stared at a spot on the seat between them. "I don't think that's a good idea." She touched his arm. "I'm not good at this—it's been a long time. I feel like a sixteen-year-old."

"Glad you feel the same. You have jarred my adolescent hormones and I'm not sure what to do." He unlocked her seatbelt wrapped his arm around her shoulders and pulled her closer. He had her full attention. He sampled her lower lip with his tongue. "You still taste like crab. I love that taste." He smothered her lips with his.

She moaned a soft yielding moan and leaned into the kiss. He explored the inside of her mouth. She gripped his shoulders. She increased the pressure of her kiss.

He pulled away. "Come in the house with me."

She retreated to her corner. "Can't. It's not that I don't want. Oh, this is awkward. I'm so out of practice. I just don't do quickies and then turn and run back home."

The soft glow of his porch light beckoned them both inside.

Who cared about tomorrow or when she returned to Seattle? He wanted her inside now. He took a deep breath. And another. The tension left his shoulders and then the rest of his body.

"I know you think your life in Seattle is what you need to focus on." He tapped the upholstery. "But you are here now. You could enjoy the moment."

"Not tonight. I wasn't prepared for this. I should have thought … known. I'm just out of practice. Can we leave it at that? I'll think about the moments here." She put the car in drive. "Long after I leave."

He had nothing to do but exit the car. He watched her retreating taillights. That's not the way he wanted the evening to end.

He poured a tall glass of ice water. He placed it next to his cheek. He stood in the darkness leaning against the kitchen counter.

Long time since a woman had tied up his insides like that. He should thank her. A part of him he thought died with Joy was alive and active. He adjusted the front of his jeans.

He had certainly satisfied his physical needs before, but he never wanted anyone the way he wanted her tonight—not since Joy.

CHAPTER EIGHT

Saturday morning, she moved the books off her library shelves, dusted behind each row, polished the furniture, then mopped the kitchen floor.

Tina would have done something. She would have awakened in David's arms in a sensual bliss instead of tossing and punching her pillow. Last night ended awkwardly with David. *I'm out of practice.* Really? What she needed to practice were her passion skills. She tossed the duster across the counter. He would never call her again.

Her longest relationship was Griscom—but that wasn't passionate. David awoke a spark she hadn't felt since her college years. Chest hairs around his collar invited her touch.

His kisses threw her brain in neutral and set her body in control. She needed to listen to her body not her brain. What was wrong with her? Why couldn't Tina have rubbed off on her more?

Talking with Tina might help, but listening to Tina make fun of her wouldn't help her morning.

As though on cue, Tina called. "Hey, can you talk? I found something you need to know about. It may be nothing. You make that decision."

She stretched in the nearest chair.

"Found what? If it's a question about any one of Annabelle's antiques, make a decision. We have so much to sort ... I just don't care if we miss a few."

"Noo," Tina's coffee press hissed in the background. "It may be a clue—a baby clue. Or it could be nothing."

Caroline held her breath. The other talk was meaningless

now. "What?

"In an old dresser buried under the basement stairway was a bill of sale for an antique washstand. The address was Lakeside, New Jersey. Also inside the drawer was a baby bracelet."

"Any identification? Hospital? Last name?"

"No, it was the kind like mothers gave—little beads with the name 'Suzanne.'"

"Whew, Tina, any connection to the bill of sale? Any names?" Caroline chewed the cuticle on her thumb.

"Nothing. May be a freak accident they were both there. Do you want me to send them?"

"No, it is probably nothing. I only found information on Jennifer."

"Have you found any more about Jennifer's family or your mother or you?"

"I'm Jennifer. She was the only baby born at Lakeside General Hospital. I'm Jennifer. I cannot find anything about my parents."

"If you only found one bit of info for your doctors or surgeons, would you have quit? Annabelle sent you there. She wanted you to go there for some reason or she would have just sold the house and never told you about it."

"I don't think ..." She had no response. She would never have been satisfied with one answer and certainly not the first one. Had Annabelle planned for her to search?

"You're quiet, what's going on?" Tina's concern was evident even through the phone. "You did fly there to find answers. Why are you backing off?"

"I don't know. "

"Do you know what you will do if or when you find your family?"

"I may never find them, but I can't just go up and say 'Hi, I'm your daughter.' I don't want to disturb anyone's life. Just want to be able to see them, watch them"

"That would make you a lurker."

Tina would be flopped on the couch sipping her coffee. The click of the spoon against a mug was audible. Caroline poured a coffee and set it on the table near the front window. She rocked back and forth. "I had Grant and Annabelle. Why would I need anyone else? Annabelle and I had a great relationship."

"Finding out your roots doesn't make you disloyal."

"No, not disloyal." Just was like making Annabelle insignificant as though she weren't enough of a mother. But she had never felt that way until this house. Then all the questions surfaced.

"Did you learn anything about Annabelle's past? Do you know why Annabelle wanted you to come there."

"She didn't tell me about this house. Or anything about her coming here? How do you get she wanted me to come here?"

"She gave you the house and let you know you were born there. She knew you. She knew you would go there. Why aren't you exploring that?"

Caroline tapped her fingers against her upper lip and walked in a circle. She had no answers.

"Doing nothing isn't going to give you any info. You always have a million questions before you take the next step. Where are those questions now? Not like you to quit before knowing you have the final solution. You have absolute proof you are Jennifer?"

She paced as she listened to Tina's rant. Just accepting Jennifer left a metallic taste in her mouth. "There is more to this story. I settled for a simple answer."

"Get out there, girl. Let me know what you find next."

She hung up, heated up her coffee and sat on the porch. Annabelle had willed her this house in a special codicil not to be opened until a year after her death. What was here? Nothing would be hidden in a drawer. Renters, the realtors could find and destroy that.

She wandered through the house cup in hand. She pulled pictures off the wall looking for papers taped to the back. Maybe that only happened in movies.

She tapped walls. Hidden rooms or holes in the wall were only in movies, too.

She searched most of the afternoon and discovered nooks and crannies, but these only yielded a pink sugar bowl, a signed book and a letter dated 1966. Nothing that explained why Annabelle owned the house. Nothing that had anything about a baby named Jennifer. Nothing that provided a single clue.

Tina is wrong. This is just a wild goose chase.

She stomped up the stairs— No clues to her past existence. *Useless. Give it up.*

She'd enjoy her time here and go back to Seattle. She dressed in the glow of the moonlight. David was right. A moonlight kayak out to see the stars would be incredible. She hadn't really paid much attention to the stars or moon in Seattle. Nights were spent walking to meetings with her heels clicking on the sidewalk. How those heels hurt her feet after a long day at work.

For fun in Seattle, she went to movies. She and Griscom attended as many of the Oscar nominees as possible. They checked off the lists of nominees. Lists again.

She fluffed her pillow. Tina. She chuckled. Tina got her into things. They attended art openings, listened to authors at the libraries and went to crazy movies off the main streets. Tina brought out the best, her more adventurous side.

She bunched another pillow behind her head. She had no trouble wheedling records, facts, studies from reluctant surgeons or doctors or office managers in Seattle to get the facts she needed. Surely, she could use those skills here to unearth records of babies born at Lakeside General.

Babies floating in cribs next to her kayak, mingled with babies with faces covered by paper and red tape, jumbled with Starbucks coffee cups stacked in the moonlight and Tina's and David's voice trying to tell her something—all interrupted her sleep. At two, she threw off the covers and fixed herself a chamomile tea and curled up on a wicker chair in the porch. She rubbed her temples. Too much.

Should she see him more and take advantage of a friend with benefits? Should she continue to look for family and the unknown past? No wonder sleep is impossible. So many decisions. Usually decisions involved others' lives—they were easier.

She stretched her neck over the back of the chair. She could go to the hospital Medical Records department to see if they stored old records, see if she could look for names. She'd bullied medical staff for answers before.

And, yes, going out with David more would be awesome. Bet she'd get better sleep if she and David took care of her needs. And why shouldn't she? The power and sensuality of his kisses tickled her fancy—her toes—her primal needs. Exploring where those kisses lead, and what response she incited ... After kayaking and certainly after that dance, it took fortitude to drive away and not go inside to his bed. But fortitude didn't fulfill any primal need and didn't let a person sleep. Less fortitude, more fun. When had she'd become such a stodgy person at thirty-one.

Sleepiness evaded her even with chamomile tea. She searched for her iPad and scuffled back to her favorite chair. A list! That helped her organize. Once again, Tina prodded her into action. She gulped her remaining tea. She was a damn good researcher, one doctors and surgeons requested. She couldn't settle for the little she had found. She would regret it once she returned.

Larkin was planning to come to the shop with the baby for a few hours on Monday. She'd double-check to make sure those plans haven't changed. That would be the perfect opportunity to go look for records. Step one, research more. Check local records.

She would also call David tomorrow, ask him out for dinner—here. Perfect. David deserved more than a name on a list. She now had a plan of action for two items.

She rinsed her dishes. Decisions made. Plans in place. Now she could sleep.

The next day, she had a colossal headache. If she'd been out partying all night, she could understand this. Just no sleep. She cut flowers and placed vases in the kitchen, on the porch and in the library. She touched the spines of the books in the library.

With her finger on the cover, she studied each title. Nothing. She pulled out a few and flipped through the pages. No hidden letters, forgotten notes. Nothing is here. She sank into the chair. Maybe there was no reason Annabelle came here.

She just found antiques in the area and bought the house for the convenience. But she left it to her.

Stephanie said she visited a cemetery. Eeww, digging

around graves? May be a clue there. She flipped through picture on her iPad and found an old one of Annabelle. She had no idea where to look in a cemetery. Maybe someone there could help or would remember her mother.

Caroline tied her walking shoes and donned her light windbreaker. Every morning, Annabelle visited the cemetery around 6:30. She 'd follow her path.

"Odd" could only describe Annabelle's actions. She disliked arising early. Who visited cemeteries? Why? Another one of the many unexplained why's since she learned she owned a house across the country.

She stopped her jog in front of Morningstar Cemetery. Although the sun peeked behind clouds, the air felt chilly. The sky darkened as soon as she stepped in front of the gate. Too many late-night readings of Stephen King novels.

Part of the cemetery was old, dated in 1830s—tall, stately trees shaded the older sections. Pathways between sections were well kept. It was easy to read names without tramping all over grave sites. She wandered down pathways lined with flowers, ivy or pebbles. She peered at tombstones, markers. Looking for … what she wasn't sure.

A man dressed in khakis and dark Henley shirt stopped. "You appear lost. Can I help you find a section or a last name?"

She focused on the spot below his right shoulder. What could she tell him?

"I'm Pete Sangfer, caretaker for Morningstar Cemetery." He looked too young to be spending his days among the dead.

"I'm doing a genealogical search." The lies came so easy. "But I can't remember the names my mother said she had found." A bright idea. She dug in her purse and produced a picture. "My mother visited our relatives buried here every year. Do you recognize her and would you know where she went?" She smiled her brightest smile. *Please know where Annabelle went in here. Give me some answers to work with.*

He glanced at the picture and then handed it back. "I just took over for my uncle. He's been caretaker of this place for over thirty years. I've helped out here and she looks familiar, but you can't rely on me."

She should have known—even this would be difficult. She

drew her zipper up and down.

"He likes to come and just hang out with me. He hates retirement and his mind is getting a little fuzzy. He remembers facts, details about the past." He leaned against the tree. "If you don't mind listening to him ramble about the people he's known who ended up here, you could come on any Monday and talk with him. Bring the picture."

She shook his hand. "Oh thank you. That would be so helpful. If he can give me any information about my past— about the relatives I can't find, I'll listen to any story he wants to tell me."

Pete nodded. "It would be good for him to think he helped someone. Meet me at the gate house. It's to the left of the main entrance. He is better in the morning."

She had a start. Maybe a doddering old man would remember. Not much to go on, but a step. At least she would know why Annabelle visited the cemetery and that should help with why she came here.

CHAPTER NINE

Monday, Caroline dressed in a pantsuit. Larkin coming in with Dylan would deflect book club's questions and interest in her leaving for a few hours.

At the bookstore, she dusted the shelves and straightened the books. Would Larkin think she'd done a good job keeping up her shop? She tossed the duster behind the counter. Who was she kidding? What did she care what Larkin thought? What's she going to do—fire you? She should be worrying about your real job miles away. She hadn't thought about that job or heard from Jean in days. She flicked on the coffee maker.

"Look at you. Irene asked as she dropped her huge leather bag on the round table. Others trickled in behind her.

She rearranged the cups near the coffee pot. "Hopefully, you all plan to be here for a while and have coffee and a snack." She faced them and crossed her hands in front of her. "Larkin and Dylan are coming for a visit."

"A visit?"

"We get to see the baby."

The women filled their coffee cups, moved chairs in a circle with an opening for Larkin and waited.

When Larkin pushed a stroller through the door, the women rose in unison. Caroline rushed forward to divest Larkin of the three overly stuffed bags Larkin pushed her way into the middle of the women, pulled back the cover of stroller, Dylan smiled and kicked the covers to the delight of his audience.

She nodded at Larkin. "You've got your audience and you certainly know what to do." She grabbed her bag with her notes. "Call me if you need me to come back earlier."

Caroline paused at the top of the stairway leading to the Records Department. What could she possibly say? She was teetering on overstepping the law. She pulled her small wallet and her Andoer ID and drew a deep breath.

A lone young woman operated the reception desk.

"Good morning." She straightened her suit jacket. "I'm Caroline." No use faking this—it would be easy to trace her. "I need your help." She flattened her ID on the counter. "I'm a researcher. We need records for births."

She tapped the top of her ID. What would sound plausible? "We need to research family records. We're looking for babies born in March, 1978."

The girl said nothing but picked up the card. Caroline's heart pounded against her ribs. This is so wrong. Are there fines, imprisonment for looking at private records? Had to be something. We have HIPAA for everything. Of course, presidents found ways to check on everyone—no privacy.

"Andoer in Seattle. I know a guy there. Glen Evenerly works there."

Glen, Glen, she knew a Glen, where did he work? Of course, Andoer's records. "I know him, nice guy." Tall guy, tiny glasses, big Adam's apple, but always happy. "Works in our records. Good friends?" *God, don't call Andoer.* She glanced at the counter. *This is so wrong.*

"Lost touch after he moved to Seattle. Heard he got married. Tell him hi. I'm Lindsey."

"Yeah, I'll tell him." *Whew, that was close.*

"You're the senior researcher. This must be important to send you to little Lakeside." She returned the ID. "I'll help you as much as I can." She swept her hand across the pile of files beside her. "They hired me just to get all the files in the computer. Come on."

She led Caroline to an adjacent room. "You can work here. I'm the only one here this morning. I'll help you when I can. I'll get files for 1978. Not all of that year is on our computer system." She pulled a sticky notes pad from her back pocket. "Good to see a real face. This is much better than sitting at the computer for hours." She bounced off.

Caroline sat at a long table waiting Lindsey's return. A

nagging guilt gnawed at her stomach. *This is so wrong.* She taking advantage of her just because she is young and trusting.

Lindsey jogged back in the room with a load of files in her arms. "You look through these. I have more. I can whiz through them."

Caroline flipped through paperwork looking for birth certificates or anything with Anna or Gram Feratti. She stretched. Her pile of rejects grew. Nothing.

Just one tidbit of information could open this up. That's how it worked at Andoer. She followed even the minutest strip of information, it opened reams of material that doctors used.

Lindsey returned. "I found birth certificates for March. This one." She waved the copy in her hand. "Was misfiled. And still isn't recorded." She handed her a copy.

Caroline placed the copy on the table and pushed the files away. "Thank you. This helps." Her voice sounded shrill. *Keep it together. Another baby. Wait until the too-eager Lindsey leaves.*

"Glad I could do something," Lindsey said.

As soon as she left, Caroline stared at the data. Her hands shook. *Suzanne Clare Kelly. March 13, 1978. Suzanne.* Tina's baby bracelet. Another baby. *Parents: Jeffrey Kelly and Margaret Whitcom Kelly.* She ran her thumb across the names. She had something. Kelly? Kelly. That last name, it had been in another file. *Where? Come on, think.*

She quickly flipped through the files. Kelly. On the third from the bottom of the stack, she pulled the marriage certificate of Margaret Whitcomb Kelly from the file. Payday. Two pieces of data could lead to more. She typed down the statistics in her iPad.

"Do you want me to copy that as well?"

She had been so engrossed in her findings she hadn't heard Lindsey's entrance. She hesitated.

Lindsey held out her hand. "I already copied the other. No one else is here today."

"Thank you." She straightened the files and slipped her notebook and the copied birth certificate in her bag. She found another lead. She used her credentials and lied to get it. Certainly not the professional woman. But this was personal.

Lindsey handed her the copy of the marriage certificate.

Caroline nodded. "I'll tell Glen I saw you when I return to Seattle."

The information waiting in her bag nagged her the rest of the day at work. Luckily, the book group left when Larkin did. She sat in the chair facing the street. She opened her laptop and typed in Margaret and Jeffrey Kelly

A multitude of links jumped for Jeffrey Kelly. She explored a few. Jeffrey on Facebook was only nineteen and wanted a woman. Jeffrey in Omaha ran a tax service. Jeffrey in Montana owned an Arabian horse farm. This could take forever. She would just have to keep a list and cross them off. Nothing appeared for Margaret Kelly.

She found one listing for Margaret Whitcom. An article about her winning a New Jersey spelling bee in 1974. The baby, Suzanne's mother had been here in 1974 and 1978. That was all she could find.

Sophia Whitcom had many articles about her accomplishments as fundraiser and volunteer in Lakeside. Chester Whitcom had been mayor in 1978. She found nothing to link Margaret to Chester or Sophia. Nothing to link any of this to Annabelle or herself.

She closed the laptop cover to help a young mother search for books for her three-year-old. The three-year-old grabbed a book and trotted to the front.

"I guess he already has opinions on reading."

The mother chuckled. "He loves books. Carries them everywhere. Good sign I guess. Buying books here makes us both happy."

The two rambled down the pathway toward town. This job was easy. She just made people smile.

As soon as she returned to her house, she covered the library table with large white sheets of paper. She wrote *Jennifer* on one side of the paper, drew a long line then wrote *Suzanne* on the top of the other side. Under each baby's name, she jotted all the information she had so far: birthdates, parents' names, weight, length, and doctor. The babies were born days apart— their parents had to have crossed paths at the hospital. She could be either one of these babies. Or not.

Dr. William Morgan had delivered them both. A great lead. If she could find him, he might remember something. Maybe he was a witness to the adoption. If he were still alive. Maybe he was an older doctor in 1978.

Two babies. Another possibility. She leaned back in her chair. A good day. Tina was right. More information was out there.

A text beeped on her phone. "Clothes arrive tomorrow. Wow, Mr. Hottie with your new look. Enjoy time you have left there."

Caroline laughed and ran her thumb over the message. Only Tina.

CHAPTER TEN

She rested the box on her hip and gripped the bags with her left hand. She had closed Readers' Haven for a few moments, walked to post office to pick up her packages from Tina. She stored them behind the counter. Every time she climbed over the boxes and saw Tina's familiar scrawl, she chuckled. Only Tina would think to send more casual—and more appropriate clothes. Of course, trusting Tina's judgement was scary.

At the end of the day, she dragged one box to Greystone then returned for the other. She piled them in the kitchen while she prepared a quick soup and sandwich supper.

She sipped her tomato soup from a cup as she unpacked the first box. Clothes. The first thing was a tiny bikini she hadn't worn in years with an attached note from Tina. "Wow, Mr. Hottie and jump in the water—figuratively and realistically." She shook her head and tossed it on the nearest chair. She unfolded her summer slacks, her capris and carried them upstairs to her bureau.

She soon filled drawers and closets. Three photos were securely wrapped within a nightshirt. A photo of she and Annabelle went on the night stand and placed the picture of she, Grant and Annabelle on the bureau. Tina sent a recent mug shot with the caption, "Don't forget me." She hummed as she placed the last of her clothes away.

When she left for work on Wednesday, she wore capris and a Henley shirt. She could get used to this change. No black pantsuits with hot, scratchy collars. Easy to wear clothes. She sat on the floor with kids, climbed on ladders to check the top of tall shelves.

She had started to water the plants when her first customer walked in.

"Good morning, where's Larkin?" A neatly dressed, white haired man entered carrying a paper grocery bag bulging with books. Caroline paused, sprinkling can in her hand.

"She and Ryan had a baby boy. I can help you." She ducked behind the counter as he hefted a stack of books onto the counter.

"I'm out of the loop. Larkin had a baby?" He stroked his chin. "I delivered Larkin. I used to know when all the babies were born." He placed a 3x5 card on the marble counter. "I'm sorry, I sound like a doddering old man. I'm William Morgan. I was the obstetrician in Lakeside for years."

Caroline dropped the watering can. A river of water poured over her shoes. She dove to the floor, and patted up the water. Anything to give herself time. Dr. William Morgan. His name was imprinted on Jennifer's and Suzanne's birth certificates. He knew facts.

The doctor peered over the counter. "Are you all right?"

She tossed the wet towel into the trash can, took a deep breath and stood. "I pinched my finger on the can. I didn't want the water to spill on any book." She picked up the index card. "What can I help you find?"

The man oozed confidence. "While we are visiting, my wife and I join other couples in a book club. This is a list of the books. Also, Mary added a few, she's interested in."

She glanced at the list. Visiting. I only have a short time to ask … ask what? Could she trust him not to talk to others? "Some we have. This series by Mallery is popular. The books go out as quickly as they come in. JoJo Moyes is also popular, but I just got two of hers in. I can order any others. How long will you be staying?"

"Just until Memorial Day weekend. Order the series. Mary wants those. You can gather the other ones and I'll be back." He glanced around the store. "Larkin and Ryan have created an inviting place here. Tea? How much?'

"You can have tea and a sticky bun for a dollar."

His grin and mannerisms exuded warmth and comfort. Bet he soothed a pregnant mom's fears. She studied him as he poured the tea.

"That's a bargain. I'll be in here often in next two weeks. All those grandchildren all at once can get to me." He bit into a sticky bun, licked the icing off his top lip. "Mary loves all the commotion. I'll escape to here. Read in the quiet." He carried his brewing tea and bun to the counter. He flipped over the 3x5 card and jotted down a number. "If you have trouble finding anything, call me."

She reached for the card and flipped it back and forth on her fingertips. She took a deep breath. "You said you delivered Larkin, you were the obstetrician here?"

He nodded. "From 1967 to 2000, I delivered almost everyone here."

"In 1978, you would have delivered all the babies."

He placed his sticky bun on a napkin on the counter. He dipped his tea bag in and out of the cup. "Yes, I was the only one in town most of my practice. Others, Thompson Wharton arrived in 1998."

"In 1978, you would have delivered a Jennifer Feratti and a Suzanne Kelly?"

The doctor continued to dip his teabag up and down in the plastic cup.

The chime on the door shattered the tension.

"Car-o-line." Irene's loud, screechy voice noted the arrival of the reading group members.

"Irene Scholfield." Dr. Morgan's scurried over to Irene's side leaving his sticky bun and tea on the counter. "Look at all of you." He glanced over his shoulder at Caroline. He then greeted each woman with an embrace of handshake.

So Doc Morgan, you know everyone and delivered everyone. You paused too long when I asked about Jennifer and Suzanne and you are hiding behind Irene. You know something.

She tried to stay busy the rest of the day, but questions she wanted to ask that doctor interrupted any sane thought.

When she returned home, she cut a few fresh flowers for inside. She should go check on Meg today. She clipped more roses. She decorated the study and the parlor with flowers, then wrapped the roses in wet paper towels and a plastic bag. She tucked a Godiva chocolate bar in her purse and headed to

Meg's.

"Meg," she hesitated at the door.

"Here, come on back."

Meg's voice was stronger. She was still seated in the lounge chair, but she sat up without being propped by pillows.

"It's good to get company."She smoothed her hair with the tips of her fingers. "It's getting a little boring around here."

"I'm here to entertain. It was getting a little boring around my place, too." She handed her the flowers and pulled out the candy bar.

"Ahh, you know my weaknesses."

"If that's all they are, you're in good shape." Caroline pulled up the chair near Meg.

"Tell me about the events at Readers' Haven."

Caroline summarized Readers' Haven Book Clubs discussion and interests.

"I just heard you and had a good time at Townline Inn."

"I'm returning home at the end of the month. Don't start pushing us together. "

"You can certainly enjoy yourself while you are here. He likes—" Meg pursed her lip. "Likes spending time with you. He needs a friend."

Caroline shook her head. "I like David. He's easy to be with. Good to talk with."

"And after you go back to Seattle, you could stay in touch and still visit."

"I live there." She enunciated each word.

"So, after you go back, are you going to forget all the friends you have made? No contact with David? Not talk to me? Larkin? Even Irene?"

It would be hard to forget everyone here. She smoothed the blanket.

"You've touched lives here." She reached for Caroline's hand. "None of us are looking forward to your leaving."

"No." A sigh overcame her frame. "I won't forget any of you." She nodded. "I'll come back to see you. I don't want to lose touch with you."

"And you will see David again. You should do more things with him while you are here. Weren't you going to go kayaking on every river and see Jersey sites?" Meg patted Caroline's hand.

"We kinda talked about events, but not seriously."

"Oh, he was serious. He wants to show you all the good parts—and they're are many, you may have to stay ... or at least come back often."

Caroline laughed. "Okay, enough."

"Hey, Meg, you awake and decent? Can I come in?" David's voice prompted Meg to sit up straighter.

Caroline grabbed the hairbrush left on the end of the bed and twirled it between her palms. This was awkward after the other night. *No way to retreat now.*

"We were just talking about you," Meg said as he leaned down to give her a kiss.

"Oh, really?" He glanced at Caroline. "Should I be pleased or run and hide?"

"Talking about rivers and other attractions. Caroline has so many rivers left to kayak and so many attractions to see." She hugged David.

He retrieved a chair and sat on the other side of the bed. He tilted his head, winked at Caroline. "Good conversation starter." He squeezed Meg's hand. "Two upcoming events could fit the bill. Next weekend is Lakeside's Summer Festival. May 28th is a Saturday night and there is a full moon. We could get great views if we kayak to the middle of Menicore Lake."

She held her napkin to her lips to hide her grin. After dinner at Townline Inn, images of David's hands, the pressure of his kiss had haunted her thoughts. She was only here a short time. David knew the limitations of her relationship. She could see him and if anything happened ... so be it.

"So will you accompany me to the Lakeside Festival? We can make plans for a moonlight kayak out to one of the islands. Great views."

"A date!" Meg clapped her hands. "You could spend the weekend together ... I mean two dates ... different ones."

She put her other hand on top of his. Both awaited Caroline's answer.

Meg looked expectedly and David leaned forward.

She shook her head. "I'm outmaneuvered. I would love to

accompany you to the festival."

Seeing the town through David's eyes would heighten to the day. Actually, just seeing David would highlight her day. They could look at anything.

"The artisans show off their jewelry, pottery, all kinds of glass items, paintings. Lots of food, music."

She nodded. Fun event. Harmless event. Before Meg could try more matchmaking, she hugged her and moved away from David's closeness. "I'll see you later. Enjoy time with David."

CHAPTER ELEVEN

The next day, she took her breakfast outside to the bench near the rose garden. Working at Readers' Haven was both a vacation and work. All so different from her job. What a reprieve from her clients at Andoer.

She had no other men in her life. She touched the delicate petals of a pink rose. She'd never dated anyone who discussed books, knew about roses, laughed that hearty deep laugh which made her laugh, too. He didn't talk about stock quotes or ask her out just to network. She didn't know how she would leave Meg. One of the women in Book Club would have to visit Meg more. Do things with her. Meg and the progression of her illness would weigh on her mind when she returned to Seattle.

She picked up a clod of dirt and threw it across the yard. She paced the length of the garden and heaved another clod at a tree. This wasn't what she expected when she came here. Going back would be empty void—a void now filled by new friends, new interests and new energy for life.

And then there were the little girls, Jennifer and Suzanne. They fit in her life, she was sure of it. She dumped her coffee into the flower bed and returned to the table in the library

On the two sheets. Jennifer had birthdate, two names and nothing. Suzanne had birthdate and two names. Not much. So much for solving mystery of her past in the short time she was here.

The doorbell rang. No one knew where she lived—at least she hadn't discussed that.

Lindsey, from the Records Department, gripped a brown envelope. One foot rested on the porch step.

"Lindsey, how did you know where to find me? Are you okay?"

A tight-lipped smile crossed her lips. "I work in records, too. I'm a researcher—or was."

Caroline bit her lip. *Was?* "Come in. Let's get something to drink."

"I found more information for you." She didn't change her position.

"Was it in Records?" The guilt that haunted her in the records department now jabbed her conscience.

"I'm now in reception." Again, the tight smile. "Guess I'll get in less trouble there."

"Did I get you in trouble? You still have a job?"

"Reception is a better place. At least I get to interact with people and am not staring at a computer screen all day." She studied her shoes. "Birth records are protected, but I guess you knew that."

"Lindsey, I—"

Lindsey held up her hand. "You're searching for someone." She pulled a paper out of the envelope. "I found this. The father listed on Suzanne's birth certificate. This is a copy of his death certificate. I hope it helps your search." She handed it to Caroline. "I have to go."

At the street, she turned. "You inherited this house, but you live in Seattle. I hope you stay here. The people in Readers' Haven like you." She grinned. "And David Montgomery is a hottie and no one has caught him—yet. I do my research, too."

"Thank you, Lindsey. I didn't want to get you in any trouble."

"I know. Good luck."

She returned to her library with the envelope. She pulled the paper and stared at the certificate. No father for Suzanne. He died even before his daughter was born. She had more information on Suzanne's side. His middle name. She typed in *Jeffrey Michael Kelly*. He graduated from high school, but not from Lakeside.

His parents were John and Katherine Kelly. She wrote their names on the white paper beneath Suzanne's name. A brother. Jason Colin Kelly. She stroked the name on the screen. A clue.

She clicked on his name.

He lived in Salisbury, Maryland. A live person who may know something. Finding information became so much easier once the one clue surfaces. She wrote down address and phone number. All she had to do is call. She studied the back of her cell phone then picked it up, dialed the first three numbers and hung up. How would she start? *Hi, I may be related to your dead brother. Yeah, I'm thirty-one years-old and just am calling now. That's real—and rude.*

She put her cell phone in her bag. I'll think about this. Maybe call tomorrow.

•

As soon as Caroline unlocked the door, Stephanie entered bearing sticky buns. After opening boxes, she leaned her hip on table. "I hear you've nestled in the exclusive circle of the book club."

"The book club women are characters. I enjoy their perspective. Are you a reader?" She slipped her hands in her pocket.

Stephanie arched an eyebrow. "I buy books on Kindle. Book Haven is a small, tight community of its own within Lakeside." She touched her lips with her index finger, then shook her head, and meandered through the shop studying the titles. "Larkin and Jim have quite a selection. Jim certainly revitalized this little spot. It was a hardware store—gone to the dogs. He saved the building and the job saved him."

Caroline waited for more of that story. She knew from overhearing conversations that Larkin and Ryan met while he was working on the store. Something bad had happened to Ryan, but she didn't know details. Stephanie knew. Caroline waited. Stephanie appeared to be like Irene, waiting for the right dramatic moment to drop information. But she said nothing more about the couple.

She paused near the bookshelves. "Now you are part of the bookstore community, you are not hooked into staying, are you? You said you would leave as soon as you sold the house. You are still here."

And one of her strong opinions was Caroline should leave. Stephanie had a raw edge to her voice. Something between Stephanie and Larkin? Someone in book club had snubbed Stephanie. She had nothing to do with their relationship, but Stephanie acted as though, she would drive Caroline to the airport if she would agree to leave.

"I'm returning to Seattle. Just staying longer than I anticipated."

"Are you selling Greystone?" Stephanie stood with her hand on her hip, staring at Caroline as though she were a cockroach.

She moved out of Stephanie's line of vision. "Yes, I'll contact a realtor. Unlike Annabelle, I can't return every year."

"No, you shouldn't." Stephanie moved abruptly and snapped up the empty sticky buns containers. "You won't need to return." She stopped at the door. "Nice to see you I'll probably stop in to check on how soon you are leaving." She left.

Caroline frowned. What was that about and what bug did she have up her ass?

When Irene and Abby arrived later, they purchased a sticky bun and then sat near the coffee table.

"If Larkin hadn't made that contract with Stephanie, I'd be much thinner. Irene said. As usual, Abby merely nodded as a chorus to Irene's thoughts.

"She doesn't leave her bakery often. She rarely mingles with any of us."

Blames it for her problems. "Stephanie left town when she was sixteen. Scandal. She was just pregnant, had the baby and returned without it."

The hair prickled on Caroline's neck. "Just pregnant? When did this all occur?"

Irene shook her head as if she couldn't believe Caroline's density. "Years ago. This was in 1978 when it was still scandalous to be unwed, a teen and pregnant."

Caroline tried to digest all of Irene's outpourings. The facts and Irene's view of the world didn't always match. One fact jumped out. "She had a baby in 1978? Where?"

Irene shrugged. "No one saw her for about two years.

Apparently, she returned home. Her parents stated she went away to help a critically ill aunt. What fifteen-year-old leaves high school to care for someone? Stephanie would have had no training."

"Where did she have this baby?" Caroline cleared her throat.

Irene put her finger to her lips, paused. "She never came back with that little girl. She died, was given to someone, the baby stayed with her aunt. We don't know the full story and Stephanie gives you a cold stare if you ask her about those two years. "

A baby. A baby born in 1978. She'd never considered Stephanie because she judged her to be in her forties … which she would be if she had a baby at sixteen. Caroline gripped the counter and avoided eye contact with Irene until she could get her racing heart and shaky limbs under control. If she were in her late forties and had a baby at sixteen, that baby could be thirty-one—my age. Calm down. Facts. She needed facts.

"Or if there ever really was a baby." Abby stood. She moved closer, but not next to Irene. She didn't nod this time. Irene scowled. Abby looked at her hands and said nothing more.

Caroline suppressed her smile. Okay, it was okay to be Irene's chorus. Nod in support, but don't interrupt or interject facts. Back to square one. A baby or maybe not. Most likely not. Another dead-end.

She could Google Stephanie later. Great, now she was a stalker in people's lives. She dumped coffee grounds and started a fresh pot.

•

It wasn't until later when the day's conversations resurfaced in her head that the impact of the day caught up with her. What if Stephanie had a baby in 1978? Did she have any connection to Greystone House? She dropped her spoon into the stir fry.

Annabelle stayed with Stephanie every year she came here. Stephanie knew a lot about Greystone and Annabelle's visits. Stephanie was eager to have her sell that house and move back.

Why? Afraid others would find out why Caroline was here? Did Stephanie recognize her and afraid Caroline would dig up her past? Stephanie didn't want her past to resurface.

She turned off the stove, pulled the chair up to the hall computer and searched Jennifer Cambridge. Bingo! A birth certificate for Jennifer Clare Hudson born February 6, 1978 in Coeur d'Alene, Idaho. Idaho!! That was closer to Seattle than Lakeside, New Jersey.

Had Annabelle and Stephanie first connected there? How had Annabelle known where to look? This could be off-track. She had no idea where Stephanie fled to or was sent to after she left Lakeside at sixteen. She had no idea how Annabelle found Homey Hearth. She couldn't let her emotions getting in the way of research and facts. She still had so little proof of anything.

Each time she thought she found a line, she discovered an entanglement. Something else to investigate. Damn.

She went back to her stir-fry now cold and limp in the wok.

CHAPTER TWELVE

Business was slow at the shop on Saturday. Caroline wandered around straightening shelves. Her cell phone pressed against her leg. Just call him. Explain you are researching, No lies there. He could be her link to her natural parent. Didn't she want to know? She shook her head. *No, this is a wild goose chase.* If she did find a real person, then what?

She beat her fist against the shelf. She really needed to get back to Seattle and the tensions and stress of her job. She was talking to herself amid rows of books. Were she home, she would be too busy to think of herself or any friend or relative.

She leaned against the books. In Seattle, no time for anything. She had three weeks left. Call and ask to meet. The worst that can happen, he can say no.

She waited until closing, then sat in a chair near the window, picked up her cell and punched in the numbers. She swung her leg back and forth.

The man answered.

Now what. She took a deep breath. "Jason Kelly? This is Caroline Ferraro. I may be related to you. I'd like to explain," She answered as many of his questions as he asked. He agreed to meet her after he looked at his schedule. He sounded both curious and recalcitrant.

She placed the cell on the table. It was something—maybe. *Think how that poor guy must feel. Some woman who could be a lunatic calls out to the blue and says, hi, I may be your niece.*

She touched the glass of the front window. She clicked her nails on the glass. *This all could be crazy. I'm Jennifer. Or I may be Suzanne.* She wandered back to get her bag and tapped her fingers on the counter. *I'm Caroline. The same person I have always been. This is absurd. I don't need to know who I was.*

An hour later, he called back. "Hi this is Jason. Jason Kelly. You just called me."

Caroline held her breath. He so far was her only physical lead and not a name on paper.

"So tell me again how you found me."

Caroline recounted her Internet search, the discovery of the birth certificate. "Look I know this is a remote possibility. You're just a lead I'm following up on. It may be nothing. I'm not after anything—except facts."

"But you may be related to my brother, Jeff."

"Yes."

"Okay, let's set up a day and I'll tell you where to meet me. I run a gardening and landscape business. If there is an emergency for someone, it may have to be on the job. But I want to see you."

"Okay. Landscaper have emergencies? Doctors get calls at all hours."

He laughed. "Someone's tree falls down, we remove it. To some gardeners, anything that affects the garden is an emergency and they want me now."

His hearty laugh did it. She wanted to meet him.

"I just have a few questions. And I'd like to meet you in person."

"Just in case, we are related."

"I guess. Look I'm new at all this. I don't have much. I just need to know." Caroline said.

"Okay. I'm not telling any of my family. They'd think I was nuts. How far away are you?" They agreed on Wednesday afternoon at his house … unless he had an emergency that day and she could meet him on the job.

"See you then. You must have some information or you wouldn't call or drive to Maryland."

"I don't know if either one of us will learn anything, but it may be the lead I need. See you Wednesday."

She could have asked him questions on the phone or emailed him. In her investigations, she didn't need to talk with medical personnel face to face. She was following her gut on this one.

She spent Saturday afternoon pulling weeds and cultivating her garden. It was hot. She stopped periodically to cool off inside. She looked at her hands and nails. In Seattle, she had a standing hair and nail appointment every second Saturday. Here, she learned she liked longer hair and she was very capable of polishing nails.

That night she went to bed more rested than she'd felt in a long time. Meg was right—she needed a garden in Seattle. Start small and add flowers. It's relaxing, good way to work off stream and made her feel good. She overslept Sunday morning.

A call from Meg awakened her.

"Meg, you okay? Do you need anything?" She sat up, fumbled with the tangled sheets and struggled to focus. She rubbed her eyes and rumbled her hair. She stifled a groan. The clock read 9 AM. She never slept until nine.

"I'm fine. In fact, very fine."

Meg's voice sounded stronger, perkier.

"I'd kick up my heels, but a major miracle hasn't occurred." Meg said. "I'm out of bed. David and I bought groceries this morning. I can cook"

"You are up and about! You sound like your old self."

"That self is still old, but I'm very tired of my own living space. I'll be at Readers' Haven early tomorrow morning."

As soon as Meg arrived the next day, she was mobbed by Irene, Abby and the rest of the club. Caroline rescued her by passing around plates of cinnamon buns and distributing drinks. She hugged Meg and whispered in her ear. "Good to see you here. You have breathing space now that they are eating."

Each had stories to tell of days Meg had missed in the shop. What a crew. They supported each other, kept up and contributed to the events in town, then yacked about it all before book discussions.

She had waited until they were all together to ask more about Stephanie and Jennifer. She needed a name and the state where Stephanie moved. She might give Meg a chance to catch her breath if she interrupted their prodding of her.

Abby walked to the counter. "That Tana French book is great. Could you order me a few more of hers?" She placed a list on the counter

Caroline nodded. Abby had a different opinion than Irene. Ask. She spun the small lined paper around the counter top with the tips of her fingers. "So you said the other day, Stephanie's baby, Jennifer, didn't return from … what was that state Stephanie moved to?"

"Jennifer, who said her baby was Jennifer?"

Conversation among the club members stopped.

Meg gripped the arms of her wheelchair. "Jennifer? What Jennifer?"

"We have no proof of any baby." Abby moved to pour more coffee. "I thought Stephanie left to care for her ailing aunt." She poured cream and sugar in her cup then the coffee. "Damn shame her mother made her do that. She just made cheerleading squad, wanted to run for student body secretary and whoosh her mother sends her …"

"Her mother didn't send her to help an aunt. She was having Jimmy Markin's baby and they hid it. The aunt was just a camouflage. Guess it worked with some." Irene stretched and looked down her nose at Abby.

Abby shook her head. "I don't think Stephanie had a Jennifer. Where did you hear that name? From someone in here?"

"Jennifer?" Meg's voice croaked. All turned to her. Caroline scurried to Meg's side. Her face was a chalky white and she gripped the sides. Maybe she shouldn't have come out her first day.

"Why are you looking for a Jennifer?" Meg's eyes searched her face.

Irene said, "Stephanie had a daughter. Caroline was just interested in Stephanie and why she avoids everyone. But I don't think we said her daughter was Jennifer. Maybe Caroline could find out Stephanie's past for us. She is a senior researcher. Must know some tricks we don't."

Meg collapsed against the back of her chair.

Caroline knelt beside her. "Are you okay? Do you want me to call David?

Meg shook her head. Her words were whispered. "Why are you here?"

Caroline paused waiting for more. Was Meg having memory problems as well? "I'm filling in for Larkin."

Meg shook her head. "Why are you here in New Jersey?"

"I inherited a house. I need to sell it."

"Greystone House, Meg." Irene said. "She now owns that one."

"Greystone?" Her voice cracked. "You have the house, not that woman from the West Coast?"

"Annabelle?" Caroline tilted her head. Annabelle must have talked with these women. They all knew something about Greystone house.

Meg closed her eyes. She dabbed a tear from the corner of her eye. "You know Annabelle."

"Yes."

Meg opened her eyes and studied Caroline's face. She placed her hand on top of Caroline's. "You own Greystone."

Caroline nodded.

"Yeah, Meg, you know that woman who showed up here once a year and rented the house." Irene moved to Meg's side.

Meg nodded. Her hand patted Caroline's hand. She took a deep breath. Her breath caught in her throat. She swallowed.

"Meg," said Caroline. "I think you're breathing as though you are having trouble. Should I call David?"

Meg inhaled deeply and the air released slowly from her lungs. She looked down. "Yes, I think I should go home." She turned in chair to Abby still sitting near the window. "Could you give me a ride home? I don't want to call David. I'll be fine in a minute." She leaned back in her chair and took another deep breath. "I think I just need to be alone at home."

Caroline watched Abby wheel Meg out the door. Meg went from eager, animated with the group to … an old woman barely able to put a sentence together. What happened?

After Meg's departure, the rest of the book club soon broke up and headed for home as well.

She still didn't find out any details. Stephanie could have had a Jennifer in 1978. Annabelle and Stephanie connected every year. She could be Jennifer and related to Stephanie. Or not. Irene was a questionable authority. Just a lot of scribbling on two sheets of paper.

She wiped down the counters and the tables. She still didn't feel like a Jennifer. She locked the doors at five and headed to Greystone.

CHAPTER THIRTEEN

Tina's sleep voice answered. "It's early. What is going on?"

"You awake? I can call later. I'm on my way to Salisbury, Maryland."

"With that I'm wide awake." Caroline heard Tina's coffee grinder in the background. "Are you going there for steak?"

"Steak? Are you awake? It's already 9:30 AM."

"Yeah, your time, East Coast woman. Yeah, I'm more alert than you. Salisbury Steak …"

"Yeah, yeah, okay I get it." Caroline chuckled. "I'm just pre-occupied. I'm going to Maryland to talk with Jason Kelly. He is the brother of Jeffrey Kelly who is Suzanne Kelly's father."

"Does he know anything? Is he the clue?"

"I don't know. He agreed to see me."

Another pause. The clink of a mug and hiss of latte steamer was dead give-away, Tina was awake.

"Do you think Annabelle knew your other parents? Do you think she went there yearly to connect with them?"

"I hope not. That would be so unfair if she saw them and never let me meet them or let me know about them. Why didn't she tell me more? Were she here …" *Why hadn't Annabelle been honest about travelling to New Jersey? Why hadn't she told her about the house? I would be so angry with her—even now.* She dug her nails into the steering wheel. Misplaced anger.

"Maybe she was afraid."

"Afraid of what? What could the other woman say?" She crossed over the Delaware Memorial Bridge.

"No, afraid you would leave and go back to the other parents."

"Why would I want to go to any other parent. Annabelle and Grant are my parents."

"Then why are you going to Maryland to find out about those parents?"

Caroline sped up and passed a truck and two cars, she tapped her fingers on the top of the steering wheel. "You're the one who convinced me I had to do this, find my family link or I wouldn't be happy. What gives?"

"I'm just playing devil's advocate." The crackling of a wrapper interrupted. "No one convinced you, trust me. You make up your mind and dig in. You know this has been eating at you since Walter told you Annabelle willed you a house that you knew nothing about—and added you were born in it. All I do is repeat your words, your ideas—then you question them."

She leaned back on the headrest. "Yeah, yeah, I'm a little nervous now. I just called him out of the blue."

"I'm lovin' this. You 'just doing something' is so refreshing. Things aren't falling in tight boxes in your life. I love these phone calls."

"Great, you're taking pleasure out of my miseries and non-comfort zone."

"Yep. Call me as soon as you leave there. I hope he gives you information you need. I do miss you in Seattle. No one to mock all the people desperately in need of coffee each morning."

"Isn't that usually us? Yeah, I'll call. Gotta go. Need to pay attention to GPS." She missed Tina. Since their preteen years, they met once a week. They managed to keep up the tradition through high school craziness and college obligations. They walked blocks until they found the perfect Starbucks—which sometimes meant meandering the streets of Seattle for a half hour. That, in turn, created a harried lunch schedule. They created life histories for those in the coffee bar and those working there. Tina lifted her spirits.

She slowed as she turned on Jason's street. *Now what? I'm going into a man's house I know nothing about at the slight chance he may give me information.*

The man waited on the porch. A Ford F150 with Kelly Landscaping emblazoned in Kelly green lettering was parked in the driveway. A small neat rancher had a shamrock attached on the front porch post. Looks like the Kellys are Irish.

"Hi, I'm Jason Kelly." He stepped forward.

"Thank you for agreeing to this. I'm Caroline Ferraro."

He nodded studied her face then stood back. "Come in. We can talk in the living room."

Iced tea pitcher, glasses and cookies were already laid out. "This is a day everyone else in my family is busy. I thought just the two of us needed to talk first."

She nodded "This may be a wild goose chase."

"You said you found me on the Internet."

She pulled out her folder. "I found two baby girls who were born near my adoption date."

He leaned forward. "Why did you start looking at your age? What do you expect to get out of this?"

She met his steady gaze. "I'm not looking for anything. I don't want to change anyone's life. I just need to know who I am." She paused and pulled out a picture of Greystone House. "I knew I was adopted and didn't really care or need to know anything until I inherited a house from my adoptive mother. The house I was born in. I didn't know it existed."

He flicked the edge of the photograph with his nail. "That's a lot to take in." He leaned back. "How can I help you? Why do you think I'm any good to your search?"

"I know nothing about Jeffrey, if he is my father. I need to find Margaret Whitcomb Kelly."

He frowned. "I don't know if she exists."

Caroline winced.

"I don't know how much help I can be. I was ten years old when my brother was killed in action. I have vague memories of him—like still action shots."

"Do you remember his wife—anything about a baby."

He shook his head. "I have postcard images stuck in my head of my brother. He was in uniform—his last visit home. We shot hoops in the side yard, he rubbed my hair with his hand, which seemed strong. He lifted me up to fix the net and it made him appear so much larger than life. The uniform made him seem distant—I have a vague recollection of him in T-shirt with the neck stretched out and jaded jeans. That had to be another day."

He stretched his fingers up and down on his thigh mimicking a giant spider's movement. "The only other thing which came to mind—I thought of last night after your call. I was coming home from T-ball practice. I had a bat in my hand. I remember a woman—blondish hair—leaving carrying a folded American flag. My mother was screaming at her." He tapped a rapid rhythm on his thigh. "The woman was pregnant. Her tan shirt ballooned out over a belly. I had never noticed a pregnant woman before and I had never seen my mother that angry."

She closed her eyes. The high-pitched squeal of a woman's voice, the heat of the summer, the anxiety. The scene stretched before her eyes as though she had been there, but she couldn't have. If she had witnessed the scene, she would have been the baby in that belly.

Her hands shook. She couldn't formulate any words. Jason handed her a glass of iced tea and waited.

"Did your mother say anything to you?"

"Not that I know of. I don't know what happened afterward. I must have blocked it out." He poured himself a tea and swallowed a gulp.

She studied slow movement of his jaw and Adam's apple as he swallowed the tea. Was she the baby in his memory or was this another dead end?

"I have another memory—years later. My mother died of cancer. My dad asked her if she wanted him to find her grandchild. She screamed at him, insisted she had no granddaughter." He ran his finger around the rim of his glass. His eyes searched hers. "That would be you. Your call jogged a lot of my memories—many questions."

"I might not be that girl." Her words came out as a whisper. She cleared her throat. "I only have bits of information."

"And maybe my mother was right—there were no grandchildren."

"But she knew the child was a granddaughter. Why would she scream at my mother … that woman? Why deny a baby's existence?" The words burned inside her chest. The denial hurt as if she were that baby inside that woman.

"My mother never got over my brother's death. She kept

his room the same. After she died, my father ripped it apart. I think it affected them both. It was my dad's idea he go in the service."

Jason held his glass tightly in his hand. "My parents and my brother had an earlier argument and he hadn't been home in a while—until the last time—the one I remember him in uniform." He swallowed more tea and then swirled the ice in the glass.

"I didn't mean to bring up painful memories."

He placed his glass on the table, spun it between his fingers. "This is a curious mystery. I never thought of going to look for that woman or that baby and you call. I may have a niece."

Caroline inhaled sharply. Jason was an uncle or could be. She had been so focused on finding out about the pasts of the babies, she hadn't thought of the present or how that past could involve the future.

"I hadn't … didn't think." She put her glass down. "We don't have much to go on."

"Would you like some blood?"

Caroline tilted her head. "Blood?"

"Don't you have to run tests—DNA—to prove a relationship?"

Her shoulders relaxed. "I'm a medical researcher. A simpler way would be to take both our hairs and have a lab run tests."

He rubbed the back of his neck. "Good. You can accomplish that?"

"Very easily. I can send it off to my company."

He formed a steeple with his fingers. "Thank God. If we had to do anything around here, my family would know. I don't want to raise any questions, or hopes until we know."

"It may take me a while usually three months. I'm not working with my company just now."

"Are you going back to Seattle?"

"Not just now.

"Will you come back for visits?"

"I don't know … I—"

"If you are my niece, I'd like some kind of contact."

The niece again. A knot formed again. If she were his niece. She hadn't thought this out in terms of real relationships. What if she found her mother and then what? Talk to her? And go back to Seattle and act as though this never happened? Not well thought out.

"I'm sure I want ..." She wiped the end of her nose with her index finger.

He handed her a tissue. "I got up last night and had to come down here. I got choked up thinking I still have family alive. Did you find anything—is your mother alive?"

"I'm not sure. The documents I found..." She pulled out a marriage license. "Lists a name, but I cannot find anyone by that name."

Jason reached for the certificate and held it. He pulled glasses from his front pocket and bent forward. "My god!" the words came out with force. "There was—is a woman married to my brother. Proof." His cheeks reddened, his eyes misted. Caroline scooted over next to him. She put her hand on his arm. "Are you okay?"

"I ... He was really married. Family—of my brother's—exist. You don't know anything about her?"

She shook her head. "Nothing about a Margaret Whitcomb Kelly."

He scowled. "I don't remember any Margaret name connected or shouted. An –y sounding name—Peggy, Maggy, Stephanie. "

Caroline jumped in her seat. "Stephanie?"

"Yeah, that might be it. Keep in mind, we are going on my memory as a ten-year-old." He ran his thumb over his brother's signature on the marriage certificate.

"Would you like me to make you a copy of that certificate and any thing else I find."

He nodded.

He gripped the marriage certificate and said nothing. Then he placed his hand on top of hers. "I hope you find more, little one." His voice was soft and distant. "I'm sorry I couldn't have given you more."

Now someone else had a stake in her search. She had a real link—Stephanie—the first person she met in Lakeside. The growly, standoffish insulated Stephanie? Irene was right. Stephanie was hiding something. *Does she know who I am?*

"You know something. You are far away and thinking. Did you figure it out?"

"Maybe." She was sharing this with a stranger—or perhaps not a stranger but someone who had a lot to lose or gain. "I'm not sure. Some pieces of the puzzle may fit together. Others could be hurt if they weren't ready for this." If Stephanie wanted her past hidden, she would not be happy for Caroline's appearance. She had just shaken up Jason's life with a piece of paper. No wonder records are kept secret. "A woman named Stephanie is in Lakeside."

"Where you were born and where," He held up the marriage certificate. "You found this."

She nodded.

"Have you talked to her? Does she recognize you? Does she know why you are there?"

"She knows I'm there to sell the house. She knew Annabelle, my adoptive mother. She hasn't indicated she knows me."

"But?"

"She is anxious for me to leave."

"You hold the power to wreak havoc her life."

"If she has kept this hidden and maybe it would effect her relationship with her husband or child."

Jason squeezed the top of her hand.

She placed her other hand on his. "But I could cause upheaval in your life. You didn't want any of your family here and didn't want them to know. What will happen if they do?"

A slow smile crossed his lips. "I have an eleven-year-old daughter. Do you know anything about eleven-year-old girls?"

She chuckled. "Only what I was like—my parents survived that year."

"You never know, and change—especially major change could be a problem. My wife—other than shocked it came up now—will be hard to convince this is not a scam. She can be overly protective. She just won't want me to get expectations up."

"Just you and wife and daughter?"

"No, an eleven-year-old son—as long as it doesn't affect his baseball playing, he won't care at all."

Great family. This man could be an uncle.

"And they would be your cousins," he added as though he were reading her mind.

"Oh," she startled. "Oh, this just keeps getting bigger."

A timer went off in the kitchen.

"We have to get you out of here." He leaped off the couch and headed to the kitchen. "That's a timer to remind me that it's almost time for Nancy's bus, my daughter." The buzzer stopped. He returned holding a small plastic bag. "Care to do the honors?"

She tilted her head. What was he thinking?

"You pull a hair out—try to get a grey one." He handed her the bag and leaned down in front of her.

She yanked a grey one. "Got it."

He held both her hands in his engulfing the bag as well. "You will keep in touch. Let me know what ever you find."

She nodded. He walked her to the door.

"You have a bigger stake. That baby may not be me, but she will be related to you."

"I think that baby is you." He gripped the door with his fist. "When you aren't sure … or you question, you tilt your head." He looked down. "Jeff always tilted his head when he asked me about homework or when he quizzed me when I got in trouble." He looked into her face. "Seeing you, watching you tilt your head—that was my brother's gesture." He inhaled. "Your Jeffrey's daughter."

She sucked in her lower lip. Was she? He certainly wanted to believe it.

He reached out with his thumb and stroked her cheek. "And my niece."

The grinding of a bus's gears made them both jump. She trotted through the door and toward her car as a light haired teen with freckles—the kind that made Caroline's teen years miserable—darted to the house. She glanced over her shoulder at her father, then Caroline and went in slamming the door.

He chuckled a low laugh. "She had a bad day. Walked head down, door dramatically slammed. She won't remember you here."

She rolled down the window of the passenger side once she slid in. "You have my cell. I have yours. If either of finds anything, we can share it."

"I still have a box of my brothers' things my mom saved. Some from his army days. I 'll find it. Maybe some clues."

She nodded. "I'll find out more about Stephanie." She put her car in gear. "Even if we're not related, I'm glad I met you."

"Drive carefully."

Caroline blinked back tears as she drove away. Even if he wasn't her uncle, she found him a family he didn't know existed. She wanted him to be an uncle. If he were that way with odd women who showed up on his doorstep with a tale of inherited houses, and possible babies and no concrete evidence—he would be a wonderful person to know if all the pieces fell together.

Stephanie. It made sense why she wanted her to sell the house and leave. *I am a reminder, a clue to her forgotten or misbegotten past. It also explains Annabelle's visits.* She smacked her palm against the dashboard. *Damn.* Annabelle was not the mother she had thought she was. Why did she start this search? Her whole world wasn't what she thought.

Images of Annabelle packing to go to yearly "spa trips." *Lies!* Annabelle visited here yearly and never talked about Greystone, the cemetery or staying with Stephanie at Homey Hearth. Yet she always returned in a week usually with antiques.

She pulled off at the rest stop and parked in the nearest space. She took a deep breath. She had stirred the cauldron and all elements bubbled to the top. She wanted to know about her past and now the results disturbed her.

She aimlessly ambled around the picnic area. White stones littered the patches of sand. She created fists, then released them. *Pull it together. Can't have my mind wandering everywhere while driving.* Leaning against the nearest tree, she watched families walk out of the rest stop. Annabelle might never have talked with Stephanie. And Stephanie may not know who she is. Get a grip.

She purchased a Starbucks Frappuccino and sat at a picnic table away from the bustling crowds.

She sipped her drink. She picked up her cell phone and put in on the table. Talking with David would be comforting.

But what would she lead with. *My life is a mess. I came here to investigate people in the town and I will change their lives forever. Oh hi, I haven't always been Caroline Ferraro. I was Suzanne Kelly.* Seeing the town through David's eyes would heighten to the day. Actually just seeing David would highlight her day. They could look at anything.

Or maybe Jennifer.

She grabbed her purse and checked. The plastic bag was still inside. She pushed it to the bottom of her black purse. Jason might not be an uncle and Stephanie may be no relation. She rubbed her temples.

She picked up the cell and dialed Tina.

"I've been staring at the phone, waiting. How did it go? Solve your mystery?" Tina's rapid-fire questions did not help the throbbing in her temples.

"Jason was only ten when Jeff died." She filled Tina in on the details. "I may have an uncle and—" She didn't know what to say about her jumbled emotions about that.

"You think is the woman remembered is Stephanie? You wondered about her. Has she shown any interest in your identity? Any recognition?"

"Only that she wants me out of there. She and Annabelle met once a year. I'm finding out about Annabelle, too. She lied all those years." Her voice rose. Others at tables surrounding her stared. She ducked her head and pulled up the hood of her jacket.

"But Annabelle loved you. You know that. There's more to this story."

Caroline swirled her remaining sips in the cup.

"Caroline, you okay?" Tina's voice rose. "You want to figure this out. I know Annabelle did everything out of love and you know that, too."

"I don't know what I thought would happen once I found a lead. I thought I would discover a few names and come home. It's not happening that way."

"What's next? You said Jason Kelly gave you a hair. Can you match DNA really—like it is on TV?

"No, it is not all solved in an hour show. I'm sure Jean can get it done quickly but it takes about three months."

"Three months. All those shows make it seem simple and instant." Tina said. "Could you get DNA from Stephanie?"

"Not the way it happens on television. I don't think it is fair. I want to talk with her.

Stephanie could be the woman I'm searching for. Jason Kelly could be my uncle or I could have no connection to either one. I could have been Jennifer." She crushed the Starbucks cup. "Or Suzanne."

"Jason thought you were related."

She tapped the cup rim on the table. "He said I reminded him of his brother. I tilt my head."

"You do when you are puzzled or want to ask a question, but don't want to disturb anyone."

Caroline grimaced at the phone.

Confidence could be hidden with a tone of her voice. But sorting through facts she had and making a decision was like remaining upright on a slippery slope. She grasped for solid ground—something provable without a doubt. She hadn't expected any of this. Her mind skyrocketed to elation, resentment, anger, confusion to determination. How could she explain this to anyone?

She had family—maybe. She'd lost Grant, Annabelle. An orphan. No family. Then connection to a house and then a town across the country. And now maybe an uncle and cousins. What a possibility—but it was just that –a possibility. Her stomach churned. Sitting in a corner sobbing wouldn't solve anything. So many questions—so few answers.

She tossed the crumpled cup into the trash. No answers solved if she just sat. Back to New Jersey.

CHAPTER FOURTEEN

She slammed her car door and paused in front of her house. Her body ached as if she had run to Salisbury. Jason was certainly a likeable man. She'd made a connection. An uncle ... maybe. Never had a real uncle. Annabelle and Grant were only children. Life had surprises.

She pushed open the door and plopped on the three-seated bench on the first landing. Annabelle considered it a rare find on one of their numerable flea market and antique jaunts. l She stretched out her legs. She was missing a blatant clue. If Tina were right, Annabelle gave her this house so she would find something.

Where would Annabelle hide anything valuable, yet findable? She had already checked the rooms. She patrolled the downstairs. The attic had antiques—Annabelle's treasures. Most renters wouldn't climb to fondle antiques. Perfect and so Annabelle. She found a flashlight in the kitchen drawer and pulled down the attic steps.

Just as every available space in Annabelle's Seattle house was crammed with antiques, this attic was full of dressers, tables, servers and chairs.

She ran her fingers along the insides of dresser drawers, searched the bottom of tables for taped notes. Nothing. Tina found a sales slip in a dresser beneath a staircase. No stairs—but a corner. Only the bassinet.

A pink bassinet was so out-of-place nestled among oak furniture. She shoved chairs, tables, and dressers aside and ripped off the plastic cover. A long skirt trailed to the floor covering its base. It was a family's bassinet. Someone had stitched the elaborate quilt nestled inside for a new baby. She fingered the raised embroidery of flowers and satin band on the edge. A note slipped out and landed on the top of the sheet. *To my baby girl. Your fingers so are so tiny and perfect. You smell like freshness.* A lump rose in her throat. Too personal, this baby bed belonged to someone who had created the ruffles, the pink trim, a quilt for her baby.

Bile rose to her throat. She was born in this house and this could have been her bed. She froze, the plastic still in her hand. No signature on the note. She picked up the quilt and sheet. No more notes.

She tugged on the lacy white cover. Names and dates were printed on the weaves of the basket style bassinet. She yanked up the cover and stuffed it inside the center of the bed. Varied inks, different handwriting were on each piece the woven wood. *James Marshall b. July 5, 1955. Rachel Marie b. January 10, 1956 ht. 16 in wt. 6 lb. 2 oz.*

She ran her finger down every interlace in the basket — each had a name, birthdate and often height and weight. Were these the babies who had slept in this? She chuckled as she read the repeats of names and the varying weights. Generations of a families preserved.

She turned the bassinet — more names and more recent dates on the other side. *Jennifer Feratti* in bold print jumped out. *That's me. My Jennifer is on this. I was in this bassinet. Suzanne Clare Kelly. Two weaves to the right.*

She exhaled and clutched her fist to her chest. Both here. Suzanne and Jennifer somehow connected. She wiped back the tears with the back of her hand. She fingered the names. The dates were the same dates she had discovered on the birth certificates. The handwriting for each name was the same.

Wish you could talk. Wish you could head me in the right direction on this.

She leaned against the arch of the attic roof and stared at the bassinet's side. Two girls born near her adoption date and both were on a bassinet in the house Annabelle owned — the house in which she was born.

The pressure in her chest increased. It was as though her body were strained through a thin straw. She leaned her cheek next to the names. *Hi, girls.*

She slid down the wall. These two are connected and she was connected to them. In her gut, she knew that. Listen to your gut, not just your research skills.

She struggled to her feet. She had to figure this out now. She would never settle in Seattle without some kind of answers. Time is running out. She touched their names again.

She tugged the coverlet down again and returned the plastic cover. She slowly climbed down the steps and flipped the staircase up, then walked to the silence of the library.

She rubbed her temples with her forefingers. Coming to NJ, selling the house, looking up her mother and then returning to her life in Seattle wasn't happening. It had become so complicated.

She added a plus sign to the sheets with Jennifer's and Suzanne's names. She pressed her fingers to her chest. Heartache. She now knew what that word meant. Her chest hurt as though an elephant sat on it. Her head throbbed. No wonder mothers hide details about adoption—it hurts. Whatever person was my mother did she know about me or wonder? Maybe her mother had blamed her for never searching. For most of her life, Caroline hadn't given that mother much thought.

She placed one sheet on top of the other and rolled them into a cylinder and fastened them with a rubber band. Maybe that mother remained hidden because she wanted no contact with me? Stephanie again. Stephanie definitely wants me to leave—a remainder of a bad choice.

She couldn't think of this any more. Her body hurt. Her heart ached. Too much. She put the rolled paper beneath the table and picked up her copy of Rosetta Stone. She tucked a blanket around her and nestled in the window seat. *Get lost in a good book and don't think.*

CHAPTER FIFTEEN

She let the shower pound away thoughts of babies, uncles or birth certificates. Today was the festival with David. Seeing Lakeside through David's eyes would muffle any plaguing of her search for answers about her past. For a day she could forget and just relax.

Once she returned to Seattle her moments of peace would disappear and she would return to her fanatic schedule and to Griscom's rants. Her shoulders tightened just thinking about Griscom and Andoer. Today, she could wash away any thoughts of Seattle and just enjoy the day.

David waited on the park bench in front of Readers' Haven. His welcoming grin lightened her step.

"You ready for an adventure?" He reached for her hand and drew her close to his side.

Bookstore as well as most shops were closed.

Garlic and sharp basil odors mingled with sweetness of maple and cotton candy. Neighbors chatted, moved in and out of displays. Stephanie was correct, she had slipped into comfortable closeness to clients of bookstore—and loved it.

•

As they toured the exhibits, David either held her hand or pressed his fingers against the small of her back. Many stopped to talk with him, most studying her. So many varied booths with artisans blowing glass, creating pottery.

Tina would love this. The atmosphere, the community of artists."

"Tina is the friend in Seattle you talk to all the time." David followed her lead as she paused before a booth. "The one Meg likes."

Caroline chuckled. "Tina is a character and has always gotten me in a lot of trouble—but she is an artist who has built a reputation and a following in Seattle. She is starting to expand thanks to the Internet."

"Paint? Sculpt? Pen and Ink? Cartoon?"

"Paints primarily landscapes. Very precise details. You feel like you can just walk down a pathway or smell the pine or flowers in her paintings."

He nodded. "I would love them."

Her hand ensconced in his was secure and sensuous. She rubbed her thumb around the interior of his palm. This was turning out to be a much better day than she thought. Listening to him talk to kids and parents offered a new look to David.

He is so comfortable in his role in the community and at ease with himself. He didn't talk with others because of what they could do for him, but because he was generally interested. Something was wrong with the company she worked for. Workers at Andoer were tight-lipped and they never chatted.

She stopped in front of a display. She didn't either. She had no idea what her assistant did on the weekends. She loved talking to patrons of the bookstore and knew what books customers wanted. But what did she know about fellow workers behind cubicles at Andoer?

•

"Although are many booths here with food, but I'd like to hold off and take you to a special spot. A Lakeside original and renown. Governors and Senators and sports figures have travelled here to eat R& J's Diner."

She bit the corner of her mouth. "The grilled vegetables smell wonderful from here." She crinkled her nose. "I'm not a big hamburger or cheese steak fan."

He held up his hand. "You can make an exception to that rule. It is worth it for an R&J burger. With secret sauce."

She raised her eyebrows. "Secret?"

"You'll just have to wait. This is unlike any experience you ever have in Seattle."

"Mr. Montgomery?" A girl about seven twirled in front of David. She eyed Caroline. "Is she your girlfriend?"

"Hi Lynette. This is Miss Ferraro."

Lynette giggled. "You were holding her hand." She stood between them. "Will you bring her to school with you?"

David leaned down. "She has her own job and is very busy. Where is your family, Lynette?"

Lynette pointed to the next booth. A woman was searching beneath tables and behind exhibits. "Come on Lynette." He took the child by the hand and led her back to her family.

A dark-haired woman approached. "You're Caroline Ferraro. I recognize you." She twisted her purse handle. "I'm David's secretary. He talks about you. I couldn't wait for him to introduce us."

"Nice to meet you. David's stories brim with amusing, sometimes painful events. Good he has you to help him and guide some to his office."

She tapped her toes on the ground, then proceeded. "It's good to see him happy. Since Joy … well, it's good to see someone make him smile again."

Caroline plastered on her practiced smile. Her breath caught in her throat, she gripped the edges of the quilt. Joy? Was there another woman in his life? Someone who left him? Or hadn't left him yet? She blinked a few times. "Nice meeting you. Take good care of David on the job."

Her stomach cramped. Of course, David had women in his life. He was sexy, good-looking and fun. What difference did that make? She had no hold on him. She needed something to drink—to wet her lips and mouth.

David walked to her side. "Sorry, Lynette is youngest of five and wanders away often. You ready for lunch? Can't leave Lakeside without visiting R& J's Diner." He linked arms.

"I—" *Well there's no woman around him now.* She could almost hear what Tina would be saying. Finishing the day, seeing it through David's eyes isn't a commitment and couldn't be honing in on Joy's territory. Okay, that's not really true, but

I'm not ready to let go.

"Okay, lunch it is."

Inside, the diner looked like a television set for an old-fashioned diner with a counter and round stools. Behind the counter, cooks and waitresses dodged each other with preparing food and carrying platters. She expected the *Happy Days* theme to start.

The place hummed with activity and aromas of baking turkey, French fries and some exotic roast odors all mingled together. For late afternoon, the place was crowded.

"Come on." David motioned to a booth near the back. He nodded to several older men parked on stools. Caroline slid in one side of the booth across from David.

"The burgers are the famous and most popular—with the secret ingredients in the sauce. Everything is served on paper—like a thin sheet." David lowered his menu to the tabletop.

"Paper? Not plates?" She peered around her large plastic-covered menu.

"Because that's how things are done at R&J's. Know what you want?" The woman who had been behind the counter when they entered, appeared next to the booth. "First time at R&J's." It was a statement. The woman flicked her eyes up and down Caroline's face.

Caroline scowled. Was she related to the woman David dated? Caroline felt the heat rise around her collar. "I'll take the cheeseburger with sauce and fries."

"My usual, Roxanne. This is Caroline Ferraro, Roxanne. She is ..."

"Took over for Larkin. I know." She took the menus from the table, but continued to scrutinize Caroline. "Heard you two were at the Festival and been kayaking." She tapped the menus on Caroline's arm. "He's a good man."

When she marched down the aisle to the grill, Caroline looked at David. "Who is she and what did I do wrong?"

"She is the owner and guardian of the restaurant, its occupants ... and most of the town. She terrifies some. She's been good to me, especially since—" He shredded his napkin in a pile.

Caroline held her breath. What? This is it. This is where he tells me there is someone else.

"I was engaged."

She sucked in her bottom lip. This was it. Ouch. She liked this guy, but not if he were engaged or even on the re-bound. A younger waitress placed a sandwich and fries in front of each of them. Caroline poked a fry with her index finger. Despite the strong savory aroma coming from her sandwich, she didn't want to eat a thing.

"Engaged several years ago." His second napkin he folded into a tiny square. "I lost Joy five years ago." He stared at the folded napkin. "She and my mother were killed in a car accident ..." He took a deep breath. "On the way home from picking up flowers for our wedding."

Air rushed out of Caroline's lungs. "David." She gripped his fingers. What could she possibly say to that tragedy? And she'd wondered if she'd stepped on Joy's toes. "David, I'm sorry. Words can't ..." What had started as an adventure had turned to an anguished memoir.

He rubbed his thumb along the back of her hand, "It was five years ago. I've carried Joy around," He cleared his throat. "I connected with you in a way I haven't ..." He gazed into her eyes. "I haven't since Joy. I feel like I can let go of her, that life. I didn't—couldn't until recently—until you."

She forced air in big gulps. How did she feel about David? She'd go back to Seattle and get on with life and ...

She held both of David's hands in her own. "David, we—I—"

"We need to talk. Just not here." He picked up his cheeseburger. "You'd better eat every bite. Roxanne is watching."

She looked at the food before her and took a tiny bite of her sandwich. It was tasty and unusual—actually delicious. She bit a big chunk. No wonder kids raved.

The sandwich gave her a reprieve. Shock, relief and the unfamiliar of awe warred inside. Eating took away the need to respond right now. He wanted to talk later, but what would she say then?

"Come on." He rose from his seat and headed to the cashier. She followed.

"You like it here, do you?" Roxanne took the bill from David but focused on her.

"Food was good, never had a sandwich like that."

She stopped ringing up the sale on the old-fashioned register. "Meant the town. Lot of people talking about you."

Caroline glanced at David looking for some clues on how to answer that. She licked her lips. "I like the town. The people. Certainly wasn't what I expected to happen when I got here."

Whoa, way too much information.

Roxanne nodded. "Nice people here. Take good care of them." She nodded toward David.

Why did that feel like a veiled threat? Had she heard part of David's comments? "It was nice meeting you."

David moved out the door, Roxanne grabbed Caroline's arm. "You've been good for David and Meg. You certainly helped Larkin out of a bad spot. Lots of people here are glad you came." She withdrew her grip. "And would like you to stay. But don't you break that man's heart. He's been hurt enough."

Caroline scurried out the door and ran to David's side.

"What did Roxanne say? She says what's on her mind."

She matched step with David. "Said many people liked me here."

"Oh yeah. Smart Roxanne." He put his arm around her shoulders and walked back to the street fair. Many vendors were closing up. They walked back to her car, which was now one of four in an empty lot. He started to open the door, stopped and put one hand on the roof so she was encased in his arms. "I like you here and would like to keep showing you around."

Five minutes ago she was panicking at his seriousness and now she found all his words suggestive. "I'd like that, too. I …"

She never finished. He captured her lips in an ardent kiss. She swirled her tongue along his upper lip. His lips pressed harder against hers, his hand played with her hair.

She tightened her grip around his body. The faint stubble of his whiskers scratched her upper lip which intensified her desire. His tongue searched the inside of her mouth. His hands played with her hair. Her senses were alive. She wanted him. She pushed away all the questions and lost herself in the kiss. He abruptly pulled away and she felt as though she were the air pushed from a balloon.

"You made me forget." With that grin, he looked like a kid caught with cookies. "You've made me forget a lot." He looked around. "I forgot we are in the middle of town." He kissed her forehead. "And I wanted you so badly, taking you on the side of the car in the middle of town seemed to be a good idea." He chuckled as if he pictured the scene.

His arms returned to either side of her anchoring her. "You are one incredible woman, Caroline Ferraro." He leaned forward. "I want to stay in contact when you return."

A deep sigh slipped through her. She felt the warmth of him even though he was inches away. "We will."

He moved away. "Great day. Call ya later."

Caroline sat on her front step. What a day. Seeing his role in the town, his secretary's comment. Roxanne's warning and Joy. Not what she expected to learn today. What did he mean by he couldn't let go of that life with Joy until he had met her? Was she the transition between her death and getting on with his life?

Transition in his life was good. She tapped her fingers on the top step. He'd been transition in hers. Going from the pain and confusion of losing Annabelle and breaking ties with Griscom to the new life she wanted when she returned. One with more friends and fun, a garden—and dating. More men were out there not like Griscom. David had proven that.

Transition. That was what they were. Both could go on with their different lives once she returned. This relationship was helping both to change. That's all it was! She smacked the dash with her fingers. All good.

He had asked her to his annual Memorial Day picnic. He tried to make it sound harmless—just his friends and part of his staff. But his father and brother were up from North Carolina and his sisters would be visiting as well. Wasn't that supposed to be significant to meet the parents? Or was that only with females' families when you are younger?

Don't be stupid. She was too old for that to be the rule.

Her parents were dead. Just meet his parents and friends. Sounded like fun—barbecue, music and then watching the town fireworks.

He also said next weekend they'd kayak. Moonlight kayaking. She didn't dare tell Tina about plans for a moonlight kayak.

When she curled up under her covers that night, glimpses of the day whirled in her head. David holding tightly to her hand as they walked through the exhibits. Watching him interact with the town. His mouth on hers, the pressure, the tenderness. And his words, "You've changed my life."

What am I going to do about that man?

CHAPTER SIXTEEN

David was still on her mind as she searched through her closet for an outfit. He'd been engaged. Losing someone on the day of the wedding, how do you deal with that?

She poured herself a large cup of coffee, then curled up on the window seat in the library. Time with David. Memorial Day picnic would be fun. Gets too tough, she could always leave. Knowing they were just each other's transition made her relationship with him easy. He wasn't expecting any permanent connection. She had no reason for any permanent connection to him.

The rolled up sheets of white paper glared at her. She unrolled them and fastened them on the table. She'd work on an equally frustrating challenge: details about the girls.

Bingo. She skimmed through headings. An article. *Yeah!* She browsed the article. *Nope, this Jennifer was born in 1988, not 1978. Misprint.*

She returned to the headings. Another one. A photo! Yes. Finally.

Nope, Jennifer Hudson couldn't be her and couldn't be related to Stephanie. *She is alive and well and winning contests in LA. Not me.* She was in New Jersey. She pushed the chair away from computer.

Both Jennifer and Suzanne are on the bassinet. Both have birth dates close to hers. She could be either one. She looked back at the sheets. She drummed her fingers on the table.

Tomorrow was Monday. Pete's uncle visits Morningstar Cemetery. At least maybe she could get answers to one puzzle. What did Annabelle do in a cemetery?

She called Larkin to see if she wanted to come in for a little bit on Monday.

"I was thinking of calling you once Dylan quieted down. I need to talk with you. I'll have to hire someone to work after you leave."

Caroline flinched. Someone to replace her. Of course, that was practical. She swallowed and licked her lips to get dryness out of her mouth.

"You there? Could you meet with me next week maybe Wednesday to come up with job descriptions and maybe what questions? You have done such a great job. I can't think of who we'll ever get."

"Someone will be glad to come in. Bet one of the women from book club would."

"As long it is not Irene. I would like that. Irene would be too much all day."

Caroline laughed. "Yeah. Love her, but I couldn't work with her all day. Sure, I'll be glad to help. Will you work at all?"

"Ryan and I think I can manage three, maybe three and a half. There's an apartment upstairs. Ryan and his daughter lived there once. I could set up a nursery."

Caroline nodded. She had heard about Ryan moving in and meeting Larkin. She had forgotten about the apartment. The stairs were in the back of the storage room led to a small living space.

"I'll come in tomorrow. I have to go check on Dylan. I hear him."

She wandered down the hall dragging her index finger along the wall. A Replacement. Larkin wanted her help finding her replacement. She didn't like that.

Monday morning, she called Pete at Morningstar, who agreed to meet her at nine.

At the gate of the cemetery, she smoothed down the front of her pants. Please make this a good day for the uncle. She brought three pictures of Annabelle. As she stepped out of her car, Pete waved to her and walked over to join her.

"Glad you showed up. I told him you were coming and were looking for someone. I had to remind him again this morning, but he's eager to help." He pointed to a path to their left.

A grey-haired man peered out the windows of the gatehouse. He stood as they entered.

"Uncle Rodney, this is the woman I told you about."

The man nodded. "You have a photo of a woman who died? You want to find her gravestone?"

"No, I have a photo of my mother. She visited here yearly to visit relatives' burial spot. I'm doing research and need to know where she went."

The man chewed on the side of his cheek as though he were chewing gum. "Okay. Let me see the picture. Maybe I'll remember her. I can't always rely on my memory."

She pulled the pictures from her bag and handed them to him.

He fingered the edge of the picture. "Yep. Annie. Came here once a year. Same place. I can show you." He grabbed a cane from behind his chair. "Come on, little lady. I can help you in your search." He stomped down the stairs. "I can handle this one, Pete, don't need you."

He ambled along the pathways at a good clip. His running monologue about the family names they passed accompanied them. He trotted down a shaded path to a small circular grave site surrounded by ferns.

"Here." He pointed to one gravestone. "Jennifer Feratti. March 12, 1978—March 14, 1978."

Caroline flinched as though someone had punched her in the stomach. Jennifer was not Stephanie's daughter who lived in Minnesota. Nor was she a Jennifer. The real Jennifer only lived two days. She crumpled to her knees.

"Sorry about your loss, Missy." Rodney mumbled. "Annie came here every year. Cleared the weeds, made sure plants were okay and stayed for an hour. I think she talked to her. Maggie May kept up the grave the rest of the time. I think she talked to her, too."

He turned and hobbled down the lane.

"Wait." Caroline stood. "Maggie May. Who is she? Did she come with my mother?"

"Annie, your mom, huh?" He tugged on his chin. "I don't remember Maggie May except when she was young. Pretty young girl. Fair skinned like you. Freckles in the summer. Whistled a lot. She talked to that one, too." He pointed to the marker. "Can't tell you who she is now." He tugged on his ear. "Sorry. I did remember Annie and remembered exactly where she went." He walked away.

Caroline stooped next to the marker and touched the cold, hard letters. She swallowed back a sob. *I'm not Jennifer. Jennifer is dead.* She so attuned to Jennifer and finding more about her, it was as though she had lost a sister.

Wish you could talk, kid. Caroline looked around the area. A small park within a park nestled among the trees across the path. Similar flowers bloomed around a wooden park bench. This is where Annabelle visited yearly.

She gripped the top of the stone. She now knew where Annabelle came. Her visit was a yearly pilgrimage to a grave. Still nothing made sense. Only more why's.

Caroline sat next to the marker. The one person who had any clues couldn't be trusted with his memories.

The connection Annabelle had to this Jennifer was unclear. And who the hell is Maggie May? The cold stone had no answers.

She pulled the weeds among the flowers. Annabelle hated weeding. She never told me about the house. She never told me about the grave. With each statement, Caroline yanked up a weed and smashed it against a nearby tree trunk. Never told me about Maggie May.

Lies, half-truths, deceptions and dead ends. She tossed the weeds and maybe a few vines into a pile. This was a tangle of misconceptions and lies. She threw stones she dug out of the sand. Each one she threw further until her arm ached. She bent forward until her forehead touched the solid earth. None of this made sense.

She didn't wipe away the tears that fell onto the earth. Why Annabelle? Her fists dug tuffs in the dirt. Eventually, the cold of the headstone penetrated her awareness. Her bones ached as much as her heart. She stood, wiped the dirt from her knees and walked back to entrance. She wasn't Jennifer. Now she had more questions than answers.

She called Tina when she returned.

"You really going to quit your search? I can't figure out your mother's role in this. She never seemed capable of lying or deceit. She was an extremely honest businesswoman. Paid attention to detail. This doesn't make sense."

"No kidding." Caroline chopped a carrot into tiny shreds as she balanced her phone on her shoulder. "How could she not share this with me? How could that much of her life be camouflaged."

"She has to be protecting you or someone from the details. So if you aren't Jennifer, then you are Suzanne and Jason is right. You've found family."

Caroline lay her phone on the counter and hit speaker. If only that were true. Making the leap would be great, but. "I don't have the proof. Jason is so counting on me being a relative ... I ... we need more. That would be unfair to claim Jason as an uncle." So many lives effected here.

"You okay? The more you dig into this the more."

"Complicated my life gets. I just don't know. So much I just don't know." She whispered the last few. In Seattle, life had been predictable ... also, boring.

"You have been attached to so many. It is going to be a tug to return. How about Mr. Hottie? Have you told him about this? Maybe he knows more about the town or Maggie May. "

"Noo," She scrapped the carrots into a pile. "I'm not ready to share this with anyone yet. I don't want news to get out about why I am here. Just in case."

"You afraid someone will run. You thought that woman, the one who bakes might be a possibility. Now what?"

"I don't think so. I don't know. The more I search, the more confusing it gets."

"Anything I can do here?"

Caroline chuckled "You are helping me by organizing Annabelle's treasures." She threw a handful carrots in the salad with her left hand. "And listening to me whine."

"Tell me about your friend, Meg. Your life there sounds full of interesting characters. I'm getting pictures of them through your stories."

A mirage of Meg images came to mind. "She has me interested in flowers and looking for birds in the yard."

Tina's laughter lightened her day. "You, in a garden or looking at birds, is an image I never associated with you. Sounds like you are taking the time to smell the roses—really. Good. Your life isn't consumed by work and schedules. You've connected with a few good people."

Maybe the moonlight kayak would be a good time to connect with David. Does his naked chest feel as good as I think—touching it, touching him.

"Earth to Caroline. You daydreaming about Hottie? You left this conversation."

Don't tell her about the moonlight kayak. "I am also making my dinner, I had to concentrate on that."

"Sure. Good to hear that Mr. Hottie is occupying your thoughts and it appears putting some sizzle in your life."

"Hey. I didn't say…"

"Nope didn't have to. Gotta go. My dinner is ready and I have my own hottie joining me. Talk to you later."

She looked at the mass of shredded carrots in the sink. Tina had made her forget for a few minutes about the cemetery. She pushed the carrots down the disposal and poured herself a glass of wine.

CHAPTER SEVENTEEN

Tomorrow, she and Larkin would discuss her replacement. She checked her notes. Even her job description was positive. She closed the door behind her.

She walked toward Greystone. Talking about finding her replacement meant finality. Her trip to Seattle loomed.

"Hey lady, want to slow down?"

David walking swiftly up the sidewalk. He was dressed in work clothes: a grey suit with unbuttoned collar and the tie pulled down. School day was over.

He stopped next to her. "I was hoping I'd catch you. Have time to take a walk along the river." He reached for her hand and they ambled toward the riverfront.

Caroline sat on one of the benches facing the water. *So peaceful here.* David yanked the tie off his neck and stuffed in his suit pocket. He leaned down staring into the water. He said nothing for several minutes.

"I'm worried about Meg. Her eyes are bothering her. She's rubbing them."

Caroline remembered her comments a few days before. "She quit reading the other day, saying reading made them blurry."

David picked up her hand. He scrolled designs on the back. "She won't let me take her to a doctor."

"She had any sign or questions from her doctors about glaucoma?"

He shook his head. "Sometimes MS can do crazy things."

She moved next to him. She rubbed the back of his neck.

He arched back against her. "That's good. Tough days at

school. Testing begins next week then it's preparing for the end of the year. Crazy time in education. And Meg, I want to help her."

She continued the massage. "You take good care of her. She's not related to you is she?"

"No, she was my mom's best friend. When my mother and Joy died, Meg helped through so much."

"Does she refuse care often?"

"She broods about things, decides she can brave it out." He shook his head. "She's so stubborn. "

"A strong woman who doesn't like to admit she needs help. Tough lady to do what she does and stand up to her disease." She kneaded the muscles in the back of his neck and on the top of his shoulders. "Good thing she has you to worry about her and look after her."

He leaned back into her massaging fingers. "You keep doing that, I could forget to worry. Forget I have to attend a PTA meeting in a few minutes. Feels so good."

He closed his eyes for a few seconds then opened them, stood up. "Thanks for listening. Especially thanks for that wonderful massage." He wrapped his arms around her waist and pulled her next to him. He kissed the top of her head

She headed home. She hummed, *Come Away with Me.* Good day. Helped a group of boys with books, read to a four-year old and helped an artist find the book she needed. And she got to touch, Mr. Hottie. She laughed. Uh-oh, she was going to get locked away. She was smiling and laughing in public and no one was with her.

But laughter felt good. She laughed again for good measure before opening the door.

Wednesday, she met with Larkin. Together they created a list of questions for Larkin to ask a potential worker. Larkin repeated how glad she was Caroline showed up at the door and how hard she would be to replace.

During the week, she listed jobs she did and notes for her replacement at Larkin's request. She didn't want to write anything down. She didn't want to think of a replacement. She left the papers next to the cash register when she locked up Friday. The store was closed for Memorial Day Weekend so she didn't have to think about it.

All she had to think about was Mr. Hottie—and he made her smile. Tomorrow was the moonlight kayak to watch the stars. Mmm, a moon, a symbol of romance. Saturday, the picnic. A holiday weekend filled with David.

Her tune changed to *By the Light of the Moon*.

At dusk the next day, she turned into David's driveway. Such a magnificent spot. Two kayaks already rested near the water. Beside them were lanterns, a small cooler and sleeping bags. Sleeping bags? That just set her body on edge. Just what were they looking at tonight?

Go for it. She could hear Tina's urging. *You know you'd like to see if he really is as muscular as he appears. Go for it.*

"Did you forget something?" David's voice startled her. She leaped out of the car.

"No. Just admiring the view."

"I brought sleeping bags to sit on and we can use them if it gets cold or windy."

Oh, so that's what the sleeping bags are for. The devilish, taunting Tina seemed to be perched on her shoulder. Doesn't mean you can't invite him to share a sleeping bag, and your warmth. Tina always prodded her into troubled waters. Tina wouldn't think twice about going after someone or have hot riotous sex just because she hadn't in a long time and needed to. A warm flush heated her cheeks.

He moved toward the house. "But I can keep you warm." She watched tight ass as he walked to the kayaks. She licked her dry lips. *Oh yeah, I bet you can.*

"You're awfully quiet." He reached for her hand. "I'm looking forward to tonight." They walked through the front door.

A constellation book and a newspaper article were opened on his kitchen counter. He flipped to a page in the newspaper. "According to the papers moon should be full, a clear night. Maybe a shooting star, if we are lucky."

Lucky. You could get lucky, buddy. Know what my wish on that star will be. What are you wishing for? She rubbed her arms. Focus. Not on his body. What was he saying about tonight?

"I packed some wine and small glasses. We can have snacks

here. We won't need to leave for a while. Not until the moon comes up." He placed chips, salsa and glasses on the table. "Would you like wine now?"

"Before I kayak in the moonlight? No, I think I want to be very alert and be able to see."

He grinned as he filled glasses with ice. "You'll do fine. The moon gives us a path to follow right to the island."

"You've done this before." She reached for a chip. How many women had he taken to this island and toted sleeping bags? Was this a practiced seduction move or was he really interested in the moon and the stars?

"I grew up kayaking. As kids, it was a great time to sneak out to the island in the dark."

"And just what did you do on this mysterious island?"

He crunched a chip. "Hunted frogs, disturbed turtles, swam naked, had sword fights with tree limbs, swung out in the water from a rope and later tried our first Thunderbird Wine." He crinkled his nose.

"Was that wince from thinking about jumping in the water or from remembering the taste of that wine?"

"The wine is an old standby, I think, for every kid here to sample illegal sip—it's 98 cents a bottle today."

She grimaced. "Didn't have those experiences. Have never heard of Thunderbird before today."

"Think it's local. What did you do to be a wild child in Seattle?"

"Tina. Tina always got me in trouble."

"And just what did Tina get you to do?" He leaned against the counter.

"We hid inside the Pacific Science Museum and wandered around after it closed." She and Tina had been frozen in their hiding spot. Afraid to go out for fear they would get caught. What a crazy time—fun time. "That was before all the surveillance equipment guarded the privacy of all those animals." She dipped a chip in salsa. "I don't know which was scarier—seeing those dinosaurs outlined in the dark or hearing the footsteps of the guard on patrol."

"Did you get caught?"

"Not on that adventure. I did touch a dinosaur bone and

stroked the fur of a seal."

He sat on the breakfast nook stool beside her. "And when did you get in trouble?"

"Tina's mom worked long hours. Often, I stayed at Tina's house a lot growing up. We got away with a lot because her mother slept through most of it. We smoked weed for the first time on her small porch. Didn't get caught."

"You don't look like one who smoked much. So when did you get caught?"

His eyes danced, his smile was infectious. She really liked this David Montgomery. Too bad she hadn't met him in Seattle. "When we were older—teens. We tried to invite boys in, thinking her mom wouldn't notice. She did. We were both grounded, our parents scandalized. "

"Do you always follow Tina's lead when she suggests something outrageous?"

Well, tonight I might. She bit into the chip and concentrated on its flavor before answering. "Not all the time. She just goads me into trying things that I'm too chicken—or just too unimaginative to think up. I need someone like Tina to spice up my life."

David's gaze lingered on her face. "I think I would like to see you and Tina together."

"You'll have to see us in Seattle."

"So am I going to be invited?"

She tilted her head. Yeah, wow she could get him on her turf. Show him her city. "Yeah," she nodded "I'd like to show you Seattle. Ever been there?"

"Nope. I've heard it s beautiful and greatest place ever to order salmon."

"You mentioned salmon before. It is a great place to have salmon, but it is used as a tourist attraction. I'll make sure you will have the best salmon ever and see Seattle."

"Visit your dinosaur?"

She frowned. "Oh, the one in Pacific Science Museum—Clyde, yes."

"Clyde?"

"Tina and I named him."

They chatted about crazy youth adventures. David rose

and cleared the dishes to the sink. "We can head out now." He handed her a device, which looked like a torture item. "This is a flashlight you can wear on your forehead." He demonstrated. She twisted it in her hands. "Do I have to? I could scare Clyde with that on. Can't I just use a normal flashlight?"

"You need both hands to paddle. No flashlight. You are going on an adventure to Machael's Island. You only turn on the flashlight if we hear movement in the water or boat whistles. You paddle in the dark."

"The moon will be that bright?"

He nodded. "Your eyes quickly adjust to the dark. You can see the water and the area ahead of you."

He picked up flashlights, constellation chart and the basket. "Time for adventure."

"What kinds of things am I going to hear in the water that I need to turn on the flashlight?"

"Lions and tigers and bears, oh my." He walked backward.

"If you start skipping down the path, I'm leaving."

"We should see nothing in the water. Snakes aren't out and wildlife is asleep. You just need to be aware. Also, to get to the island, we cross an open waterway. Bigger powerboats can cross. They're noisy. We'll hear them. Then we turn on lights and stay out of their way. We have right-of-way, but that doesn't mean they will look for us or move."

The moon sparkled on the water. "It does look like a path." The moonbeam highlighted a channel in the river just for them.

"Didn't believe me, huh? It will be a wonderful night, believe me on that." He handed her the PFD and used it to pull her closer and kissed her.

Already a wonderful night. She flicked her tongue over his bottom lip. Salty. He leaned into her. His hand caressed the back of her head. His tongue danced across her upper lip.

He released her and stood looking as though he'd been hit by a thunderbolt.

Maybe the same bolt hit her. She had forgotten where she was. This isn't over. She wanted more. That island is private, dark. Time to explore—David, not the island,

"I guess we'd better go. Paddle now." Her voice squeaked.

He nodded and yanked up the zipper on his PFD. "Once we both get our boats moving, you can pull up beside me. It is quiet water till we get closer to the island."

She stepped in her kayak as he held the side. He gave her the paddle and pushed her in. He loaded the cooler, sleeping bags, pushed off then, jumped in the boat. Soon he was beside her.

The water was quiet, serene. The stars shone brightly and also gave a twinkling radiance to the water. The drips of the water from the paddles were the only sound.

"You okay," his voice was soft, muted.

"Yes, I'm just admiring. It's so quiet. Do you paddle much at night?"

"Not by myself. It's like swimming by yourself. Too dangerous. Too much unexpected in the water. I do love it on the water. I sit outside at night." He dipped his paddle in.

"Your turkey friends let you do that undisturbed?" Her fingers loosened on her paddle.

"Yeah. They aren't out to chase me away."

When they crossed the channel, he pointed out rocks and branches as they paddled closer to the island. The island was a patch sticking above the water. Small scraggly pines stuck finger-like branches into the sky. The island was maybe the size of three football fields. He aimed at a clear spot between two fallen trees, pulled his boat in then signaled her to follow.

He offered an arm as a steadying board as she scrambled from the kayak. The night air smelled like pine candle. The air was moist with humidity.

He handed her the sleeping bags, "Can you manage them and the paddles. I don't like to leave them with the boats."

They walked single file between the pines to a clear space on the edge of the island. He spread out the bags, put the cooler beside them and piled paddles and PFDs together.

She put the paddles down and he shook out a tiny square plaid tablecloth. He placed a tray and then two plastic wine glasses, a bottle and crackers. "I have white or red. I wasn't sure which."

"Tonight I'll take red. I really like both." Griscom had taken a wine-tasting course and had made buying and tasting wine a science. He discussed the wine's flavors every time someone opened a bottle. She had given up drinking it because of him.

David tugged on the edge of the sleeping bag until he turned her completely around so she faced the water. He handed her a glass of wine and scooted behind her and stretched his legs on either side.

"Now, if you look that way," His voice and the warmth of his nearness caressed her neck and her cheek. "You will see stars. And over there," He stretched his arm across her to point to the left. He dropped his arm so it rested across her shoulder. "That's Machael's Cove, one of my favorite spots."

"Is this where you swam naked?"

His deep laugh rumbled against her back. She snuggled closer into the comfort and warmth of his chest.

His cheek brushed hers. "Look up there, you can see Big Dipper." He tightened his hold around her waist. "Get your wish ready. I've seen multiple shooting stars here."

The sky was dark and filled with stars as if she had climbed to the top of Mt. Rainier in Seattle. If she reached up she could touch one, they looked so close.

"Oh. Oh," She jumped up and pointed as a shooting star crossed the sky in front of them. He grasped her hand and raced to the edge of the water.

Leaning against a nearby pine, he enclosed her in the warmth of his arms. He whispered in her ear. "Make a wish." His breath caressed her cheek, his hand rested on her shoulder. As if he read her mind and knew her wish, he wrapped his arms around her. He leaned back against the tree and they stared silently at the sky.

The night stilled. The rustle of small animals darting in the scrubs behind them, the waves quietly lapping the shore all magnified. A wish is a dream unfulfilled. Actions fulfill dreams.

She slipped her hands beneath his T-shirt, her fingers stroked his chest hairs, her palms pushed into his abs as she ran her hands down the inside of his shirt. His tight muscles, the silkiness of his hair tickling her fingertips was so much better than any fantasy about him. A low moan rumbled against her palms. Ah, he liked this, too.

She pushed his shirt upward and flipped it over his head and tossed it onto the nearby bush. She rubbed her cheek against his nakedness. Yes, this is what wishes were about. "I've been thinking about your pecs."

He striped her of her shirt and hung it over his. He unfastened her bra and she let it slip off. They melted together. She rubbed her nipples against him. His erection pressed into her pelvic bone.

"I've been thinking of more than your pecs." He leaned down pressed his mouth against hers. She rocked her hips against him.

With no warning, he flipped her up into his arms.

"David, you can't carry …"

He tightened his grip. "But I am. Pretend you are a princess. In fairy tales, princesses like to be swept off their feet."

Laughter erupted deep from within her. She curled into his arms.

He gently placed her on the sleeping bag and knelt beside her. "You have too many clothes on." He tugged her jeans. She shimmed out of them and pushed them away with her hands.

David stroked the curves of her belly, slowly exploring her sides, her hips. His fingers both soft and hot created sizzling strokes along her body. He drew erratic patterns around her nipples. She clenched the edges of the sleeping bag as the heat rose within.

More of him. She wanted more. She unsnapped his pants and slid her hands on his warm skin as she peeled his jeans down. His erection bounced before her. She painstakingly ran her nail down his shaft. A quick intake of David's breath. With two fingers, she ran two fingers down the length of him and flicked her tongue across his tip. He closed his eyes. His chest rose in short, quick breaths.

He stroked the curves of her belly, then moved down and tickled her pubic hairs with the tips of his fingers. "I've wanted to touch you since first day watching slowly slurp Chinese noodles down the back of your throat."

His hands encircling his glass on that same day inspired graphic thoughts about what those hands might feel like on her naked skin. She licked her lips. Now she knew—magnificent!

Hot sensations electrified her body. His finger exploring her and her fingers touching the softness and toughness of his chest his legs set off sparks of heat and need within.

He thrust two deep within her, this thumb continued his torment. She arched against him driving his fingers deeper.

She held onto his shoulders to keep herself grounded. "David, please." She tugged on his shoulders pulling him on top of her. Deftly, he flipped onto his back and she sat on top of him. Her wetness embraced him.

"The ground is too bumpy and sharp. I'll stay underneath."

"You are so princely."

"Princes aim to please." He seized his jeans, pulled shiny squares from a pocket. He's prepared, well-prepared. He rolled a condom down. Placing his hands on her hips, he guided her down the length of him.

A sharp cry rang out as heat spiraled through her body. She rocked her hips the length of him. They reached a rhythm. With each rocking movement she tightened her folds against him, tried to hang on, but exploded with cries then whimpers. The whole world was reduced to one sensation. The pressure of David's body next to hers and desire overwhelming her. She lost herself in sensations, lost her hold of realty and the earth beneath them.

When her body calmed and she floated back to earth, she lay beside David's warmth. His breathing was labored, his eyes closed.

"I don't remember ever being like that. I was noisy."

A low chuckle shook his chest. He didn't open his eyes. "It's okay, I heard all the animals slip into the water and swim off the island."

She jabbed him in the arm. He leaned up on his hand and faced her. "I'm glad you made noises. I liked it. All of it." He leaned back on the ground and she snuggled next to him, her head resting on his outstretched arm.

She awoke to the stillness of the moment between darkness and dawn. The stars had faded, a faint pale glow rose along the horizon. She was naked lying on her back on some island in New Jersey. Satisfied couldn't begin to describe this. A rock poked her shoulder, but she didn't want to tarnish the moment. She couldn't move.

The sensuous, exciting man with muscular arms and long magical fingers lay close beside her. His quiet breathing caressed her ear, his body warmth still peaked a glow. His touch brought her to heights she had never even imagined or even wished for on that shooting star.

"You're smiling, so that's a good thing." He stretched his fingers out and covered her hand with his. "Good night?"

"I don't think I've ever had an evening like that. In so many ways," She rolled toward him and touched dark hairs around his temple. "It was a memorable night."

"Stick with me, honey, and many more once-in-a lifetime adventures are in your future."

She chuckled at his very bad Bogart imitation.

He snuggled closer. "It was a wonderful night."

Squeals of high-pitched laughter pierced the quiet.

"Kids! Quick!" He jumped up. He hopped on one foot yanking on his pants. "Kids here. Grab as much as you can. Go to the boats. I'll grab our shirts." He stopped. "Put on something."

She shook her pants that were inside out balled up at the end of the sleeping bag and pulled them up. Grabbed sleeping bags, wine bottle and the PFDs. David swooped up the paddles, his picnic basket and they jogged down to the water's edge. "Here." He tossed her clothes to her, threw things in his boat.

Caroline threw her bra in the bottom of her kayak, tugged on her shirt and jumped in. He handed her the paddles and pushed her into the water. She paddled as fast as her arms could move. The wine bottle rolled around the boat. She kicked her bra out of the way. The sounds of the children's voices faded behind them.

She turned slightly. A shirtless David paddled erratically, the edge of a sleeping bag trailed in the water beside him. His rumpled hair stuck up randomly. She placed her paddle across her lap. Laughter spilled over. Her sides shook, tears clouded her eyes. Like two characters in a cartoon, they had darted around, dressed and raced away.

David slowed his kayak down beside her. "I feel like a twelve-year-old caught skinny dipping."

"Where's your shirt?"

"In the cooler, I hope. We can shower and dress at my place."

She paddled beside him. Her glow within matched the glimmer surrounding them as the morning light spread across the horizon. "Thank you." She rested her paddle across the "Memorable evening."

"Not often you see shooting stars out there. Hope you get your wish."

My wish and then some. Alive. The morning light, the freshness of the air and the tingle lingering inside. Alive. Had she ever felt so alive?

After they returned, they worked side by side emptying kayaks, and coolers. David whistled as he hung wet clothes on the line. She carried the wine glasses and picnic food inside.

David yanked towels out of a closet. "We've been in the woods all night. Time for a tick check.'

"Tick check?"

"New Jersey woods have dangerous ticks." His words were serious, but his eyes twinkled. With his hand on her shoulder, he guided her to his bathroom. "I have to examine every square inch of your body—your sexy body—to make sure it is not marred by even the tiniest tick." He pulled her shirt off and threw it in a pile on the floor. Her kissed her forehead and nuzzled her temple with his beard stubble. "Every inch of you." He flicked his tongue on the inside of her ear.

Her body tingled. Her nipples hardened. Oh yes, a wonderful day. Alive.

"A tick check, huh? Guess I have to inspect you." She ran her fingers across his chest. Yesterday, his skin against her fingertips sizzled with heat. Today, touching him, the warmth of his body, the hardness of his muscles answered an ache within.

"Every inch." His tongue moved from her ear, down her neck. He bent down and kissed her breast, coaxing her nipple in his mouth then rolling around with his tongue.

"David." His name came out as a gasp. Her fingers dug into

his shoulders.

He reached behind her, flipped on the shower. He tugged her pants down and tossed them to the pile. "We can do a much better check soaping each other in the shower."

She clung to him as he stepped under the water soaking them both. She groped for the soap, poured it into her palm and washed him from his shoulders to his penis. The moan from David spurned her on. She stroked slowly from his balls to his tip. She fondled his balls in her palm. "Nope, no ticks there."

He flattened his palms on either side of the shower stall. She encircled his cock with her fingers and gently moved the length of him. He lifted her and pushed her into the furthest corner of the shower, then kissed her, his stubble scratching her lips. His kisses sent shivers down her spine. Her breasts ached with need.

He could kiss her forever. The fullness of his lips pressed hard against hers. His tongue teased the top of her mouth, her cheeks. He rolled her nipple between his thumb and forefinger. She scratched her nail across his nipple, and then gently tugged on the hardened tip.

He sharply inhaled. "You're driving me crazy."

"That's a good thing."

"Oh, ye-s-s." His answers came out as moans as she leaned down and pulled on the other nipple with her teeth, then flicked her tongue across it. She wanted him, wanted him inside her. "David, condom. Now."

He flung open the shower door slamming against the wall, rummaged through a drawer and returned ready. She yanked him back in the closeness of the shower

He lifted her up, she wrapped her legs around his hips and he drove his cock deep within her. Her breath came in pants. She rocked against him as he pounded inside her again.

"David." Desire spun out of control as wave after wave of exotic sensations travelled throughout her body leaving her shuddering and shaking.

They collapsed against the shower wall. Neither moved. She still held onto his shoulders. She had dug her nails in his arms and left red marks. No one had ever made her crazy with need or made her climax with intensity.

He leaned on one leg. His hands dangled at his sides. He smiled with the same infectious smile which made her fall in— which attracted her the first time he entered Readers' Haven.

"Guess we are tick free and ready to play in the woods again." He said.

"Today?"

"No," He slid open the shower door. "No more today. My sisters arrive in three hours to help get ready for tomorrow's picnic."

"Sisters? The picnic. I forgot all about that. I need to get out of here."

He helped her out of the shower and into his arms. He wrapped a towel around her back. "We have plenty of time." He rested his chin on top of her head. "We're good."

She rested her cheek in the hollow of his chest—it fit as though the spot were made for her. *Yeah, we're good.*

She dried off in the guest room put on David's sweatshirt and clean jeans she had packed. The sleeves hung long past her fingers and the hem stretched halfway to her knees. She hugged it. It smelled earthy like the outdoor smell of the island and David.

Oh, come on, she was no longer the teen wanting the boy friend's sweater. She ran her fingers through her wet hair.

The smell of bacon drifted into the room. David starting breakfast. She'd slept in the woods with a sexy man, she had crazy sex in a shower and now that man is making her breakfast. Could she convince him to come to Seattle with her so she could repeat this day? Move to Seattle? It has schools.

David walking through the bustling streets of Seattle amid the traffic and irritating smells didn't fit. Even if they could escape to the mountains of Idaho's Coeur d'Alene, that was only some weekends at best. She looked out the window at the moving river, his kayaks. No, she couldn't paint a person into the landscape of your life. David didn't fit in her frame of life.

She touched the letters on the front of his sweatshirt. He said he wanted to visit.

"Breakfast!"

David had two places ready on the counter and bacon, eggs

already on each plate.

She bit into the bacon. Ah, it tasted as good as it smelled. "Thanks for breakfast. How soon will your sisters get here?"

"They will be late." He placed a plate of toast on the table. "Carrieann flies in first and is picking up Gloria who flew in yesterday. She stayed at the airport hotel. Gloria is never ready." He rolled his eyes. "They will be late."

She laughed.

"You have no siblings to argue or laugh with."

She shook her head.

"Best of world and worst of world. My sisters are great… and aggravating."

"I need to get out of here before your sisters arrive—late." She picked up her plate and took it to the sink. "You sure you want me here tomorrow?"

"Very sure." He scrapped his plate in the sink. "Very. Want you here every day. Want to move in? We could shower daily."

"David!' She poked him in the ribs. "Enough." She tried to wipe away her grin and be serious, but that didn't work. "Of course, not. I mean I'll be here tomorrow, but no, not daily showers."

He placed his hands around her face. "See you tomorrow. I'll take one day at a time."

CHAPTER EIGHTEEN

Caroline packed ice around the tortellini salad in the Styrofoam container. Relax. David said a few friends came to his annual Memorial Day picnic. An annual event. Then you add siblings and his dad. Did that mean something when he wanted her to meet his family?

So when she met them, she'd lead with, "Hi, I'm Caroline. The grin I can't wipe off is because of David's talented fingers and tongue." That would get his friends' attention. She bit her lip. Can't go anywhere near that bathroom. Showers will never be the same in his house. Focus. His relatives. His friends. Not sex.

She checked her outfit one more time. Capris, navy blue tee shirt and red hairband. Appropriate, not overdone. She patted left side of her curls. Hair down long, didn't frizz today. Her Seattle hairdresser worked to keep her curly hair short and in control. Now she designed her own style and her hair was past shoulder length. She tossed it over her shoulder. And she liked it long. She smoothed the front of her shirt.

Okay, she was as ready as she would ever be. Just a few friends and his sisters, and a brother and father. She could do this.

She turned onto David's street. Cars lined the sides. A few friends? She parked and paused at the end of the drive. The front yard had setups for badminton, a corn hole toss and croquet dotted the front yard. Many different color kayaks lined the shoreline and overflowed onto the grass.

The smell of hickory-smoked barbecue and coconut lured her a few steps down the driveway. Music blared from speakers somewhere behind his cabin. Now what?

She knew no one but David and he was nowhere in sight. She was holding a dish and gaping like an idiot. She gripped her plastic container and marched to the kitchen.

A tall, lanky woman with light hair greeted her when she reached the kitchen. "Hey, you're Caroline. I've heard about this salad." She dropped her spoon on the counter. "And about you. I'm Carrieann, David's sister." She took the container from Caroline's hands and placed it atop the covered bowl on the top shelf of the refrigerator.

Great, start out with the relatives. "Should I worry about what you have heard?" Did that sound enough like a joke? Her palms were sweaty. How could she get out of this without saying the wrong thing?

The woman had David's open, inviting grin relaxed her. "Miriam called. She saw you on a date with David and reported it right away."

"Oh, well, we're not really dating. I mean I like him." She grabbed a pretzel from a nearby basket and shoved it in her mouth.

"David doesn't appear in public with women. That made it a noteworthy event, so Miriam called." She licked the icing from a small bowl, covered it and pushed it to the corner. "That doesn't sound good. He dates. Not many. Certainly none he has shown any interest in until you. I was curious, wanted to meet you." She flushed. "I'm digging myself in deep." She pointed out the window. "David is supervising the grill. Go see him."

Caroline headed to the group of men. "Nice to meet you," she shouted over her shoulder.

Chicken pieces, ribs, hamburgers, and hotdogs lined one grill. Shrimp, trout, seafood kabobs filled another. The tempting smells of garlic, hickory smoke grew stronger the closer she got. *If that tastes as good as it smells, no wonder why so many come to this event.*

David wrapped his arm around her and led them away from the group. "Hey," he said softly in her ear before he kissed her. "I thought of you while taking my shower."

She edged away. So many eyes on them as they kissed.

"Want me to introduce you around? I could get everyone's attention by kissing you the way I want to, then just say, "This is Caroline.'"

Her eyes widened. "Don't do anything like that. I just met one of your sisters."

"Uh-oh. Which one?"

"Carrieann."

David's body relaxed. "She didn't grill you. Don't get anywhere alone with Gloria. She's the overly protective big sister."

"What did you tell them about me?"

He grinned and guided her to the nearest picnic table. He sat next to her and wrapped his arm around her. "I'm interested and don't want you to leave."

Caroline inhaled sharply.

Car doors slammed and noise peaked. David glanced over his shoulder. "I'll come get you in a minute. My dad arrived and I need to help Cliff." He tugged on her hand. "Meg is over under the tent in the shade. She has been asking about you. I'll meet you there." He walked with her to the tent, let go of her hand and scurried off.

Meg waved from her lounge chair in the corner of the tent. A glass of iced tea and a small plate with carrots, and grilled vegetables rested on a table beside her.

"Quite a crowd." Meg said. "Glad you came. He will be back once he gets his dad settled."

Caroline pulled up a chair.

"Poor Bentley—his dad. Such a wonderful man. Gentle, generous. Such a shame. Some days are good. Some days he is lost to a world the rest of us don't know." She shook her head. "I miss him. His wife and I were best friends. Suzanne would be so upset."

"David told me about losing his mom and fiancé just before the wedding. Such a tragedy."

Meg bit her lip. "I didn't think he'd ever get over it. Broke his heart. Changed him." She sipped her tea. "Then he closed up his feelings. Reached out to help others like the kids in that school. That's where he has directed his life and his emotions."

David pushed a wheelchair toward the back porch. A man

the same size and gait as David walked on the other side of the white haired man bent over in the chair.

"It is important to David you are here. He likes you. You need to get to know him better."

"Yeah, I know." She jumped as though someone had pricked her. "I mean, I like David. We have fun. I'm going ho—Back."

Meg nodded. "Spend time together. Are you going to stay in touch when you go back?"

She liked his hands, liked the feel of them on her skin, her cheek.

Meg paused with a carrot halfway to her lips.

What had Meg just asked her? The movement of David's hands interrupted any sane thought. Think. Meg wants an answer. Ah, keeping in touch. "David and I haven't discussed if we will talk after I return." An ache closed its fist around her heart. He would be a hard man to leave. But they had two different lives on opposite sides of the country.

"I would hate to see David in anguish again in his life. He just started to trust life."

She shook her head. She was not in charge of that. I just met him. We have no commitment. "I don't know, Meg, we will have to see with that." She didn't want to get into this with her. "Can I get you anything? That barbecue smells wonderful."

"Maybe later. David is coming." She nodded toward the front lawn. Caroline stood as David ambled toward her. That smile gave him an impish look. He would be a hard man to leave.

"Excuse us, Meg, I want to introduce her to my dad." He took her hand between both of his. "You okay? I haven't spent much time with you yet." He wrapped his around hers. "Come on."

His father was ensconced in the corner of his back porch. No mistaking the resemblance between him and the two men near him. All three had that long, lean look and green eyes. David brought her close to his side and introduced her.

Bentley shook her hand and grinned. "Good to finally meet you." He leaned forward. "What a beauty." Grasping her other hand, he added, "You going hold onto this one? You need a woman in your life."

Cliff moved next to the chair and straightened the pillow behind him.

"Dad, no matchmaking. She lives in Seattle."

"Seattle?" He leaned back in the chair. "I visited around there. Bainbridge."

She smiled. "My mother's house is on Bainbridge Island."

"Beautiful spot. I fished there."

David squeezed her elbow. "I'll be right back. Grill's smoking too much." He trotted away.

"I travelled there by bus. Before I met Suzie." He looked over toward the water and the kayaks.

Cliff patted his shoulder. "Good day. He can talk with someone and hold his own. Doesn't always happen." His father studied the kayaks as three women ventured into the water.

"You returning to Seattle soon?"

A heavy weight descended on her shoulders. Soon. She shrugged off the feeling. "I came to sell a house. I stayed longer to help a friend. I have to return to a job, my life."

"Maggie May," Bentley clutched her hand. "You're still beautiful."

Caroline shuffled backward and grabbed the chair back to steady herself.

"You did the right thing. You are a brave, amazing woman, Maggie May. You haven't changed a bit." His eyes brightened.

She knelt down beside him. "I am not Maggie May."

"Changing your name gave you a fresh start, but you will still be Maggie May to me." He patted her head. "Damn shame we listened to that woman. You're a strong lovely girl, don't you forget that!" His voice raised an octave.

"I'm not Maggie May, do you know her?"

"Don't you contradict me, young lady." He stood gripping the sides of the wheelchair and wobbling on his thin legs.

Cliff held him up. "Easy, Dad. Sit down." He helped him back in the chair and handed him pretzels on a plate. "Let's get you something to eat." He turned to Caroline. "Sorry, sometimes he loses reality."

"He compared me to Maggie May. Who is she? Why did he

say that?"

Cliff shrugged. "Sometimes he just mixes people up. Goes back in time. Or just creates a memory. I'm sorry if he upset you."

"No, no, it's okay. I don't want to ruin his day. Does he know Maggie May? Is she real?"

"I don't know." Cliff turned the wheelchair around. "He could be back to normal later. You could try talking to him. I don't know."

She wandered to the back yard. Maggie May again. How does he know the woman at the cemetery? She clutched her stomach. A girl? He called Maggie May a girl, but didn't Rodney call Maggie May another woman?

David met her halfway. "Hey, pretty lady."

She blinked. David. She could ask him.

"They are starting up the band. Care to dance with me. Great way to get close. Then I can be with you and not get interrupted." David grabbed her fingertips.

She'd ask him later when so many weren't around. "Been a long time since I danced." She hesitated. When had she just danced for fun? Business associate's wedding? Dancing with David their first time together in his house— that was memorable.

"Just follow me. We did great with John Legend. No one in this crowd cares."

A small band of two guitarists, keyboard player, fiddle and flute were setting up in the side yard. Boards stretched in a horizontal line adding a dance floor to the yard. This was a well-planned party with lots to do.

"Come, they're playing our song." The band started Legend's *Slow Dance*—the one they had danced to in his kitchen. She slipped into the cradle of his arms.

He spun her out catching her by the tips of his fingers, then spun her back then drew in close so their bodies molded together.

Her head fit perfectly in the hollow of his chest. She closed her eyes, inhaled deeply. She had no desire to leave his embrace

"You feel so good next to me. Do you think I could bribe them to just play slow dances?"

"We could hope."

The music changed pace and they danced to anything the band chose. They ad-libbed steps from hip-hop to country line dancing. Her sides hurt from laughing as they tripped over feet and bumped into each other and others. David spun her high in the air or they awkwardly flapped their arms in the *Chicken Dance*.

When had she felt this free, free to act goofy, to flap my wings, to be flung in the air like a rag doll and laugh so richly. She bent in half trying to catch her breath after their awkward attempt to keep up with *Jump on It*.

David leaned down. "Don't go anywhere." He trotted to the guitarist, chatted briefly, then returned. "Come." He led her to the middle of the floor just as the band played the first bars of *Sweet Caroline*.

He swung her into his arms and sang along. The crowd formed a circle around them and joined in the "Sweet Caroline, Bum, bum, bum." In the closing bars, he picked her off her feet, held her tight to his body and swayed to the closing bars. "You're wonderful!"

They stopped dancing to the riotous applause of his friends and family, then sank on the nearest picnic table bench. Her feet, her legs, even her arms ached, but her heart sang. No wonder everyone came to his Memorial Day picnic. Maybe next year, she'd fly out. *I love this!*

His sisters brought two plates loaded with ribs, salad, grilled vegetables and a pile of napkins. Carrieanne flopped on the bench across from her brother. "You need to recharge after all that energy. That was great." She chuckled. "I haven't heard you sing in years." She poked David in the arm. "Of course, now I know why. When did you learn to dance like that? What have you been doing this year that we didn't know about?"

David stopped eating, held the dripping rib in his fingers. "I haven't danced ... since Joy." He wiped the rib drippings off the table. "And never like that." He winked at Caroline. "I was inspired."

She inspired him to come out of his shell? She inspired that craziness? A giggle escaped. "That was so much fun." She hugged David's arm and kissed his cheek. "I'm so glad you invited me."

Gloria scowled at her. What had she done? Kissing her brother brought that glower?

"The tortellini salad was awesome. David also raves about desserts you've made. You cook for a big family?" Carrieanne scooped up another mouthful of salad.

"No, I had the time here to try more things."

While she chatted with one sister, she avoided the pointed glare from the other, very silent and stony sister. What was with that one? She didn't like the flagrant throwing out the rules when one danced? Doesn't like the food? She turned to avoid the pointed stare. Talking with Carrieanne was easy.

"David, Cliff is signaling you. I think he needs your help with Dad." Gloria gave up her scowl to point in Cliff's direction. David patted her on her arm and jumped up to help.

"Why don't you get desserts for all of us." Gloria stared at her sister.

"You didn't eat food yet."

"Now Carrieanne." As soon as her sister scurried away, Gloria faced Caroline.

Caroline shifted in her seat. This sister had an agenda.

"David is happier than I have seen him in years." She didn't have to add in the ending, "since Joy" but Caroline heard it. "Singing, dancing, laughing with such exuberance had disappeared from his life."

Exuberance, laughter were good words, but Gloria spat them out as though they were incriminations.

"We have fun. I'm glad I met David." She forced a smile, but gripped the bench with her fingers.

"You enjoy your time? My brother is in love with you."

"No, no he can't be. We haven't known each other long enough for that to happen."

"You can't be that dense. You don't notice how he looks at you, how he reaches to touch you, to kiss you. You can't tell how he feels when you are close to him?" Gloria half rose from her chair and leaned forward on the tips of her fingers.

She looked down at the table. David's hand as he stroked her nakedness, the warmth of his body close as they danced, the joy, the laughter he elicited. She loved all that, but …

"You are involved with him," Gloria persisted. "You snuggle too close, kiss his cheek, radiate when you are with him. He doesn't matter? You are involved with David." She tapped her nails on the table.

Involved. Sex. Fun. But involvement required commitment and emotion. But they were transition friends. Even David said that. She pushed her plate to the center of the table.

"What are you going to do about it?" Gloria stood up and glared down at her.

"I have to go back, back to Seattle. That's where I live."

"And then what? When he's not there to hold you, not there to kiss, not there to laugh and tease? Then what?"

"I ..."

"What do you want from my brother?"

She opened her mouth to answer Gloria, but just blinked.

"You need to decide." She rapped her knuckles on the table. "Decide what he is in your life and make the right decision." She stomped away, caught her approaching sister's arm and steered her toward the house. "They don't want dessert."

David walked his father to the car. He gently lifted him from the chair and placed him in a seat.

What did she want? She sat rooted watching him interact with his brother and sisters clustering around the father's side of the car.

She needed to be polite, say good-bye. Then she needed to leave. David wasn't in love with her. She wasn't— She just needed to leave. She pressed her fingers to center of her abdomen. Lunch didn't agree with her. That's why she needed to go.

She joined David to say good-bye to his family. Bentley stared blankly at her as if he had never seen her. No more information on Maggie May.

"Nice to meet you." Cliff hugged her. "Sorry his day was confused. We can't predict what comes to his mind." He moved to his father, checked his seatbelt, squeezed his shoulder, then got in the driver's side and waved goodbye.

David rested his arm around her shoulders as they watched them leave. His sisters disappeared into the crowd in the back yard.

"I need to go."

"Now? Thought we could dance more and maybe paddle out in the kayaks and disappear for a while."

"I need to go. I open tomorrow and need to be alert." That was a lie, but she would call Larkin and convince her opening when people were off for a holiday weekend would be good for business. Focusing on other things and not thinking about David's arms, his words and the touch of his fingers would be good for her.

He walked her to the car and pulled her into his arms. "Best picnic in my memory."

She smiled and leaned against him. His heart beat a steady rhythm, his fingers massaged her back. "Yes, it was the best picnic ever." She bit her upper lip, then pushed herself away with the palms. "Talk to you later."

"Caroline?" David's hands hung at his sides. "We... Don't leave."

She shut the car door to silence his words.

CHAPTER NINETEEN

Monday morning, she was glad to have a job to go to. She had a restless night. She dreamt of sleeping under the trees in David's arms and Gloria had become an owl in the trees above them hooting "Decide, decide." She had no life here. He didn't love her. They had established that. How unfair to even think about a relationship.

She put off calling Tina. Describing the picnic and all the events was too confusing. She yanked books off the shelves and wiped the wood, then replaced the books. She couldn't share that with Tina yet.

She rearranged books and dusted the wood. She even climbed on the ladder and cleaned the ceiling fans. She read over her list of questions for her replacement. That's what she should focus on—returning to the house in Seattle.

She wiped down the coffee table and cleaned all of the mugs. A gang of middle school boys came in needing help with a school project. She spent most of her afternoon pulling out details of the assignment and helping each find materials. It was exhausting, but gratifying. It banished Gloria's scowl and refrain. "What are you going to do …"

The store emptied. She packed her iPad and papers in her bag. Dr. Morgan entered carrying a bag of books. "Hi Caroline."

"You bringing in books before you leave?" Caroline had not expected to see Dr. Morgan again especially in an empty store. Although he had been in several times, it was always when the store was crowded and he avoided her. He was leaving for Arizona tomorrow carrying all his knowledge about her with him.

He rocked on his heels with the bag hanging in his hand. "I came to talk with you."

Caroline reached for the bag then stopped in midair. "Oh," came out in a whisper. If she said anything more, would he bolt for the door?

"I delivered Jennifer and Suzanne."

She inhaled sharply and tucked her shaking hands under her armpits.

He dropped the books on the floor and sat on the stool in front of her. "I couldn't in good conscience go back to Arizona without talking to you. Too many years I have held an ugly secret." His shoulders sagged.

"Secret?" Her voice crackled.

"I've waited for my past to catch up with me. Waited to lose my medical license. Waited. And." His closed fist covered his mouth. He paused as if the words were weighed and would be difficult to cough up.

She gripped the edge of the counter. Secret? Lose his license? Did she want to know this? In two and a half weeks, she could be home in familiar territory. "There is a connection between Jennifer and Suzanne?"

He nodded.

"Did you know my mother?" She had no voice. She took a deep breath.

He tapped his lip with the index finger. "When do you close? Can we go somewhere to talk?"

She glanced at the schoolhouse clock behind the counter. "I can close up now. I need to finish here—it will take five minutes." She could come in early the next morning and straighten up more before opening. She closed out the register.

"I didn't know your mother. I met her. I delivered her baby." He walked over to the front windows.

She dropped the can of coffee grounds on the floor. "Her baby?"

He plopped into a wicker chair.

"You never discussed this with Annabelle? What do you know?" He rubbed his forehead.

"You delivered Annabelle's baby?" That mother. What had

she missed? "We didn't discuss anything about her having a baby. I thought I was adopted. We discussed that. I inherited the house—the house I was born in, so I thought. That's why I came here."

She grabbed the whiskbroom and dustpan. She leaned down to collect her thoughts. All these years she thought she was adopted? *I was simply born here? Why would Annabelle hide she was my mother? Grant wasn't my father? More lies?*

She vigorously swept the grounds and dumped the dirt into the trash.

"So Annabelle changed my name, what was the problem? I don't understand what she did and she isn't around to ask. I came here for nothing."

Dr. Morgan's face was ashen. He looked as though he'd stabbed Annabelle, not helped her. Why all the secrecy and why would he lose his license … unless— Her world swirled. She reached for the coffee table to steady her. "Jennifer. The one buried in Morningstar Cemetery is Annabelle's baby."

He nodded.

She plopped on the floor. The broom and dustpan flew across the floor. "Her baby died." She clasped her knees with her arms. She had all the clues wrong. Annabelle had a baby, but not me. Jennifer. All those years she'd kept that a secret. She lost a child. A painful loss? Or just more lies. "How? What happened?"

He sighed deeply settled back in the cushions. "If Annabelle and Grant aren't here, what I tell you can't harm them."

She stood. "I'm here." She picked up the dustpan and slapped it on the counter. "I'm here. I deserve to know. How I became Annabelle and Grant's. Who is Jennifer Feratti? Annabelle and Grant are not listed on her certificate. Why not? I'm here for answers."

Annabelle had lied about so much. He knew. She deserved the truth.

"Can I help you do anything? We need to go where we won't be disturbed." He pulled a cell phone from his pocket. "I need to let my wife know where I am and what I am about to do."

"We can go to my house. No one visits there."

He stopped tapping numbers on his phone. "Greystone?" He studied her face. "Return to the scene of the crime."

She sucked in her upper lip, waited, then asked. "You've said some things. Scene of crime. Should have lost your license. Is there something very bad in my past? Something I did or family did that was wrong."

"They were innocent—both your mothers. Just manipulated. We were all manipulated by a scheming, selfish woman. They were naïve, and scared." He looked up at the ceiling. "I, however, just didn't have the backbone to take the moral road. " He shook his head and looked down at his foot. "I've regretted those actions and worried about the consequences." He touched her arm. "And then you asked those question, brought it all back. This time I couldn't walk away and not do anything."

"Do you have a car? I walk here every day. "

"I went out for a walk and ended up here. No car. My wife can pick me up after our conversation."

She locked the shop door behind them.

She ushered him in and he studied the rooms and ran his fingers over the historic tables and decorations. "My wife has always wanted to see the inside. This is an antiques lover's paradise."

"Annabelle collected, restored and loved old furniture. We were always out in search of the best, the savable, the real finds." She placed her bag on the counter.

"Apparently my wife, Mary knew all that. Maybe she filled me in and I didn't pay attention. Maybe I heard the name and blocked out the rest."

"Would you like some tea? Where would be the most comfortable spot for you to talk?" The doctor's color had not returned. His shoulders stooped. But he was willing and eager to talk.

She served tea on the porch. The soft fragrance of roses filled the room.

He sipped his drink, crossed his leg over the other. "What do you know? Have you found your natural mother?"

She shook her head. "I found the birth certificates of Jennifer and Suzanne, the death certificate of Suzanne's father and Jennifer's grave. I know my mother visited there." Her stomach churned with her day's coffee. All she found were bits and pieces. Nothing matched. "Not much. I found Jeffrey's, Suzanne's father's brother, Jason."

"His brother? I didn't even know he had one."

He placed the teacup on the wicker table. "Annabelle and Grant were here for something happy—a wedding, a reunion. They were on their way back. They were hit by a drunk driver." He folded his hands, then unfolded them. "Your mother wasn't in a seat belt and hit the dashboard. Then, seat belts were optional and thought to do harm to pregnant women. She ended up with a gash in her forehead."

"She always had bangs to hide the scar. When angry, she'd rub it."

"She had a concussion, was out of it. The baby sustained injuries. We waited, but decided to do caesarian. Your mother was injured and bleeding internally. We thought we could save them both. Jennifer lived forty-eight hours."

Her mother had a baby and it had died, yet she never shared that. Her chest compressed as though a monster coiled it in a ball. She rubbed her chest. How had she missed so many clues?

"Your father held up—he was a great support. Your mother was dazed from the concussion, not prepared for sudden loss of a baby. The witch was persuasive and persistent."

Dr. Morgan babbled about events and people. Who was the witch? This didn't make sense. Caroline frowned. "I don't understand. How did I come into this? Wasn't I born the same day?"

"You were born a day later."

She poured more tea for herself and filled the doctor's teacup. Lacing it would vodka or any liquor made sense. All her research, all her conclusions flew out the window. She paced. "Wait."

She yanked her folder of information off the long library table and returned. "The facts don't match."

A deep sigh compressed the doctor's frame. "A distortion of the facts. That's what I have had the hardest time living with. I was an accomplice. I went along—accepted Cruella's scheme."

"Cruella?"

"You know in that Disney film—the evil woman." He stood beside her. "Not either parent. Your grandmother." He paced the width of the porch. "Politics became more important than two babies—and the mothers. I didn't stand in the way." He stopped his rant. "You haven't discovered your natural mother? She hasn't come forward?"

"She's alive?" She clutched his arm. He knew. He knew. She was this close.

He swallowed. "I can't—won't reveal her. If she hasn't been discovered or hasn't told anyone up to this point." He shook his head. "I've complicated her life. I won't add to it." He patted her fingers digging into his arm. "She's alive."

"Come." He led her to her own loveseat as though he were her dance escort. "I'll tell you the story without revealing two names. Maybe that will give me some peace and may rectify some of the past."

She sat next to him. Her hand rested on his arm. His hand patted the top of hers. "Annabelle had the baby, was devastated by the accident, the loss of her baby and had a concussion. She and Grant were vulnerable."

He tapped the fingers of his other hand on his knee. "Your mother had you. She was very young."

"She was twenty-one. In 1978, that wasn't …"

The doctor shook his head. "She was 17, would have been a senior in high school."

"But. The marriage certificate …"

He shook his head again. "She lied to marry Jeff Kelly. Then a woman had to be twenty-one to marry without parental consent. They married on an army base. Got away with changing her license." When Caroline attempted to argue again, he held up his hand. "The birth certificate—both babies' birth certificates were false." He hung his head, his voice continued low and soft. "I changed them and signed them. A doctor—an honorable doctor I tried to be that rest of my career."

"The evil one convinced me—persuaded us all. The best for everyone was for Annabelle to take Margaret and Jeff's child to Seattle. Annabelle and Grant would have the baby they wanted so much. And could raise her better than a widowed seventeen-year-old without a college education could do."

Caroline took a deep breath. She removed her hand from Morgan's arm. Her cell phone rang in her pocket. She didn't touch it.

"My mother—natural mother didn't want, couldn't raise me. It makes—" *No, it doesn't make sense. If I had a child, I would never let go.*

"Then, having a baby when you were still in high school was still scandalous. Her grandmother wouldn't allow it."

"Allow it? A grandmother?"

He tapped his lip with his forefinger. "She and her husband were powerful people—on a grand scale. Powerful in the state. She didn't want a scandal. She had originally sent ..." He bit his lip. "Sent her granddaughter away to have the baby. But your mother." The doctor chuckled. "Was as stubborn and proud as her grandmother. She decided she wasn't a shameful woman. She was married and pregnant. Then Jeffrey was killed. Your mother was devastated, defeated. She came home. Alone. Sad."

Caroline swallowed. Were this a book, she would quit reading. Sad, depressing tale of so many mistakes and pain. At seventeen, would she have been able to stand up to family and friends? At seventeen, she was more interested in dances and music and sneaking out with Tina. But other girls had babies. She rubbed her wrists.

"You want to hear all this? It's an old man's unburdening."

Her doorbell rang. She startled dropping her folder. She scurried to the door. *Please don't be Irene who saw Dr. Morgan come here and just has to know.*

She flung open the door and blocked the entrance with her body. A short, white-haired woman clung to the straw purse in her hand,

"You're the girl." She pushed back her hair over her left ear. "I'm Mary Morgan. I'm William's ride and—" She leaned on the doorframe. "I thought he might need me. I didn't want him going through this alone."

Caroline gripped the frame. "Come in, please. We're having tea. Come join us."

"Oh," She stopped in the entranceway. "Oh, this house is exquisite." She glanced in the parlor and up the stairs. "Look at all the antiques."

Caroline's shoulders relaxed. "Your husband warned me that I may never get you out once you saw the antiques."

Mary looked up at Caroline for a minute. "Suzanne- all grown up."

A tremor went through Caroline's body. Suzanne. She felt like a Suzanne. Now she had proof and they were in her house.

"Oh!" She covered her mouth with her fingers. Wait until she called Jason. She had an uncle and cousins. What a confusing day. She rubbed her cheeks.

Dr. Morgan hugged her as soon as she entered. He patted his wife's shoulders. "She doesn't know all of the story. We can't tell her names of her mother or grandmother, but I am telling her what I did."

Mary scowled.

"We are having tea. I'll get all of us hot water and teapot." She left them to talk.

In the kitchen, she leaned against the counter. Tears flowed down her cheeks. She didn't wipe them away. No wonder her mother never talked. What a loss for her. And her natural mother—seventeen and a widow? Her hands shook as she held the teakettle under the faucet. Tears still streamed uninterrupted.

I was a Suzanne. My father is dead. My mother doesn't want to be found. She placed the teakettle on the stove.

I have an uncle. I have discovered family. She fumbled with the box of teabags. *Jason! He's a wonderful person. I like him. An uncle. I have an uncle.*

She poured the hot water in the pot. *But mother, who was she?* William Morgan hadn't finished his story. How did Annabelle end up with her? Why the secrecy?

She returned the hot tea and more cups. Mary and her husband sat side-by side. He looked rumpled and tired. Mary took the cup offered to William and placed it on the small table. "Your mother—your mother and her friend –were brave. It was a difficult situation for her. I don't know if she were ever convinced it was the right one."

Caroline studied the roses on the outside of the teapot. Why had she wanted to learn of her past? This wasn't a fun, interesting path, it was tortuous.

She handed a cup to Mary. "You know my mother? You knew she was pregnant? You knew she was married?"

Mary shook her head. "I didn't really know much about her until you were born." She glanced at William who nodded. "She called our house that night. A terrible angry storm raged outside. We, luckily, still had power." She patted his hand. "He left immediately. I stayed on the phone with your mother's friend and talked with your mother to keep her calm—and when you decided you were coming before William could possibly get there through downed trees and power lines. I coached them both through your birth."

He nodded. "My wife had attended and helped with many an emergency birth. I usually took her if we weren't going to the hospital to help keep mothers calm. She knew enough from watching and hearing me to get your mother—and her friend through it."

"My father was dead." Where was her mother or grandmother? What friend? Did my mother replace my father that fast? This threw a different light. Maybe she shouldn't have been so fast to feel sorry for her. "Who helped? Grandmother? My mother had another friend replacing Jeffrey?"

Mary shook her head. "Luckily for us all, your grandparents were attending a state function in Trenton. She—your grandmother didn't even know." She cleared her throat. "That her granddaughter was home, let alone having the baby. Your mother's best friend throughout her life was by her side. The girls had been inseparable since childhood."

Girls. Could have been her and Tina. She nodded.

"By the time, I could get through the storm. You had arrived and were wrapped in a towel." He snorted. "But the wind also blew in the wicked witch. Things changed."

Mary shook her head. "Appearances were important. She was used to having her way and people doing what she ordered. They were powerful people in this town."

"We didn't realize their influence was only that strong

here in town. That authority dimmed the farther away you travelled."

Mary patted his leg. "That's hindsight." She turned to Caroline. "She hounded your mother to get rid of the baby. Find someone to take it ... you." She patted Caroline's hand. "Then your grandmother learned of the woman—the woman who was not from here—who had lost a baby. How convenient for your grandparents." Her nose crinkled and her face scrunched as though she had eaten a bad pickle. "She badgered us all into thinking this was perfect solution for two women's pain. Annabelle could still have a baby—go home with one. It would help with her loss."

He rested his head on the back of the loveseat and stared at a spot on the wall. "She nagged your mother relentlessly. Ma ... your mother couldn't have the baby. Your grandmother wouldn't let her see you. That other mother, Annabelle would have the money, the time, the lifestyle to give you things your mother wouldn't be able to."

Mary butted in. "She said your mother would be on her own if she kept you."

He shook his head. "She had lost her husband. Was devastated. Her grandmother was a formidable adversary. She agreed to a better life for you."

This couple were sketching in the picture of her beginnings. The facts as well as the innuendoes. Details she had missed or situations which hadn't even crossed her mind. "Did the mothers talk? Agree to this?"

"No, wicked witch brought the baby."

"Brought you." Mary said.

"Paid for their flight back."

"What happened to my mother? Did she ..." Now she wanted more than a name. Now she wanted to know if she had loved her and wanted her. But if she did wouldn't she have tried to contact her before now?

Mary leaned across and squeezed Caroline's hand. "I don't think she ever got over it."

"You still have contact with her?"

Mary and William exchanged a glance and nodded simultaneously.

"I've been here a month." She bit her upper lip. "Would I have seen her? Run into her in town?"

Dr. Morgan nodded. Mary tapped his knee.

An invisible force squeezed the air from her lungs and tightened a viselike grip around her chest. No words came forth. She sat glued to her chair—numb.

Mary stood and reached for her husband's hand. "You need to digest all this. I'll leave our number in Arizona. We need to make a flight tonight."

Caroline moved next to them. They had filled in so many gaps.

Mary wrapped her in a tight embrace. "People make difficult decisions every day." She patted her back. "She did give you a better life—one she couldn't have managed then."

Caroline walked both to the door. She hugged the doctor. "Thank you. Thank you for telling me. Not letting me spin in confusion, never knowing the truth."

After they left, she collapsed on the stairway, gripped the newel post and let the tears fall. She had wanted the truth. Your mother is here and doesn't want to acknowledge you.

Annabelle lost a child and found another. Annabelle visited yearly. Had she missed that baby? Annabelle and Grant always loved her. That she knew that her whole life. Her mother was Annabelle.

Margaret and Jeffrey were baby donors. One never lived to get excited over a baby and one didn't care she existed. Her birth mother was alive and here. They had passed in the town, but that mother made no effort to contact her.

She wiped her tears from her face with the back of her sleeve. She retrieved the teacups and teapot from the porch table and then rinsed them in the sink.

Prior to Annabelle's lawyer announcing she owned a house in New Jersey, she never thought about another mother. Her life in Seattle was simple. She went to work, worked long hours so she had no time for book clubs, or gardening or festivals. She had a productive all-encompassing job in a big city. Both her parents had died, but she had Tina. Annabelle and Grant were all the family she had or wanted. Life there was calm, regular. No emotion roller coasters. Simple life.

Until she came here. She had wanted answers. Now she had them. But the knowledge squeezed her heart. Be careful what you wish for.

She shut off the faucet and rested her hands on the counter top. Annabelle had left out details, but life hadn't been easy. Morgans had helped her fill in the puzzle of her past. Bless Doc Morgan. She had been Suzanne. Answer to one of her questions. The knot between her shoulders eased.

She had an uncle. She rinsed her face with cold water. An uncle she had to contact.

CHAPTER TWENTY

Wednesday morning, she called Jason with her news from Doctor Morgan's visit. "If he's right, I'm Suzanne."

"You know he's right. You are my niece. I knew it! I knew it." His excitement crackled through the phone.

"We still don't have the DNA proof."

"You and I don't need that." He cleared his throat. "That's a lot of information to take in. What do you think now?"

"I think," She paced the length of hall between the entrance and the kitchen. "Both mothers were so young. I don't know what I would have done. But—"

"You think your mother, Jeffrey's wife, knows you are there?"

"Maybe, yes. I just don't know what to believe or think."

"I'm looking at my calendar. I have the weekend off. I can be there Friday night."

"Jason, I don't …"

"That's Uncle Jason to you."

She laughed. "I hope so."

"I can stay one night. We can go see that woman, the one who wants you to leave. Maybe I'll recognize something." He paused. "I'm telling my wife. We'll tell the kids after the weekend."

"Oh." She stopped in the middle of the hall. "Oh." An aunt and cousins. She had never had aunt, uncles or cousins. "Yeah, sure."

"My wife is going to be very confused. I never told Robin much about Jeffrey except that he died. You brought my brother back."

Her phone buzzed. Another call from David. He called yesterday, but hadn't answered when she called back.

"Jason ..." She smiled. "Uncle Jason. I have a call I need to get. Call me when you are on the way. I'm glad you are coming."

She clicked over to David. She had so much to share with him. Time to tell him the truth about her reason for arriving and staying.

"David, I tried to call. Can you ..."

"I am at the hospital with Meg." He sounded worn out.

He filled her in with details. Meg's vision problems had progressed. She now could only see vague movements. The hospital was running tests and that would determine the next step.

"I'll be there in a few minutes." She locked up, prepared few sandwiches. What else can I do for him?

David waited outside Meg's room slumped on a bench. His scruffy and worn appearance was out of character

"Hey." She slid in next to him and wrapped her arms around him.

"Need a friend?"

He nodded and leaned his head on her shoulder. "I need a shower and need to get to work. Meg is in with doctors."

"Work?"

"State testing starts. Need to double-check the school, the paperwork. My job ..."

"I can wait for Meg. This is your busy time?"

He nodded. "Testing. I have to be there tomorrow when it starts. I've dealt with problems on the phone and Sandy kept me posted."

David summarized what he knew. The blindness was part of her MS and could be temporary or permanent manifestation. They wouldn't know that for a while.

She would be released Wednesday. Until they could renovate Meg's house, she would stay with David.

"She insists that she can go to her own home and she will learn to adapt."

She squeezed his shoulders. "She always insists. Her home health aide could be there more."

"She has Jillian wrapped around her fingers. She'll convince her she can manage. The hospital wanted her to go to rehab for a few weeks, Meg won't stay there. She will only go daily, then less. But she has to be released to be on her own."

Meg can't do this on her own. David is worn out and torn between school and Meg. She would be here for two weeks.

"Why don't you let me convince Meg to stay at my house? That will give you a reprieve to finish school. Will give you both time to have the modifications done to her house."

David tapped the guest pass against his knee. "You can't take that on. You will be leaving."

"I'll be here long enough to help out. I love Meg and would do anything. You know she isn't going to give me as much of a hard time as she is you. You are family."

"She does listen to you." Taking her hands in his, he faced her. "If you are sure you can manage that it would help me. She will have an aide who can take her to therapy, doctors, come in and help. You don't have to be there caring for her."

It took most of the day talking with Meg, doctors and her aide to set up the move. Meg, although she didn't want to disrupt anyone's life, was delighted to spend time with Caroline.

Caroline used the rest of her day arranging her house. Jillian and Meg arrived Wednesday afternoon and set up Meg's room.

As expected, Meg shooed Jillian away as quickly as she could, explaining, "I need time to wheel around the house, get my bearings, bump into things until I learn the house."

Meg refused any help from Caroline. "Just let me wheel around. I'll run into things until I imprint a floor plan in my head."

Meg maneuvered her wheelchair the same circuit several times. She touched the backs of furniture, ran her fingers across chair backs as she memorized the lay of the downstairs.

Caroline was mesmerized by her actions. What a brave incredible woman. Another hindrance faced without a whimper. Very stubborn woman to boot. She didn't ask for much either.

She moved closer after Meg bumped into a table leg.

"I'm fine, Caroline, I can hear you worrying. Let me figure this out on my own. I need to visualize the setup, set up patterns in my brain so I can get around."

"Should I rearrange the furniture? We could set up a clear path throughout the downstairs so you don't have to memorize the floor plan."

Meg waved her hand as if dismissing the thought. "No. You've already done enough just letting me move in until David can get the contractors in to rebuild my downstairs. And that," Meg slapped her hand on the wheelchair arm. "That just irritates me."

Caroline grinned. Well, even Meg could get pissed at someone. But she didn't want her fretting about staying. "I'm honored to have you as a guest. I love talking with you and this will give us plenty of time. You can really teach me about rose care."

Meg paused, a smile replaced her determined scowl. "I'd like that." A deep sigh transversed her entire body. She looked in Caroline's direction. "Please." Her voice was soft. "Take me out to the roses."

"Gladly. How about if just this time, I wheel you there. Once you learn about the dips in the floor and where the temporary ramps are, you can do it yourself."

Caroline wheeled her across the metal room divider.

"Are we heading to the kitchen and is there still a family room." She cocked her head as though listening. "A family room to the right?"

"Yes." Caroline paused before crossing the threshold into the kitchen. "You know this house?"

Meg gripped the wheel stopping the chair abruptly. She took a deep breath. "I played here with friends."

"Okay, David and I attached two ramps. This one leads into a porch. The next is one from the porch to the outside. We need to fix this door so you can open it yourself."

"You don't need to go to all that trouble. Oh," She touched her lips with her fingers. "The roses." She inhaled deeply. "A small rose bush ... should be ... if you were looking out the library window to the left. A pink rose bush."

"There is." Caroline walked toward it. "Only it's not small.

It's about three feet high. Many buds. A few open."

Meg reached out and Caroline guided her hand to the bush. Meg cupped a bud with her palm. She stroked the petals.

"It looks very healthy from what I can tell from the rose books I've looked at in the store. Its leaves are dark green and shiny. The buds have no sign of bugs. No sign any of those ugly borers have damage the stems."

Meg fingered the petals, reached up to judge the size. "I planted this rose. Many years ago. Over thirty."

Roses here? She played here? "Did you plant as a project?"

Meg closed her eyes and took time before answering. "It was a commemoration rose." She dropped her hand.

"Why don't we sit on the porch? We can enjoy the garden, I have fresh tea and you can tell me how to plant roses."

Meg tilted her head. "You adding to the garden here? Or you going to do something besides work when you return to Seattle?"

Caroline chuckled. "Actually, Meg, you have been a bad — or big influence. I think I'll plant a flower garden outside my Seattle house."

"Glad you are taking back good habits and memories from here." She clapped as though she were a child.

Caroline maneuvered her chair to the porch. "I'm taking back a lot from here. More clothes, good thoughts, and lots of memories." She repositioned a chair and adjusted the shades. She wheeled Meg's chair in the vacated spot beneath the windows and across from the screen door. She'd still be able to smell her roses.

"I don't want to be a burden. You have company coming tomorrow. I could go home for the day."

"Don't be ridiculous. It's not company, it's …" Meg had too much on her plate right now. She would love to share her real reason for being here and the unfolding mystery of her past. She'd wait until Meg adjusted to her new life. "It's Jason — we're sharing research."

"I'll be at that first therapy session. The doctors insist I attend. So I won't interfere."

"He's only here for a night. We're investigating the same thing. We need to run out, but we will do that while Jillian is here."

She was getting so good at half-truths. She couldn't make this a habit. Once she figured all this out, she could tell them all. Tell them what? Tell them she'd happily lied to them all?

She excused herself and escaped to the kitchen to get drinks and a snack for Meg. She had stooped low. She liked Meg and David. Not telling or telling them partial truths are still lies. Friends didn't do that.

She poured the tea on top of the ice and headed back to the porch. One who lies and leaves. Maybe it is good she was leaving. They deserve better.

Caroline tried not to hover around Meg. In two days, they established a routine.

Saturday morning, she waited in the family room for the arrival of Jason's or the return of Meg from therapy. She tapped her foot on the rung as she rocked in the corner rocker. The boards squeaked as she eased her tension with the frantic rocking. *Come on, Jason, get here.*

Jason's car arrived first. She wanted a few minutes with him.

He overpowered her with a big hug and swung her in a large circle. "I just knew. You're Jeffrey's daughter. I have a connection."

Laughter rippled through her. Yes, she also had a connection—to this big, huggable man. He was worth the trip to New Jersey.

He put her down. "This is your house? The one you inherited which started all this?"

She stood with her hands on her hips. Her place. She didn't think even Annabelle knew how coming here would change her look at life. "This is it. Come on. Something else has happened since we talked."

"More? You found out more about your mother?"

"No," She led him inside the house. "Meg. Remember the friend I told you about?"

"The older woman."

Caroline nodded. "She is staying here until her place is fixed up."

He paused in the doorway. "Great place." He placed his

hand on her arm. "You are helping her. You talk about her; she's important. Will I get to meet the man you are so interested in as well?"

"David?"

"You talk about him as well. I am your uncle. Shouldn't I meet him?"

She chuckled. "Not as an uncle. He is busy with school. You may meet him. Then we can decide what to do while you are here."

"I want to meet that Stephanie woman—the one who you think wants you to leave. Maybe I'll have a feeling or see something in her. We can decide if she is the one—Jeffrey's wife, your mom." He paused at the landing with his suitcase.

"After you settle in, we'll go. A couple clues make her a possibility, but I have been wrong on so much."

"I'm the uncle not the aunt. All I need to do is put the suitcase in my room. Were my wife here, she'd unpack and want a tour. That can wait."

On the way to the bed and breakfast, they rehearsed their story on Jason's appearance. Every available space in Stephanie's kitchen overflowed with cooling sticky buns or rising bread loaves.

Stephanie straightened from her perch over large open stove. She pushed a lock of her reddish hair off her face. "What are you doing here? Your friends at Readers' Haven let you go?"

"Hi," Jason moved forward, clasping Stephanie's hand in his. "I'm Jason Kelly. Caroline has raved about your cinnamon buns."

"Seattle? Follow her here?" She turned her focus on Jason. "You moving into Greystone?"

"I'm from Salisbury, Maryland." He leaned on his back heels and folded his arms across his chest.

"Not far. Why are you here?"

"As I started to say, Caroline told me about your baking, I'd like to buy two dozen. I'm hosting a breakfast."

"Here in Lakeside?"

"No, no, he just stopped to visit. He's meeting family." Caroline interrupted. Jason startled. That wasn't the story they had planned.

She reached for two white cardboard boxes then lead the way down the hall. "Have tea while I pack these up." She handed each a teacup and pointed to a table with an electric teakettle and teabags.

Jason gripped the fragile teacup in his hand. The teacup disappeared. "I like your downtown. I think it would be a wonderful town to grow up in."

Stephanie studied first Jason, then Caroline before filling one white box with sticky buns. "Thinking of staying?" She glared at Caroline. "Staying or selling."

"I'll return to Seattle as planned."

"You've said that before."

Jason stood and reached for the box already tied. "Thank you for selling us just two boxes. Your reputation will spread beyond Lakeside."

He waited until they were back on the sidewalk before stating, "Certainly hostile toward you. Does she want to buy Greystone?"

"Oh, I never thought of that. I just assumed she wanted me to leave."

Jason scowled. "Something's up her butt about you."

"What did you think? Look like anyone you remember?"

"Nothing. Nothing in holding her hand. Nothing in her voice. She didn't react when I said Salisbury."

"But she doesn't like any questions about her past."

"I think she likes to control everything."

Jason nodded. "Something is eating at her. But she is not the one." He pounded his fist in his hand.

Caroline pulled on the Goldenrod weed closest to her. She dusted the sidewalk with the Goldenrod flower heads as they walked back to Greystone.

"We can't rely totally on my gut level reaction. I was only ten when I saw her. I only have a vague image. A pregnant woman standing next to a car clutching a folded American flag."

"The flag?"

"That's what started the violent argument between my mother and the woman. That was Jeffrey's flag, which went to his wife. My mother wouldn't recognize your mother because she wanted that flag."

Caroline bit her upper lip. How do you respond to that? That's my mother with me. She hesitated. Jason reached out to steady her. She shook her head. Not necessarily her mother. She and Jason hadn't proven anything.

Once inside her house, they flopped side by side on her couch. She tapped her fingers on the denim on her knee. "If not Stephanie, then we are back to square one."

"You're going back to Seattle." He rolled up the magazine he had picked up from the coffee table. "Tough to find anyone when we are nearly the furthest ends of the country."

"Farthest would be Maine. We have the Internet." Caroline winced. Her words came out too sharply. "I came here just to sell the house. I didn't—"

"What? To find a relative?"

"No," She tapped Jason's leg. "I'm glad I found you. I don't know, we just don't know yet."

"I do." He placed his hand over hers. "I'm trusting my gut. You are my niece." He wrapped her arm around her shoulders. "You said you have to leave." He rolled his eyes. "To return to Seattle. Now that I discovered a niece, I don't want to let her go."

She had no ready response. She'd just found him. Dr. Morgan said her mother was alive and still in Lakeside. Her mother gave her up. She was young. Getting pregnant had been a mistake. Then she wouldn't want that daughter to appear years later. She had a right to her life. She should go back and not disturb her life.

The front door squeaked. Caroline hurried to help Jillian push open the door to accommodate Meg's chair.

"How did it go?" She stepped aside. Jillian walked beside Meg as she maneuvered her way to the living room.

Meg turned her head in direction of Caroline's voice. "I learned how to use utensils better so I don't look like a fool spilling food all over when I eat." She wagged a finger at Caroline. "You will tell me when I have crumbs or even glops on my shirt."

"You show me what you learned and we'll practice and

get it down." She squatted near Meg's knees and patted her hand. "Then I'll treat you to the fanciest restaurant in NYC to celebrate."

Meg sighed, looked down at her hands. "Better learn quickly. You will be gone in fourteen days."

A stab of guilt lanced her gut. She wouldn't be here to help Meg through this. She needed someone to encourage her and just be there when the home health aide wasn't.

She sucked in her upper lip and chewed on it with her front teeth. "We'll work together until I leave. Then I'll fly back to take you to New York." She had airline miles from flying for Andoer. She now had a reason to use them.

Meg focused on Caroline. "Maybe." She sat straighter then turned her head to the center of the room.

"Hi, I'm Jason, Caroline's friend." He walked forward and into their conversation

"I'm sorry. Meg Ottinger, this is Jason Kelly."

Meg gripped the wheel. Her knuckles whitened. "From Seattle?"

"No." She stroked Meg's arm. "Remember we are researching together. He's from Salisbury, Maryland."

"Kelly?" Her face whitened to chalky paste.

"Meg, you feeling okay." Caroline signaled Jillian who also leaned down next to her.

Jillian felt her hands, then her temple. "Meg, what's wrong?"

"That therapy too difficult for you?" Caroline grasped her hand.

Meg blinked and turned her head in the direction of each voice. "The therapy?" She looked down. "Yeah. The therapy, that's it." She moved her wheels. "I need to go to my room to recover."

Jillian glanced at Caroline above Meg's head. "I'll stay with her. Check with you later."

Jason waited until the two disappeared into the back room. "That's quite a lot to take on. She's a close friend?"

"Yes." She had never seen Meg that way. She filled in Jason on Meg's illness and her usual stubborn, persistent demeanor.

"Good. I thought I made her sick."

"No, she's not like that usually."

Jillian came out. "She's lying down." She shrugged. "I'm not sure what started that. Give her a little time. Maybe that she couldn't tell there was another person in the room and the enormity of her blindness. Call me if she gets like that again. Or if you notice anything else."

Jason and Caroline chatted over dinner. Jason entertained her with stories of his children, Nancy and Eric. Like the sand in the clichéd hourglass, time was running out. She'd really like to go back to Salisbury and meet his wife and daughter.

They cleared the table together.

David was not able to come over which disappointed Jason. He and Caroline sat in the family room after clearing the dishes. He brought pictures of his family as well as his parents. He had very few of Jeffrey and of course, none of her mother.

"I have a friend who has a photography studio. He made me a copy." He handed her a black and white picture of Jeffrey Kelly in his uniform. "This is a few months before he died."

Caroline hugged it to her body. She choked out the words. "Thank you."

At night, before she crawled into bed, she propped the picture on the dresser across from her bed. Her father. She snuggled under the sheet. And an uncle in a room down the hall. This wasn't what she expected flying here.

Skype, phone calls, emails, all the modern media, would keep her in touch with Jason, Meg and David. But a Skype call would not compare to Jason's hug.

Although Jason had to leave early the next morning, he'd agreed to share breakfast. Caroline awakened early to make pancakes and was surprised when Meg joined her in the kitchen.

"Feeling better? You scared me last night. You lost color in your face."

"I was out of it—out of my element." She cracked eggs and whipped the batter as Caroline set the table. They sat together in the kitchen.

Jason moved next to Meg. "Caroline told me all kinds of stories about you. I think you are an amazing, inspiring woman."

Meg turned her head slowly to face Jason. "Inspiring?"

"You sound as though you could conquer anything."

Meg looked at him as though she could see him. Finally, she said. "Some things ... some things you never conquer."

"Caroline has talked about you a great deal. I'm so glad to have met you."

"Since I'm at a disadvantage here, I'd like to know you more. Describe yourself so I can see you."

His laughter was full-hearted and infectious.

"Oh that laugh!" Meg reached for his arm.

"You know that is tough for a male. I have light hair—dirty blonde is the word, I think. Blue eyes."

"Eyes blue like Caroline's—the blue eyes like ocean blue?" Meg tugged on a strand of her hair. "Or blue eyes like steel?"

Caroline said, "He has blue eyes you can see across the room."

When Jason startled at her comments, she added. "Your eyes stand out for a male. His hair, Meg, is sandy colored. He is about 6' 1.'"

With each detail, Meg nodded. "Any facial markings—like dimples?"

Jason groaned. "Yes, I have a deep dimple right in one cheek. Been teased about it my whole life."

Meg clutched Jason's hand. "And a dimple, too." She looked down at her lap. "I like dimples."

"Here." Jason grabbed both her hands. "My friend's grandmother is blind." He placed Meg's fingers on his cheeks. "This is how she gets to know people."

Meg ran her fingers across his cheeks, down his nose and across his dimple. A tear ran down her cheek. She quickly wiped it away, dropped her hands to her lap. "You've become a wonderful man, Jason Kelly." She leaned back in the cushions. "Quite a gift at my age to meet you."

Jason stretched out his legs. "It's good to be here. I've learned a great deal." He leaned toward Meg. "I, too, will miss Caroline and would love to encourage her to stay."

A deep sigh over took Meg's tiny frame.

Jason held Meg's hand and glanced up at Caroline. "We're united. We don't want to lose you in our live."

Caroline squeezed her hands together to quiet the ache in her chest. She didn't want to lose them either. "I'll return. I'll keep in touch."

Jason stood. "I have a long ride." He bent down to Meg. "It has been a pleasure. I hope we can visit again. If Caroline keeps her word, I'll see you again."

Meg rose. Jason held her arm to steady her.

"Jason Kelly, you have given me a gift just sharing breakfast." She touched his cheek. "A memory to savor."

"See you soon." Jason walked with Caroline to his car parked on the street.

Jason reached for the doorknob, and then dropped his arm to his side. "You will come back? You just can't leave and that's it. We never see each other. I'm attached."

She rubbed the side of her head. Why did she start all this? Just coming in and selling the damn house would have better. Leaving those who had become part of her life was tortuous. In her heart, Jason was an uncle, not matter what the results said. "I'll keep in touch. I'll return."

She sucked in her upper lip. When she returned to her own environment, became wrapped up in her Seattle life would she want to come back?

Her view of that life had turned upside down here. She was a different person, what would happen when she went back?

Jason placed his hands on her shoulders and gazed directly into her eyes. "You have to make up your mind what you want. You have touched and changed many lives here from what I witnessed." He let go and backed away. "You will have to decide how that changed your life."

He kissed the top of her head. "Stay in touch. Call when you return home so I know you are okay."

A strange warmth, as though she were wrapped in his enormous hug, settled around her.

Jason wanted her to check in when she returned. Her college friends had to call home, but Annabelle fostered independence and didn't require checking in. Now she had someone who looked after her.

She rubbed her chest. An uncle. An unexpected blessing arising from her impulsive flight to New Jersey to view her inheritance.

CHAPTER TWENTY-ONE

She returned to the family room. Meg still sat on the loveseat.

"You doing better today?"

Meg nodded. "Your friend is returning to Maryland?"

"Yes, he just came up to share notes on ..." More lies. She would have to break this habit soon. "Research notes before I go back."

Meg hung her head and picked at spot on her pants. "You are going back." The mournful tone in her voice tugged at Caroline's heart.

"Yes, I have to—not yet."

"I'm moving into a rehabilitation center."

Caroline knelt on the floor before Meg. "You are?" When did this occur? Did David know? He never said anything to her. Of course, she wouldn't be here. But still it hurt. Meg in a facility not home.

"Tomorrow, I am moving to Generate Rehabilitation Center until my house is ready."

"What changed? I thought you were staying here until the renovations were complete. Jillian will be here while I work. You wouldn't have to worry."

"I can't wait here until you choose to leave us. We can't hold our breath until you break off the connections." She fumbled until she closed her hand around the arm of the wheelchair and pulled it closer. "The opportunity to move in a rehab facility opened up. There I can concentrate on skills and learn not to depend on others."

Caroline winced at her words. She couldn't guarantee she would be here until Meg was resettled in her house.

"But tomorrow?"

"An opening at the rehab hospital, well, it's there. I might as well take it." She tugged her chair closer and moved into it. "Jillian is coming tomorrow. I need to pack. I have my dinner."

She left Caroline curled on the floor.

It was as though her insides had been scooped out and a void left behind. She really loved Meg. She rubbed her temples.

The upstairs Grandfather's clock chimed seven. How long has she been here? Just reminiscing about moments since her arrival. Many memories and many people here Her existence in Seattle seemed to be a lifetime ago. She stretched to remove kinks from her neck and back.

She opened all the cupboards and the freezer door looking for something for dinner. Nothing looked good. She settled for a cup of tea, a plate of crackers and cheese.

She curled up in the window seat in the library with the latest Susan Mallery book which had just arrived at Readers' Haven. Read now. When she returned, she would rarely have time to read. No time for walks or tea. Just time to jump to Griscom's dictates. She propped her feet up on the seat. And she didn't have a comfortable library seat either.

Escaping to Mallery-created characters didn't hold her attention the way it usually did. At ten, she gave up and went to sleep.

Early Monday morning, she tapped on Meg's door.

"Come in, Caroline."

Meg sat on her bed with her bags beside her. She certainly was becoming independent without the rehab center. She had packed without even asking for her help.

She leaned against the door frame. She swallowed the sobs that wanted to overwhelm her. Wouldn't see her unless she ...

"Caroline,"

She jerked her head up and choked back the tears. Don't upset Meg. "I'm here in the door."

"In the kitchen, in a glass container is a cutting from the pink rose bush. You should take it home."

Taking back flowers. What a good memento. "Thank you for thinking of that."

"Keep it in water until you leave. Wrap it in wet paper

towels, then plastic wrap." Meg waved her index finger as though she were lecturing Caroline. "Keep it in your bag, but don't let anything crush it." She took a deep breath and slowly exhaled. "You should have ..." She took another breath. "You should have part of that rose bush."

"Thanks for cutting it and getting ..." She hadn't heard Meg go outside. She insisted on her independence.

A cutting. She hadn't thought to do that. Start a garden from a cutting here. "It can be the first rose bush I start my new garden with."

That brought out Meg's smile.

Her departure was awkward. She hugged her frail frame then stood on the front lawn watching Jillian's car moving away. Moving Meg to a cold, sterile facility, not a house or home. That wasn't fair.

•

She created jobs at Readers' Haven to bury her thoughts about Meg. The book club was as noisy. Trying to get twelve women to agree on twelve books took three hours and several pots of coffee. The only book everyone agreed upon was Meg's choice which she had called in to Abby.

Abby was adamant "Meg said she can keep up. She can listen to books on tape. She likes *If You Dare* to discuss."

Caroline jotted down the titles, too. It would give her good books to read on her Kindle at night. Amazing, Meg wasn't giving up on this part of her life either.

Caroline said, "You know Meg. She's stubborn, She'll find a way."

"But how long can she keep this up? First, she was crippled, now she can't see. How long until her MS kills her?"

"We never know if she's really sick or not. Look at her before the blindness. First, she couldn't leave bed, then she's wheeling down the street like before. People don't heal like that."

Caroline came out from behind the counter. "You need to understand her and the disease. It doesn't kill you—it's not fatal, at least not the type Meg has." She faced the woman with negative comments. "MS is just like that. The symptoms come, seize your life and then can go and your life goes back to normal. That's one of the tragedies of living with it. It changes. Her blindness could be temporary."

She sat on a stool and faced the whole group. "I contacted the MS society. There is a very active chapter in Philly. They are sending brochures to the group." She zeroed in on Irene. "You can pass them out. Decide on ways you can help Meg without being obvious." She empathized the last word as she studied Irene's face.

Irene nodded.

Caroline retreated to her counter. Where had that come from? She just lectured grown women. She needed them to know about Meg. Meg wouldn't accept help easily. If she had a relapse, someone would need to visit. If her blindness wasn't temporary, these women needed to keep her in this group. Keep her as a friend.

Irene stopped at the counter as the rest filed out the door. "You are very protective of Meg." She tapped her 3 x 5 card on the counter. "That was helpful."

"Irene, you are the leader of the group." Caroline paused. "You need to reach out to Meg. Read those materials."

"You really are leaving."

Caroline gripped the counter. Of course, she was. Hadn't she made that clear the whole time she was here?

"You renting like Annabelle and coming to visit?"

Caroline hesitated. It would give her a reason to come back and see David and Meg and even the book club. "I'm talking with the realtor about selling. I'm not sure which would be the best route right now."

"I'll check on Meg. She is part of us—this group. You taught us about caring for each other when you took the time to visit Meg and take her chocolates and books." Irene dropped her heavy bag on the floor. "We will all miss you."

When she returned to Greystone, the house was quiet. How easily Meg had been part of her life. She dug her sneakers from the back of her closet and laced them up as she sat in the kitchen. She walked down Sassafras and ended up along the river near the bench she had discovered her first day in

Lakeside. She stood next to the park bench and rested her foot on the edge of it.

This is where it started. If she hadn't explored the streets, hadn't discovered Larkin on the floor, where would she be now? Easy answer, she would be in Seattle without new friends, or new interests. She would never have had the overnight with David. She wouldn't trade my time here for anything.

Changes in her Seattle life were coming.

Taking the extended leave of absence and staying here had left its mark. Gardening — the yard in Seattle was small, but she could have a few rose bushes.

Friends and fun. Other workers at Andoer get together for some holiday every month. She never went. Jean, her assistant, knew her birthday, knew her needs. Loyal Jean kept you up on office changes, Griscom's rants. Her weekly news notes were funny.

She has been your assistant for three, no four years, but she knew little about her. She reads. A book is always in her drawer — the right hand one and when no one is demanding her attention, her nose is buried in a book. She didn't know what books she liked or what she did on the weekend.

She rose and leaned over the railing and watched the swirling waters below. She needed to find a gift for Jean before she left. Maybe a glass paperweight.

She chatted with women here, know people in the supermarket. That doesn't happen in Washington state. She needed friends besides Tina. Certainly more friends and fun. Life is more than work. Andoer had taken over her life.

She kicked a stone into the water. Only eleven more days in Readers' Haven. *Irene will look after Meg. Larkin and I meet tomorrow.* She tapped her fingers on the railing.

Perhaps Larkin could get Stephanie more involved with the book group.

She didn't want anyone looking after David. She pulled leaves off a nearby branch and slowly dropped each leaf one at a time into the water. David. He said he would visit. She turned away from the water and looked up Sassafras toward town. She would come back and visit Meg, David, Uncle Jason.

She pushed herself off the railing and marched to the arts

district businesses. She bought glass paperweights for both Jean and Tina. She could tell them how they were made. She had heard and seen that process. She found two pair of earrings for Tina and on a whim, picked up flyers on upcoming events. Tina would love to see the shops and talk with the artists and craftsmen. That would be another excuse to come back. She could bring Tina to the arts district.

Two clay mugs were too tempting. She needed souvenirs, too. This had been the best vacation—that's what it was a respite, a vacation from her normal life. She needed something to remember.

She held the mug. All the other memories— David's kiss, the touch of his fingers. Meg's friendship. Jason's laugh. Irene's orders—no souvenir could replace any of those. She could think of them all each morning when she drank her Starbucks. That's a reason to go back. A real Starbucks everywhere.

At home, she prepared a dinner, but pushed her vegetables and chicken pieces around her plate. Now what?

David called, "Hey,"

"David, Meg left."

"You know how she is. She felt she was in your way, interfering with what you needed to do."

"I miss her. I wanted her to stay."

"She's stubborn."

She heard him move around, a glass click.

"I miss you. How about dinner Friday night—here."

Oh that held possibilities. "Should I take a shower here?"

A deep laugh. His laugh was warm, inviting. His fingers could be inviting, too. "I would love dinner. How about I prepare something special and bring it."

"How about dinner and an overnight?"

She laughed. "That sounds good to me."

"Crazy time at work these days. Testing is crazy. By Friday, I'll need a friend. Want to be that friend?"

"I give good back rubs. I could add that to friendship extras."

"I may fall in love. Just thinking about it makes me want to head over right now."

Her heart skipped. Her fingers tingled. Touching him,

giving him that rub would feel good to her in so many ways. "I would do that, but I would fall asleep on the way."

So much for her daydreams. "I'll keep my fingers flexible for Friday."

"Oh, I'll so look forward to that."

She hung up. To Friday. No, she didn't want to have someone else watch out for him. Friday, she would get him to promise to visit. Set a date for him to come out so they wouldn't lose touch. She wanted to see him again. And again.

She woke late on Tuesday morning. She rushed around throwing on clothes. She'd get coffee there. She met with Larkin this morning. By the time she got there, Larkin had opened the doors and started coffee.

"Oh that coffee smells so good. I overslept. The first time."

"I'm not worried. I hear the town rave about you everywhere I go. They love you and hate to have you leave." She handed her a cup of coffee. "They encourage me to stay on childcare leave."

"Where is Dylan?"

"In the children's area with his sister. Have you met Dylan's big sister, Madison? Come on,"

A ginger-haired little girl about seven bent over a stroller. She held up books to Dylan's face.

What a picture. Satisfaction and pride showed in Larkin's face.

"When are you returning to work here?" She asked.

Larkin's shoulders sank. "I have been over and over applications. No one seems right. We are booking an agency to acquire more applicants." She headed back to the coffee bar and poured herself a cup. "Ryan and I talked. I would come back part time. Hire someone to run the bookstore. I could have an office upstairs."

"Upstairs?"

"Yeah, the steps lead to an apartment. Ryan lived there once. We could make it an office."

"Sounds good. Is it a place you could let Dylan sleep near you?"

"Maybe. I want to expand." She sat. "I've been thinking of this while I was on leave. Ryan and I have looked into this. I want to add something to attract e-book readers and maybe set up an online research spot. Place we could help others find info." She looked up at Caroline. "Wish you were here to help get it started."

She sat down across from Larkin. "Great idea. Would expand the store. Bring in others." She sipped her coffee. "I could help from Seattle."

Larkin posed, her spoon in the air. "You could? We could?"

"Email, Skype. I could help with links. Research links." She refilled her coffee. "I would love it. I could keep contact here. Help the store."

"May-b-e-e. Wait until I see how it works with working and Dylan."

"You're not looking forward to it."

"If I could find your twin, or someone who helped, or who could understand and put up with Irene."

Dylan wailed. Madison wheeled the stroller to her mom.

"We need to talk before you leave." Larkin chatted and changed Dylan while he lay in the stroller. "You are irreplaceable." She fastened a strap around him and attached his bag to the handle.

She hugged Caroline. "We will miss you. I'll never find anyone like you." She sighed. "I need to get him home. We'll talk again."

She cleaned up the children's section. The day dragged.

David opened the door. "Hey, how was your meeting with Larkin?" He paused in the doorway and glanced around the shop.

She waited. This was unexpected. Why did he hesitate in the doorway?

He entered but paced in front of the window. He didn't hug her or kiss her hello.

"You've touched so many lives. Meg, Abby, Larkin even Irene." He stopped, studied her face then walked in front of her. He wrapped his arms around her and nestled her close to him. "And mine."

Her head rested on her spot. His heartbeat beat a steady rhythm in her ear. She snuggled closer and closed her eyes.

"Don't leave us. Stay until we know what this is between

us."

Staying here within the warmth of his arms. Oh, yes. Nowhere else on earth made her this secure, this happy She loved the closeness of David's arms around her.

No! She jumped away. Where had that word come from? Certainly neither one mentioned it. Like. Like his hands. Like his kisses. Really like the feel of him inside her. Like not love. He held her gaze. His hands roamed down her arms, he held her hands in his. "Stay."

She gasped as if a hardened blow had connected with her belly. "David. I can't."

He squeezed her fingers.

"I can't. I have a job."

"Is that job more important than the people here?"

She opened her mouth, nothing came out. Nothing. Nothing came to mind that she could grasp about her job carried the same weight as Meg or David.

"You have no answers?" He waited.

What could she say? Pain seared through her heart. A rip tore her in half the same way one tore a paper in half.

He turned and walked out the door.

She stared at the blank, solid door—now closed. A fist tightened its hold on her heart. She gripped the nearest bookshelf until the sobs died.

CHAPTER TWENTY-TWO

She dragged herself from her spot between the shelves. She rubbed her cheeks vigorously with her palms. *Go home. Get out of this shop.*

Outside it was cool. The evening was settling in. She headed to the river and sat on her bench overlooking the flow below. This is where it had started. From the bench she had meandered to a bookstore and a pregnant woman needing help—and she had stayed.

Their world had become hers. She willingly nestled in a small town with a noisy book club with an older woman who imparted wisdom, friendship and asked for little in return. She helped Meg and fell into the arms of the good-looking, compassionate David.

But their world was not her reality. She worked in Andover with Griscom's rantings and the frantic demands of medical professionals as the setting.

She wound the end of her T-shirt in a tight ball.

Her everyday existence didn't include chattering women discussing books, didn't merit the close friendship of a Meg in her life, nor did it include the passion and adventure of time with a man like David.

Words of Jason, Meg, David pounded on her head. *Stay... need you ... what do you want ... more important than the people here.*

She couldn't do it. She couldn't be all that to all of them. She didn't live here. She stayed to help a pregnant woman who owned a bookstore. And all else just happened.

She had no answers for questions from Jason, Meg or even

the one from David's sister. She didn't know what she wanted to do about David. Her job wasn't more important than people, but she worked in Seattle. Helping Larkin was just helping. It wasn't her career. She couldn't just take David back to Seattle and continue their relationship.

She rested her head on the metal railing. She couldn't just let the same thoughts run round and round like a gerbil in a cage.

Home.

She walked with her head down to Sassafras Street and paused at the gate. The house looked different than the day she arrived. Then she had no idea what changes would occur. If she had known, would she have immediately left?

She puttered in the kitchen. She didn't feel like dinner. She strolled to the rose garden. The pink rose bush had more flowers. She pinched off the spent blooms. She'd have to remind Kevin at the realty to hire a gardener. What should she do? Sell? Rent?

More problems. Her cell phone buzzed in her pocket. A text from Jean? Did Jean know how to text? *Read your email!*

She frowned. She tapped the edge of her phone. She hadn't checked emails since … she couldn't remember when. She talked to people here. She called Tina. Emails were Griscom's communication.

She returned to the house, poured ice water and sat in the library with her laptop. Five messages from Griscom all in caps. *Not doing it.* She deleted them all.

Jean's subject line was also in caps screaming her to read messages. The first line caught her attention. *Griscom posted your job and is interviewing next week.* She glanced at the date. Jean sent these three days ago. She leaned back on the window seat pillows and read the rest.

She crossed her arms. She still had two weeks until her leave was up. He said he would only interview if she hadn't returned in six weeks. He had the nerve to post her job? She threw the pillow across the room.

Too many wanted pieces of her. Both here and in Seattle. She rubbed her temples. She closed her laptop and headed upstairs. Tomorrow, she would deal with Griscom. And talk to David about returning to Seattle.

She tossed clothes on the floor, pulled on a nightshirt and crawled into bed.

She awoke hours later it was still dark. She rubbed her eyes and then the side of her face. That didn't help. Faces of Meg, Irene and David were interspersed with a screaming Griscom in her dreams. She ached. Her head throbbed. She was losing her job—her real job. The one that pays the bills. Reality was in Seattle.

She picked up her iPad, searched online, then closed her eyes and hit send. She had no other choice.

She picked up her cellphone and dialed Tina.

"Hey, I need a favor."

Tina's shaky voice answered, "You do know it's two o'clock in the morning?" A shuffling noise cut off the rest of Tina's words. "Are you okay? What's wrong?"

"Nothing is wrong. I'm coming home and I need you to pick me up at the airport tomorrow." She looked down the list of flights on her laptop. "I … Damn—no direct flights. I can leave here by noon, be there late tomorrow. I'll let you know a time. Just wanted to see if you were available before I booked."

"Are you on something? You're babbling. No explanations. Just that you are leaving? What's wrong?"

"I'm flying to Seattle. I …" She yanked a suitcase from the back of the closet. "I have a job." She couldn't add to that.

"Now? You decide in the middle of the night? Something's up. You've been goofy over Mr. Hottie. You talk about those people there all the time and now you're ready to leave? You have two weeks until your deadline."

"Griscom listed my job."

"That's it. You woke me at two to tell me he listed your job and you're flying back. You're going to explain all this when you get here."

"Maybe." If she had an explanation. "I'll text with the flight number and an accurate time." She threw clothes on her bed and emptied drawers. *Damn.* Too many colorful outfits added. The black suits still hung in the closet. Why did she think black was sophisticated and my color? How dull. She fingered the teal outfit on the bed. *My life has become more colorful. The black outfits stay.* By six AM, she had her bags packed and lined at the door.

She meandered through the house, stroking furniture, and sitting in each room. Using her iPhone, she took pictures of rooms, several shots of the library. The early morning sun added a shine to the rose bushes in the backyard. She ended her goodbye tour in the library on the window seat.

No place in the Seattle house could fit a window seat, especially a seat with a view of a rose garden. She fingered a few book spines. She could transform an upstairs room to a library in the Seattle house. She didn't need that many guest rooms. *What guests? Add that to your list. Library. New friends as guests.*

Of course, if David comes out he will be a guest.

David. He is at work. The state testing. Can't interrupt his day. What would she say? You frighten me? You're getting… I have to leave. I have no reason.

She kicked her feet against the wooden base. How could even face David. A note! She'd explain in a note, wouldn't interrupt his work. Then she wouldn't have to face him. She jotted a short note and sealed it in an envelope.

She called the realtor and made arrangements to list the house. Before she loaded the rental car, Caroline labeled a few pieces of furniture and the bassinet in the attic with red duct tape. The realty would ship these after the house sold.

In a large sling purse, she placed the rolled white papers with her notes on Jennifer and Suzanne. She tucked the pink roses wrapped in wet paper towels and a plastic bag inside of the roll.

She jingled the keys in her hand. *Get this day over.* She threw her bags in the trunk.

The front door shut with a definitive thud. *Bye house.*

She drove slowly through town. So many memories in such a short time. The river, a book shop, center of town and the street fair. R&J Diner. She drove down a side street and walked the rest of the way to Jennifer's grave site.

Goodbye Jen. We're sisters of a sort. Certainly our lives are connected. She touched the gravestone. *No more yearly visits. Need to pay Pete Sangfer funds to keep up the park and the flowers.*

Bye.

She walked back. At least she knew why Annabelle visited. *Still have no idea who Maggie May is.*

She drove out of town to David's. This was the toughest. A short note. That's all. Just explaining a job crisis. What could she say? She couldn't explain her feelings. She couldn't even explain them to herself.

She sat in the driveway. No kayaks near the water. Quiet and still. *Add kayaking to the list of things to do back in Seattle.*

She flicked the note back and forth with her index finger as she walked to the front door. She slipped it between the front door and the screen. *Bye David.* She leaned her head on his door. *You don't know how sorry I am you don't live in Seattle.*

She maneuvered out of his driveway without looking back. She gripped the steering wheel until her fingers ached. Meg. Another tough one.

No one was in Meg's room at Rehabilitation Center. She paced the perimeter of her room. Five minutes. No Meg. Meg's nurse who said she would be in therapy for an hour

She couldn't wait. She had to catch a plane. Borrowing a pen from a nursing station, she jotted a long note to Meg. She propped it on her pillow. This was so cruel. She wanted to talk, to explain and she needed to hug her goodbye.

She dragged herself out the door. A vacuum sucked out her insides. Empty. She leaned her head on the steering wheel and closed her eyes. Tina waited in Seattle. A confrontation with Griscom was inevitable. Time to return. She started the car.

At the airport, hailed a baggage handler to take care of all her luggage, handed over the keys to her rental and sat near the gate. Others hustled on and off planes. Changing places. Changing lives.

She flung her carryon in the compartment. She was heading home. She winced. Images of Greystone appeared with the word, "Home."

She took a sleeping pill as soon as the plane started down the runway. She never took sleeping pills, but she didn't want to think. She arrived in Seattle at nine, tired and cranky.

Tina awaited her at the baggage turntable sitting on a cart. She bet Tina guarded that cart like a territorial bear. Carts were gold at Sea-Tac airport. Tina jumped up and waved when she sighted Caroline.

After a quick hug, Tina stepped back. "You look different. Hair style is complimentary. I don't remember you with hair that long and straight. Not since high school days. But something is very different about you. Long flight, huh?"

"Unbelievably long trip."

They loaded the car with luggage and boxes. Caroline gripped the armrest as Tina whizzed around cars and flew down side streets on the way to the house. Tina drove through the city like a mouse racing through a maze to get a tidbit at the end.

At the house, she dumped the boxes and bags in the hallway. Later. She had forever to unpack. She slumped in the flowered loveseat in the living room. All the furniture in this house was Annabelle's, too. She just moved in when Annabelle needed help after her stroke and never took the time to add my personal stamp to the house.

Her townhouse never had much of a personal stamp either. Griscom had lived with her and didn't like "clutter," which meant anything she wanted to add. It had been black and white starkness—kinda described her life then.

She needed to get rid of some furniture in this house and add pictures and treasures. Like the two paintings she had picked up at the festival.

"I think I'm going to add a garden in the yard. It gets great sunlight. Maybe change things in the house."

"Okay, that's not the lead-in I expected." Tina stretched lengthwise on the other loveseat. "What prompted the sudden flight home?"

Caroline studied the designs in the Oriental rug. Why? Everyone closed in and if she didn't leave, she would be caught in their ensnaring— What compassion? Interest? What had anyone done except like her? But this was home. She had to return to this house, to her job, to her friendship with Tina.

"I've never known you to run away."

"I didn't. I'm home. I have a job to salvage. I live in Seattle. I need to get back to my life. Need to find answers to some unresolved issues here."

"What about unresolved issues you left in New Jersey?"

She leaned back on the loveseat. She left them all notes. What a coward's way out. If she had only received a note from David as a goodbye, she'd have been crushed. She hadn't shared why she had really arrived in Lakeside. She just dropped half-truths about who she was. She certainly wasn't the friend everyone thought she was.

"Your conversations were filled with David, Meg, Irene, Stephanie, book club and Larkin. Now you have discovered family in Maryland. And you just left?" Tina sat up. "That's not the Caroline I grew up with."

"I had to leave. They were all taking pieces of me. Molding me like a sculptor. Wanting me ..."

"Wanting you to stay as part of their lives?" Tina shifted. "I want you in Seattle. I need my best friend nearby, but—" She rested her chin on her hand. "You won't be content here until you decide what's important. And keep those connections in a way you can deal with." She leaned against the cushions. "Maybe you should be like Annabelle, and just go back once a year."

Caroline threw a pillow across the room "I can't be like Annabelle." She slumped on the couch. "This is home. But it feels empty. I just don't know. Yet."

Tina stood. "We can talk tomorrow. You look as though someone dragged you here—not flew. We have days to talk. You're home. I'm glad you're back."

"I haven't even asked you about your life. How are you doing? How is the art career?"

"I have lots to fill you in on. Staying here has been inspiring and productive for me. Art career is moving—moving ahead. Tomorrow, I'll show you."

Caroline dragged one bag up to her room, glanced around. *Changes needed here.* She flopped on the bed and didn't even bother turning down the sheets or cover. She was back.

She hadn't even had the guts to say goodbye. She had fled. She closed her eyes to shut out the recriminations. Faces from Lakeside floated behind her closed lids. They were part of her.

She needed to make amends. She buried her face in the pillow.

Sunlight streamed though the window as Caroline awoke. No smell of lavender or roses wafted in through an open window. Seattle. This should be the familiar smells and sounds. She closed her eyes.

The strong smell of coffee was evident. The steady beat of music and Tina singing off-key meant somewhere in the house, Tina was painting. She had missed her.

Up. Face your day. She was home. *Oh, have to see Griscom today.* She flopped back down. *This is your world.* She had a job, which includes working with Griscom. *Get up and get on with your life.*

She stumbled downstairs, poured a big mug of coffee and followed the sound of music to the basement. Tina had converted a section of the basement into an art studio. A mixture of turpentine, oils and strange plastic smell of acrylic paint woke her up more than the coffee.

Tina's back was to Caroline. She swayed to the music and belted out lyrics to whatever song was beaming through her earphones. Brushes, sketches, paint tubes were strewn across the long table. Caroline unplugged the iPad. Tina jumped.

"Hey! You're up. Did I wake you?"

"Nah, slept enough. I have to face Griscom today. Need time to get ready for that."

Tina grimaced. "Ah, Griscom, I haven't missed seeing him."

The longer she stayed in Lakeside, the fewer thoughts she had of Griscom.

"Welcome home. Jet lag? You're quiet."

"I guess that's it."

Tina put down her brushes. "You need to talk. I have to explain all this." She swung her arm around to indicate the addition of an art.

Caroline sipped her coffee. "Yeah, I need to figure out a couple things first."

"Like gee, I'm in love with Hottie and I left him behind. That's what you need to figure out."

"I'm not in love with David." *Just hurts to think about him.* "He was just a passing Hottie."

"Phew, right. What about the relative you found? And left."

She put down the cup on the edge of the table. "I did. I have an uncle who is … just wonderful. Warm, funny. You have to meet him"

"He's in Maryland. You are in Washington?" She arched an eyebrow. "You left an uncle behind."

"We can Skype. Visit. Relatives do that. We could show him, his family Seattle. David wants to visit, too."

Tina opened her mouth, closed it. She rocked on her heels. "The mother you wanted to find. You gave up?"

"She didn't want me. She doesn't want to be found."

"We have lots to discuss."

Caroline grabbed her cup. "Later." So much happened in New Jersey. Using Tina as her sounding board usually helped with any problem, but she had no idea where to start in explaining her confusion. She tapped her nails on her cup. "I have to meet with Griscom in an hour. I need to get ready. I want to be early and talk with Jean."

Tina wrinkled her nose. "I don't know how you left Mr. Hottie for—" She made a face as if she had swallowed a rotten orange. "For eewe, peeuee Griscom."

Caroline laughed. "Gotta go. Tonight when I get home, we'll sit down with a bottle of wine or two." She hopped up the stairs. She went straight to the closet and yanked out all the black pantsuits and dresses. *This is going to change as well.*

Time for new outfits. More color. Outfits to wear out because I'm going to start a life here. Life with friends, books, and gardening. Not a cookie cutter one, but an independent one with people interact. Find one this week. She showered, dressed and flew out the door.

She'd forgotten about Seattle traffic. She stopped quickly for a Starbucks grande cappuccino. Now that was great. Good things are in Seattle. She slipped into her parking spot at Andoer.

A life-time ago she parked here. She twisted her neck to assuage the kink. Her head throbbed as though someone had stretched a wide rubber band around her forehead.

Men with strained faces nodded hello, lowered their eyes and darted past. Women hurried past with arms loaded with files. They smiled, but didn't stop to talk. As she walked closer to her hallway, the men and women in the halls mumbled greetings. "Hey, great to see you." "Thank God, you are back."

"Get a handle on him, will you."

Caroline walked through glass doors to her office. Jean darted in behind her and shut the door. Nothing had been touched. Her orderly wire shelves were orderly stacked on the cabinet behind her deck. Her burgundy desk blotter lay squarely in the middle.

This is a dream. She was physically here, but it was as though watching this through a gauzy screen. Through the glass windows, others moved along as though they were robots. She heard the grating sound of Griscom's high, bleating voice coming down the hall. She gripped the edge of her desk. No, this was a nightmare.

"Welcome back." Jean remained in the doorway. "You look different. She moved closer. "Haircut? Something is new."

Caroline pulled out her desk chair, but didn't sit down. Even the sounds of Jean's voice coupled with the distant cry of Griscom had a surreal, unearthly sound.

"Griscom obviously hasn't learned you are physically here or he would be yelling his demands." Jean rocked on her heels. "Many of us are glad to see you back. Griscom has been out of control without you."

Caroline wrinkled her nose. Tina was right. Eewe peuee, Griscom.

Jean held up most of the conversation. "Dr. Hardesty left a detailed message of how you have to find a nugget of info for him. He's needed you and you weren't here. He's in the business of saving lives and you neglected and yadayada." Jean waved her hand in the air.

Her assistant had distinct opinions about these docs. She had never noticed that when they had worked together before.

"Jean, how are you? I don't think I ever thanked you for your emails updating me on the company and the crazy requests. Thank you for relaying messages to Griscom and answering his rants. I'm sure that was a difficult position."

Jean shrugged. "Everything about Griscom can be difficult. It's a fascinating job—finding information about diseases that aren't the common knowledge, but he can be a hindrance to the job. I don't know how you work closely with him. I ... Are you okay? You seemed distracted. Tough to be back?"

Caroline focused on the top button of Jean's cardigan. Actually, she had taken a retreat and mentally escaped to Greystone's garden with the smell of lavender and roses and the quiet of birdsong. Tension in the building was palpable.

"It is tough." She opened her middle drawer and glanced at the pens lined up and scissors in the right slot in the desk caddy. Voices rose behind the glass wall. Griscom would invade her office any minute. The band around her head grew tighter. *Okay, if he is going to create a scene, let's get it over.*

As soon as he saw her, he started. "Have you come to your senses and returned. You won't get a pay raise or any special treatment since you have been gone. You need to catch up on cases. Doctors are disturbed you left them high and dry. Your pay was docked for all that time that you just left." He glanced at the heads of office staff now peeking over the cubicles.

Griscom halted in the middle of the office hallway. Office personnel was silent. No one talked on the phone. No one moved. "All ears" applied to the entire office.

The office was barren. How had she not realized that before? No one was allowed to put up any posters or decorate their cubbies except for a family picture. Dull elevator music was low in the background. The cubbies were arranged so no one faced another worker. The office lounge was near the custodian's office and had one long table. No one ever delivered fresh sticky buns. Workers didn't cluster together to chat.

With his arms folded across his chest, he paused in his tirade as though waiting. Waiting? For what, an apology for taking time off?

"I had plenty of unused sick days and comp time. We both know I wasn't docked any pay for the time off I deserved." She stated that clearly so the office wouldn't ever be afraid of taking their time. "It does the office staff good to take a break. Vacation is a refreshing change from here."

Some office members grinned. Others nodded. Griscom tapped his foot. "Vacation? Who takes off? You don't get ahead dawdling in a small town. New Jersey? You left here to go there, really?" He nodded at the members of his office. "Tomorrow." He looked directly at her. "Tomorrow you will report to me at 8 AM sharp so we can get you back on track."

"No, Griscom, I won't." Her words came out calmer than she felt.

"Your vacation is over." Spit flew his mouth as he barked his words. "You are back in Seattle and you will listen to me. You will be back here ready to go tomorrow morning."

"No, Griscom, I came in to resign." Whew. That felt good. That thought hadn't entered her head until she heard his voice and the white sterile environment of the room overpowered her. She didn't want to be here anymore. "I'm going to HR as soon as I make sure I have everything out of my office and it is ready for the next person."

"You what?" Griscom 's face contorted. "You'd leave? For what? I groomed you for big things as this company grows. Where are you going to find that? You will have no power, money."

"Griscom." She grabbed one of his flailing arms. "You gave me my start. Taught me impeccable research skills. I'm grateful for that. But I want something else."

Griscom studied her face as though she had morphed into an alien. He folded his arms. His face darkened. "You will be sorry if you walk out. I won't give you references. Where else could you possibly go?"

She shrugged. "Just not here."

Jean gasped. Others ducked behind their cubicles.

Griscom glared at her. When she didn't apologize or add anything, he stomped down the hall to his office and slammed the door behind him. Jean and Caroline were the only ones left in the hall.

"Jean, I'll pack up the few items I have. I'll jot down notes for whomever takes my place and email it to you."

Jean said, "I'll get you a box. Would you write me a letter of recommendation?"

"You're leaving? Where will you go?"

She shrugged. "Not here. Not if you are not here. "

"Don't let my insanity lead you astray. I ..." She didn't know how to express her feelings. "I changed" sounded too clichéd. Until she walked in and the white walls closed in and the tight smiles of other workers appeared as though they were in a zombie mode, she hadn't thought about leaving. She wanted a job where she connected with real people and workers weren't afraid to laugh and smile.

"I was looking forward to seeing you. I like working with you. But things have changed for me." She looked down at the blousey shirt she wore. "I'm pregnant and I don't want to work in this toxic environment." She looked up at Caroline. "However, if you find a job and need an assistant."

Caroline said, "In an instant. But maybe it's about time you took a job where you need an assistant." She returned to her office. "I don't even know where I'm going to look for a job yet. Hadn't really thought this out."

Jean touched her elbow. "Are you okay? What happened to you out there? You aren't as tense and frazzled as you always were here. But—" Jean shrugged and put her hands on her hips. "You always have a plan, a list, a check-off. You ask questions, then do."

She chuckled. "I guess I learned checklists and plans don't always work on people and real life."

"I'll get you that box." Jean trotted down the hall.

Caroline headed to HR. She felt light on her feet and avoided the urgency to jump in the air and click her heels. She had savings and a small inheritance. Her mother's house was paid for. She would sell Greystone. This wasn't a completely rash act.

She needed to find something else in her life. She leaned against the wall. She grabbed her cell out of her pocket and texted Tina. "Get ready for celebration dinner. Call ya later." She clicked her phone shut.

The business in HR took less than an hour. She would receive pay for her accumulated comp time. She had a lot of that. Why had she ever worked so many overtime hours? She needed a new job … and she needed a real life.

Jean rushed down the hall toward her, her high heels clicking on the floor.

Oh no, what did Griscom do now to torture someone else?

"Caroline, there's a man waiting for you in your office. Wow." Jean paused to catch her breath. "He's eye candy."

She paused waiting for an explanation.

"Is that the David you talked about from New Jersey?"

Caroline stopped mid-step. "David? Here?"

Jean leaned against the wall. She nodded.

Caroline removed her high heels and jogged down the hallway. She arrived a little breathless with her shoes still in her hand. David rose from a chair as she entered.

"David, what are you doing here? You came all the way from New Jersey to Seattle?"

The slow smile, which had turned her to mush the first day she met him, greeted her as he looked from her face to the shoes in her hand, to her stocking feet. "You left Lakeside in a hurry with many things unsaid ... unsettled. You left me a note. That simply isn't enough. When do you get off from work?"

"Right now. "

He moved forward until they were inches apart. His heat warmed her whole being just by standing next to her. David was here.

Griscom pushed in the office almost hitting David with the door.

"He can't be here. I didn't give him clearance." He curled his lip. "You are leaving me ... your job for this?" His eyebrow arched and he scrunched his nose as though David smelled like rotten eggs.

David moved to Caroline's side. "You really are leaving your job?"

"That's a surprise to you, teacher?" Griscom dragged out each letter so it sounded like a child's taunt. "She's giving up a career here with upward mobility and benefits that you can't even match in a school." He waved his hand as if he were fanning away smelly odor. "You can't give her the things I ... the things she could get here."

David faced Griscom. "I haven't promised her anything. She makes decisions and choices for herself." He picked up an empty box. "I just came to carry the boxes."

Caroline chuckled as she took the box from David's hand and moved to her desk. "Griscom, David and I were talking. Would you close the door as you leave?"

Griscom humphed and muttered as he left.

"Nice guy. He was your boss?" He leaned against the door. No one would get in again. "You left? You didn't say you were quitting. You talked about the job you had to get back to."

"I didn't know until this morning. The thoughts of walking in here every day were more than I could handle." She picked up her books. She needed to keep her hands busy. She wanted to grab David, and run her fingers down his body to assure herself he wasn't a figment of her imagination. And she sooo wanted to kiss him. "One thing I learned in New Jersey was I think I want to work with people. Helping people, having direct contact with people."

"What else did you learn in New Jersey?" He locked the door. He moved until he stood inches from her.

The temptation was worse. Taking him on her desktop would be crazy.

"We have things to discuss. Like why are you here?" She reached for the box and placed it on top of her desk. "I need to pack and get out before I slug Griscom."

He tapped a closed fist in his palm. "I think I'd be glad to take care of that for you."

"Let's go before we both get in trouble." She tossed two books, a handful of pens and calendar in her box. He hefted it into his arms. "Anything else. You don't have much here."

She shook her head. "I just need to talk with Jean." She pulled Jean's paperweight from her bag.

"I have a rental out front. I'll meet you out there. If you are not there in five minutes," He looked at the clock on the wall. "I'll come in and punch him."

Laughing, she pushed him through the door. David here. How had he found her? Probably Tina.

She made plans with Jean to go to lunch later in the week. She watched the clock and was out before the prescribed five minutes. David leaned against a white Honda facing the entrance to the office.

"You can follow me to my house." She jotted her address on a piece of paper. "This is it, if you have a GPS. That's my car." She pointed to a red Mini Cooper.

"I won't lose you in the traffic." She watched for the white Honda with every turn. Tina had chili bubbling on the stove.

The smell wafted throughout the house. Caroline could hear her humming in the basement studio.

"This is my mother's house." She paused in the hallway. "I have a lot to tell you about my family."

"Is that why you left like that? You didn't say goodbye. Explain anything. I know you said you had to be home by …" He dropped a small suitcase near the door. "I didn't think you would leave like that."

"It became too much. I had a job here, my home. Meg, you, Irene, I felt like everyone was closing in."

"We didn't mean to make you so miserable you would flee." He rubbed his fingers along stubble on his cheeks. "But none of us wanted you leave. You became part of us."

"Hi, I'm Tina." She paused when they both turned. "I've talked to you on the phone."

"You told him where I worked!"

"Yeah and that came out okay. You are both here." Tina looked at Caroline as if just seeing her. "Here? You left work for him that's a good sign."

"I quit."

Tina grabbed the back of the nearest chair. "You quit? You?"

A bubble of giggles erupted when she pictured Griscom's face when he left her office. "Yep. Told Griscom I was done with his cramped, claustrophobic, mean-spirited organization. I never want to hear his high pitched nasal whine again."

Tina walked to David's side. "I don't know what you did with my best friend while she was in New Jersey, but this is not her."

He leaned down to Tina's level and whispered. "I hid her in New Jersey so she wouldn't leave. I just came to fetch her clone."

Tina poked him in the arm. "I like you."

"Ah yoo-hoo. I'm standing here. Are you two done?"

Tina wandered to the kitchen. "I think this calls for a celebration and an explanation. Is it too early for champagne?"

David flopped in the nearest chair. "I took a night flight in and had a layover in Minnesota. No champagne for me."

Tina jumped over the back of the loveseat and stretched out the length of it. Caroline sat down in the other loveseat.

"Okay, you first." Tina pointed to Caroline. "You quit? Describe Griscom's face in detail. I want to savor that one."

Caroline studied the swirls of the rug below her. "I'm not sure what started it. When I entered the building, the walls closed, sterile, stifling. I worked there for a lifetime. I grew, learned—for years loved the research." She looked down the hallway toward her mother's kitchen. How could she explain that cold, hollow pit in her stomach when she walked in that office.

She leaned toward Tina. "I just don't think I'm that person anymore." She frowned and squeezed her forehead between her fingers and thumb. She sounded like the women on those abhorrent talk shows. "What I liked best about Readers' Haven was seeing the faces of the ones I helped. I liked the interaction and reading people."

"Larkin posted an advertisement for a part-time worker and manger. You could apply." David said.

Caroline shook her head. "I love Meg and many in the book club." Her eyes flicked over to Tina and back. "I met a relative I didn't know I had. I'll come back to New Jersey to see everyone, but I live here."

Tina pointed to Caroline. "So you lost your job." She turned to David. "And you followed her here. Good for you. What now?"

David shook his head. "I don't know. I just got on a plane."

"This could get interesting."

"My home is here." She enunciated each word. They looked skeptical.

Caroline wet her lips. So much she had neglected to say or just plain lied about. How would that change when she did confess her motives?

His cell phone rang. "Wait." He held up his hand. "I've got to take this." He opened his cell and walked away. "Doc Barker."

Caroline stiffened. Meg's doctor?

Tina moved Caroline's legs off the loveseat and curled beside her. "You didn't tell him why you were really in Lakeside?"

"I did. I was there to sell property."

Tina curled her lip and shook her head. "That's not a lie, but it's not all the details either. You didn't ask him about others. About your mother? He lived there. He could have helped."

"I can't just blurt out facts. The truth changes people's lives."

"Yeah, your life." Tina muttered. She scurried back to her seat as David walked in. His ashen face coupled with the steel grip he had on his phone prompted Caroline's leap to his side.

"David?" She placed her hand on his arm. "What? Is it Meg?"

He closed his eyes. "She's in the hospital." He took a breath. "In a coma."

"Oh David," She wrapped her arms around his chest. "David, is she— What did Dr. Barker say?"

"Irene hadn't been able to reach her on the phone and luckily went to see her."

Caroline closed her eyes. She had gotten through to Irene. Irene checked on her.

"How bad is Meg? What do you know?"

He leaned his head down on hers. "Her vitals are good. She has minimal response." He kissed the top of her head. "Still so many unknowns."

"I have …" She leaned back. "Connections through the company. I'll see if I can get us tickets out tonight."

He touched her cheek. "You're coming home with me?"

"I'm coming. It's Meg. You can't go yourself."

"I'm coming, too."

They both turned. "You coming too?"

Tina nodded. "You've talked about the town. It's an arts district. I'd like to see it." She stepped closer to the couple and touched Caroline's sleeve. "I can help you with family research."

Caroline moved away from David. "Get bags from the attic. I'll call Reuben, see what he can do for us. See how soon he can get us all a flight." She poked David in the arm. "You take a nap. You've been up all night. I'll wake you up a couple of hours."

He mutely nodded.

"Come on," She led him to a room on the second floor. "Sleep in here. The bathroom's attached." She pointed to a door.

He plopped the small suitcase on the bed. "And where are you sleeping—how close?"

"You're too tired. I am down the hall."

"You won't let me sleep long."

She shook her head. "I'll let you get a couple of hours. I don't know what's available. If there's any question, I'll get you a flight first and Tina and I will follow."

He reached for her hand. "I would rather we'd go together."

"Okay. I can't promise anything."

She dialed two friends while he slept. The best she could manage was three together the next morning, but it was a direct flight. They would be in New Jersey by Thursday late afternoon.

She folded underwear, a T-shirt in a small suitcase. Tina rolled her packed bag in and flopped on the bed. "He flew all the way here for you. Impressive."

Caroline placed another T-shirt in the top. "I don't know why. I didn't expect him to come here."

"I think the element of surprise was planned. Maybe he was afraid you'd tell him 'no' if he alerted you."

"Well, I would have. We made no plans ..." She sat on the bed.

"You did run away from some things, didn't you?" Tina picked up Caroline's jeans, rolled them into a tight cylinder and tucked them in a suitcase corner. "You ran from him. He's certainly not Griscom."

"No, but he thinks I have changed his life, turned it around. I can't get my own life where I want to be. How can I influence his? It's all so complicated and entangled."

"Time to get it untangled. Time to share the truth with David. He cares for you, which he proved by his arrival. He's not willing to let you go." Tina pulled out the handle of her small suitcase. "I'm going down to pack some art supplies. I can't let some of this work go." She paused. "I want to see this town. Talk with the artists. Think I'm going to love it—maybe not as much as you do."

"Love it? I ..." She looked a Tina. Tina tapped her fingers on the top of her suitcase handle and gave Caroline one of her classic eye rolls she had perfected in high school.

"Okay," said Caroline. "I miss the place. It's so different from here."

"I don't want you loving it so much you move there, but I think you need to admit your attachments to the people there, find a way to let that grow." She paused at the doorway. "Maybe we should get a bite to eat."

Caroline nodded. "I'll wake up David. He can sleep again on the way to New Jersey."

CHAPTER TWENTY-THREE

She pushed David's door open a crack. He was sprawled across the bed with one arm flung across the top of the pillow and his legs extended in opposite directions. His breathing was heavy.

"David." She stroked his arm.

He blinked as though he were coming back from a far away land. "Hi." He touched her cheek with the back of his hand. "Good to see your face." He leaned on one arm. "Did you get the flight?"

"The earliest we can go is first thing in the morning. We are all on the same flight."

He nodded.

She held his hand. "You flew all the way here. Why?'

"You left." He traced a pattern on her hand with his thumb. "You left an empty hole. We need to figure out what this is between us." He reached for her and she stretched on the bed beside him. "What's bothering you? Why did you leave—so abruptly?"

"Life was closing in." She picked at the bottom sheet. "I left out ... didn't tell you important things about me and why I was there." She studied the design in the sheet. "They weren't all lies. They were just details left out."

He fluffed the pillow behind his back. "Are you going to fill in those details?"

"I inherited a house. I planned to fly in, see it, put it on the market and fly back to Seattle and my familiar steady life." She rubbed her forehead with her fingers. "I didn't expect to find a pregnant woman in labor, meet you, Irene, Meg and the reading group gang and stay. And like it. Life doesn't always follow your expectations."

His boyish grin complemented the twinkle in his eyes. "Remind me to buy Dylan a big present. I like that kid more. He started all this."

She pressed her fingers on her abdomen to relieve the churning. When he found out the little lies she told, would he still be grinning? She pressed on. "The house. I was born in that house. I inherited it from my adoptive mother."

David scowled, and sat up. "Run that by me again. You were born in New Jersey? You got the house—how was your mother involved with a house in New Jersey?" He pressed his fingers together. "Did you know all this before you came here? Did you come looking for your mother and father?"

Caroline filled him in on her search and her discoveries along the way. "I know Jeffery Kelly died—even before I was born. I found his brother living in Maryland. I don't know who my mother is. She doesn't want to be found."

He continued to frown. "You and your mom—the one who raised you—sounds like you had a close relationship." He punched the center of the pillow. "But you had questions about your birth parents. And looking for birth parents didn't work out."

She spread her hands on top of the sheets. "Yeah," She sat up. "I did find an uncle. I'm happy with that. I don't need to find any one else."

"You never told anyone. Meg, Irene," He tossed the pillow to the side of him. "I could have helped you look or may have known something."

"My search. I didn't want to start rumors or upset anyone. Once I met Jason, I realized how I could turn my natural mother's life upside." She arched her fingers then flattened them. "I could cause her pain." She rested her hands on her lap.

"Meg knows most in town. I know Greystone. My mom grew up in that house."

"Your family once owned Greystone?" She sat up straighter, the churning in her stomach turned to a hard lump of lard instead. "How long?"

"I think my mom ... I think she lived there through her

teens, maybe younger."

Caroline chewed on the corner of her mouth. What did David's family have to do with this? Her mother might have known David's family.

He stroked the side of her face with his index finger. "Is that why you left? It changed what you thought you knew about your history. Will returning to Lakeside upset you?"

"I haven't processed it all. I fled to Seattle because everything was changing." She shrugged.

"Adjusting to new ways of thinking and looking at yourself and your needs takes a long time. Joy died five years ago. I couldn't let go of her, couldn't go forward." He cupped her face in his palms. "Not until you. You came into my life. Everything opened up."

"That's too much put on my shoulders."

Tina's banging on pans interrupted their thoughts. "Soup's on. Come on out."

Caroline jumped off the bed. "Dinner. You ready for Tina? Great cook, crazy friend."

David followed her to the kitchen. Tina had ladled out chili in bowls. Traces of warm yeast bread spread through the air.

Tina peppered them both with questions about Lakeside throughout dinner.

David dipped his crusty bread into the chili sauce left in the bottom of his bowl. "You will be able to see it soon." He paused with his bread clutched in his fingers. "Good people there. Lots to do in the Arts District."

Tina pushed her bowl away from her. "I'm sure I'll spend plenty of time there talking with other artists, making connections." She sipped her water. "But I also want to explore —ask questions Caroline couldn't. See if I can find her mother." She rubbed her fingers along the rim. "Even if she doesn't want to make contact, at least Caroline can end a chapter."

"If." He tapped his fork on the plate edge. "When Meg comes out of the coma, she'll help. She knows many, knows about families."

Tina reached for another piece of bread. "So tell me again, why you don't think it's Meg."

Caroline and David gasped. David's fork clattered on his

plate.

"Meg." Caroline dropped her spoon in the bowl. "I never even thought of Meg. Can't be." She swallowed to dislodge the lump in her throat. "No, Meg would be too young. She couldn't have had me. Besides." She looked from David to Tina and back to David. "We're close. I ... if she were my mom. No, can't be Meg."

David focused on the wall. "No, Meg and my mom were best friends." He scratched the side of his head. "I would have at least heard of some hint of that."

The conversation shifted to the chili. Dinner churned in her stomach as she helped Tina clean up.

Tina tossed the dish towel on the counter. "Come on downstairs. I'll show the studio. I needed a place to work so I requisitioned a section of the basement. You said you wouldn't mind."

Caroline nodded.

"I took over and painted daily." Tina led the way.

Tina's career had grown. Others artists clamored to work in the studio with her.

The overcrowded, dark basement had become a colorful display of her work. Tina described the artists' group, which flourished there.

"Impressive." Caroline walked down the row of vivid landscapes. "You helped me sort through Annabelle's antiques and rejuvenated your career in the six weeks I was gone."

"I often sleep down here," Tina said. "I paint at night and early morning. I just crash." She rocked on her heels. "You can have the whole upstairs just to yourselves. I won't disturb you or hear you."

"Jeez, Tina." Caroline flush rose up her cheeks. "Enough."

She and David climbed both sets of stairs together. David stopped outside his room. "Well, I guess ..."

"I have a queen size bed. It's softer, too." She grabbed him by the belt, pulled him in her room and shut the door with her foot. David. He had wandered through her thoughts and her dreams since she left. She palmed the hardened hills and valleys of his upper body beneath his shirt.

She closed her eyes. With her fingertips, she swirled

indiscernible designs around his nipples and across the hairs of his chest. If she had remained in Seattle, she would never have touched his skin, or felt his taut ready body beneath her fingers. Never—too harsh a sentence.

She wanted this man. She pushed the shirt over his head and tossed it to the floor. He yanked off her shirt and added it and her bra to the pile beside the bed. David kissed her tasting the inside of her upper lip with his tongue that sent chills down her spine.

"All. Off. Now." Pressing his hands down the back of her pants, he pushed them to the floor. He unsnapped his jeans and yanked them off and kicked them to the pile.

He swooped her up and dropped on the bed. When she bounced, giggles erupted. This man, this day were unlike any other.

He straddled her legs. He wiggled his eyebrows. "Want something?"

"You." Caroline rubbed her thumbnail down the inside of his bobbing penis and was rewarded with sharp hiss from his compressed lips. *Yes!* Exciting this man was a heady experience. She continued her torment swirling her fingers around the ridges of his tip.

David trapped her arms on either side of her head and captured a nipple between his lips. The onslaught of his sizzling, torturous tongue drove away any coherent thought. Every nerve, crackling and alive, drove her desire to high alert. Release was an urgent call.

"David. Now please." Her voice, raspy and tight, sounded like an old record.

As he leaned across her to grab the foil pack from the floor beside the clothing pile, his shaft brushed against her moistness. She clutched the sheets.

He rolled on the condom and plunged deep within. She dug her fingers into his hips increasing the rhythm and pressure of each thrust. Relief exploded as though she were the center of a fireworks rocket.

Her breath slowed to ragged pants. She closed her eyes and pressed her cheek on his chest willing herself back to the reality of earth and a bed and David's warmth.

Her body calmed, her nerve ending soothed. No longer on fire, her breathing and heart rate lessened—her needs sated.

David wrapped his arms around her. He inhaled deep breaths. "I hope Tina had earphones on and loud music playing."

"We created a song of our own."

She snuggled into David's warmth. He drew the sheet over their bodies.

The alarm rang much too early. She slammed down the button and flopped back next to David. "Hey," she whispered. "We need to get up—plane leaves early."

"Mmm," He rolled over and tugged her body until she nestled in his arms. "Five more minutes. Waking up holding you. One of my dreams."

She snuggled closer. Who could refuse a request like that?

Tina's singing and banging dishes disturbed their peace.

"She's a whirlwind. Throws herself into something, it's a hundred percent, isn't it?"

She laughed. "Oh yes, she just jumps in. She wants to see Lakeside. Certainly is your big fan."

"You talked and described us, did you?"

"We talk about everything. I toss out ideas. We argue, discuss politics, job, family." She poked him in the ribs. "And everyone in Lakeside, not just you." She kissed him on the forehead. "She knows all my secrets. We have been friends forever." She ran kisses from his forehead to his cheeks. "We need to get ready to get that flight."

"Keep kissing me and we will miss the flight." He rolled her away from him and stood up at the end of the bed. "Think I'll sit with Tina the whole way to New Jersey and ask her about stories about you."

She stretched. "Oh, she will tell many—not always true, usually embellished. But we're sitting together and Tina is across the aisle—next to me."

After quickly devouring the breakfast sandwiches Tina prepared, they loaded carryon suitcases and boarded their flight. Caroline rested her head on David's shoulder and wrapped her arm around his. He dozed. Tina sketched on the pad she carried.

Please be okay, Meg. She had to be. Tina's question about Meg being related considering still buzzed in her head. She reconsidered all the facts she accumulated researching her birth mother. Nothing pointed to Meg.

Meg had to be okay. She stroked David's arm. For all their sakes.

She was looking forward to seeing Larkin and even Irene. She leaned her head back and closed her eyes. She'd have to thank her for checking on Meg. If only she could talk with Meg. So much whirling in her head.

Mid-flight, she stretched her legs, walked the aisle and headed to the lavatory aboard flight. When she returned, David and Tina were seated together. She heard their laughter before she reached her seat.

"Hey, no conspiring while I'm not here to defend myself."

David leaned around Tina. "She's just filling me in on your childhood and teen years."

Tina winked at David. "I promised pictures next time he visits Seattle."

Caroline groaned. "You need to move." She poked Tina's arm. "I need to defend myself and you need to shut up."

They switched seats, she asked David. "Do I want to know what fabrications she told you?"

He chuckled. "I have a new view of the trouble you two got into. I want to see pictures of your hairstyles when you were fifteen." He paused then reached for her hand. "She also said when you called from Lakeside, when you talked about the town, the people, you were happy. Happy like the carefree, adventurous child she knew. She likes the different person being away brought out."

"Lakeside is a very distinct place. Brought out a—new side of me. One I didn't even know was there." She leaned her head on his shoulder. "Liked a log cabin away from everything. Liked kayaking and listening to birds. None of those things were ever part of my world."

He rested his cheek on top of her head. "I need you there." His voice cracked.

"Meg is going to be okay. She has to be. We can wait until she awakens together."

"Together. I like that sound." He kissed the top of her head. "I hated that note you left." He softened his voice to a whisper. "I need to know if you feel as I do." He nestled as close as he could with the armrest between them.

All three dozed the rest of the trip. At the airport, they parted company. David got his car and travelled straight to the hospital. Tina and Caroline waited to rent a car, then Caroline gave Tina a tour of Lakeside before going to Greystone.

"Look at this! Looks as though someone captured it from a small town picture. Look at the coloring of the doors and shutters." Tina wiggled around in her seat to catch varied views as Caroline drove through the main street of town.

"I thought the same thing. Small town takes adjustment. Close-knit communities exist within the whole town." She turned toward the river. "The bookstore gang is a community all their own." She parked and pointed to a bench. "That's one of my favorite spots here. One I found the first day."

Tina nodded. "I can certainly entertain myself while you visit Meg and friends." She turned toward Caroline. "Galleries. Did you see how many there are on that street? And things to sketch. That one tall building with green shutters and tones of brown in the building. Part brick, part wood. Love it. And this." She waved her hand across the expanse of the windshield. "This is a dozen paintings at different times of day."

"It's a great place." She started the car. "Come on, I need to check in on Larkin and the bookstore."

As she pulled in a parking place, a large yellow poster tacked to the door of Readers' Haven. Her stomach tightened. Not open? No lights flickered inside. No one moved in or out. She twisted her bracelet as she read: *Bookstore Closed. Limited Hours. Open Wednesday and Saturday noon to four until further notice. Sorry, folks. I'm working on it. Larkin and Ryan.*

She tugged on her lips with her fingertips. Larkin couldn't do it—couldn't keep it open with Dylan here and obviously, hadn't found someone to help.

"That sucks." Tina stood beside her. "I really wanted to see this place." She put her hand on her friend's arm. "You okay, you look green."

"That's really bad for business. Bad for everyone. So many

rely on this. Larkin can't afford to lose loyal customers. Must be hard." Nagging guilt pricked her conscience. If she hadn't left, Larkin could have kept it open until she found a helper.

"We can come back when Larkin is here."

They drove to the house. Tina toured the inside with an open mouth. "Oh my God, this is the best of Annabelle. All the antiques, but not all crowded together for storage as they were in her house." She spun around in the middle of the living room. "What a great place."

"Come on, show you my two favorite spots." She led her to the library. "I wanted to move this space with me."

"So cozy, inviting. Almost makes me wish I were a reader."

"One more." She led her to the garden.

"This is why you want a garden." She inhaled. "Smells wonderful. So many varied flowers."

"All roses." Caroline corrected her. She touched the pink flowers of a bush. "Meg planted this. Her commemorative rose. She loved this one, knows a lot about roses."

Tina walked to the rose and stared. "Meg planted this rose?" She turned toward her friend. "Doesn't that strike you as odd?" She fingered a green leaf. "Meg planted a rose here at the house Annabelle owned. Did they know each other?"

Caroline frowned and sucked in her bottom lip. What else had Meg said? "It was a long time ago. Think before Annabelle owned this." She moved away from the garden. "I never asked Meg about Annabelle. Never talked to anyone about her except Stephanie."

Tina walked beside her. "David may be your best source for finding your mother. Still odd Meg planted that rose. More to that story."

They walked inside. "After I unpack, I'll meet you in the library." Tina chose a room on the corner of the second floor.

CHAPTER TWENTY-FOUR

Caroline cut pink roses from the garden and arranged them in a vase in the library. The petals were soft with slight raspberry fragrance. A restlessness enveloped her. It was as though she had been sucked through a time machine vacuum back to her old life in Seattle and then transported immediately back to New Jersey. She didn't know where she belonged.

Tina bounced down the stairs and flopped on a seat. She tucked her knees beneath her and leaned back against the cushions in the library window seat. "You can't take this with you to Seattle, but you can a lot of other things you got here."

She nodded. "Can't take the people back either."

"I like David. He's funny, fun-loving and he flew to Seattle to get you. Flew there!"

"I like him, too." Warmth flooded her being every time she thought of him and instant images came to mind. When he arrived at the office. And then last night curled up next to him. *Yeah, I like him, too.* The glow grew.

"What are you going to do?"

Tina's voice jolted her from her musings.

"I don't know." She stood, walked the length of the library, turned and paused. "I woke up next to him. It felt so right."

"You can't do that long distance."

"I don't know." She walked to the side window, tapped on the glass. "I know. But I belong in Seattle."

Tina kicked her heel against the window seat. "I hope so, but you." She sat still. "You are not the same person. Would you be happy in Seattle?"

"My family is there. Annabelle and Grant. You."

"Annabelle and Grant are dead. I won't like you leaving, but life changes. We'll still be friends wherever you are."

"David and I could still be friends."

Tina's breath came out deep loud sigh. "He's your lover—that's not just friends."

The door clicked. David's hello echoed in the hall. Both scrambled to the hall. David's face was tired and worn.

"Come." She led him to family room. "Drink? Alcoholic? Water? Tea?"

He sank in the chair. "Cold beer? Do you have any?"

She nodded. "Not much of a selection." She brought him a cold Sam Adams. She and Tina opened a bottle of Merlot, poured glasses and sat in the high-backed chairs.

"What did you find out? How is she?"

He took two long swigs. "She looks like she is sleeping—a light sleep. But no response."

Caroline sat next to him, placing her hand on his thigh. "What's the doctor say?" Her words stuck in her throat.

He gripped the neck of the bottle. "They're watching her. Tests. Hopefully, we'll know something." He seized her hand. "Something good."

"What happened?"

"Meg fell at home. Looked like she tripped over her rug." He took a sip. "Stubborn woman. Had to go back to her house. She knew her way there. Jillian came every morning, stayed overnight. Meg chased her away daily."

"She fell at home?"

"Irene broke into the house."

Thank god for Irene. "How can I help?"

He ran his finger around the tip of the bottle. "I sat there today. I talked with her."

Tina edged forward. "Talking to her?"

He nodded. "Talking to anyone in a coma might help keep the patient alert or help. Internet wisdom." He shrugged. "But it is at least something I can do."

"I can come in with you or stay with her while you work. You don't have to do this alone." She reached for his hand. David's tension radiated through his fingers.

He nodded. "That's a good idea. Jillian came in today. She

sat with her while I had lunch. She's coming in at noon daily, too."

"We can set up schedules so someone is always there."

Tina added." I don't know her, but I'll help." She stretched. "I'll look around during the day tomorrow. Look at your family research, then I can come in at night and you two can catch dinner together."

"We can all meet back here each night—compare notes."

David looked from one to the other. "Thanks for coming back with me. It helps. I ..." He looked down.

Caroline stroked his arm. "Why don't you stay here for the next few nights? It's closer to Meg if you get calls and need to be there."

"Stay here?" His eyes widened then a slow grin crossed his face.

Caroline suppressed her laugh. *What a great idea. He would be closer to Meg—but he'd be here with her every night.* "It would be more convenient."

At least she could still make him smile. Tina stayed downstairs with her sketchbook on her lap. David followed Caroline upstairs.

Each paused outside the adjacent rooms.

"You are welcome to sleep in here," She stood in the doorway. "If you need your own space, it's okay."

He shut the door. "Sleeping in your arms is just what I need. Been an exhausting day, but I need your warmth."

She opened her door wider. He fell asleep almost as soon as he lay down. She stayed awake watching him. She gently stroked his hairline with her index finger. "Good night, David Montgomery. I'll share my warmth any time." She snuggled down under the sheet.

The next morning, David left early to talk with the doctors. Caroline searched the Internet for job possibilities in Seattle. None looked promising. She shut her screen. Nothing. She didn't know what job she wanted. She knew about medical research, but she liked working and talking with people in the bookstore.

Tina was bent over her sketchpad with her pencil rapidly drawing with quick strokes. She watched her for a few minutes.

The building, the one which attracted Tina's attention the first day, slowly filled in the space on the page.

"You were impressed with the town and the buildings."

Her pencil stopped mid-line. "Oh." She sat up, put her pencil aside. "I took photos yesterday. So many fresh images. I made interesting contacts." She stretched her neck from one side to the other. "Today, I'm asking questions, researching in the library for you."

"Thanks for taking over the search."

"Do you need company when you visit Meg?"

"No, I want to see her. I'm going to change and leave early." Tina nodded and returned to her drawing.

At the hospital, Caroline watched the numbers on the way up in the elevator. David reassured her Meg looked good. She wanted to see her. If she had convinced her to stay at Greystone, she wouldn't have fallen. Caroline leaned her head back and closed her eyes.

She paused outside her door, took a deep breath. David rose as she entered. "You sure you want to stay?"

"No, no, it's Meg, I can stay with her. Talk with her."

He kissed her, a slow, gentle kiss. "Thank you for being here." He looked down at Meg. "Hopefully, she will awaken and …" He swallowed and looked at the chart on the far wall.

She reached for his hand, "She will waken and—be her old self." She sat in the chair next to the bed that he had just vacated. *Meg just has to be okay.*

She brushed a hair from Meg's face. "Hi Meg, it's Caroline. I'm back." She rested her hand on her arm. "Wish you were able to talk. I'm confused about—about a lot of things. I'm glad to be back. Being in Seattle was just out of sync. I can't be in both places."

Talking to an unresponsive woman was silly. *Wish Meg could talk.* She needed her wisdom, her insights would help.

"It's about your David. He certainly has enlivened my life." She bit back the wanton grin. The thought of David, the sensuousness of his kiss, the feel of his skin beneath her fingers brought out a restlessness and giddiness. Starting the day curled beside him made the day brighter. He was different than anyone she knew. Fun, responsive and they had a phenomenal connection in bed. Might be a good thing not to talk about David. Bedtime with David was not discussable with Meg.

For the afternoon, she alternated talking and just sitting and thinking. She called Uncle Jason and related the latest news.

She tapped her fingers on the bed frame. "I need coffee or water, Meg, I'll be back." Maybe she could call Larkin while she was here.

She heard familiar voices as she walked out of Meg's door. Irene and Stephanie sat side by side in a waiting room chatting. Irene and Stephanie together?

Irene waved her inside. "How is she doing?"

Stephanie added, "I came to see you. I have something for you."

Irene winked. "Tonight we will sit with her so you and David can have a quiet dinner together."

"Here." Stephanie handed her a mug. "I brought hot coffee and sticky buns."

"Oh, I missed them. Thank you." She bit into a bun and sighed. They were so good. No Starbucks store display of processed bakery items could match this. "How long have you been sitting here together?"

Stephanie and Irene made eye contact, then both laughed.

"Guess we have held a grudge for too many years." Stephanie said.

"A grudge?"

They nodded. Irene started the explanation. "Stephanie left town. I think …" She paused. "I think, I was responsible for gossip and ill-will toward Stephanie."

"No, we both said evil things. I never forgave anyone. Blamed the whole group." She refreshed Irene's cup with hot coffee, then offered more to Caroline. "We never said more than a few words to each other since we were in our twenties." She sipped her coffee. "Very childish."

Irene nodded to Stephanie. "She reads a lot, has read most of the books the Readers' Haven Book Club has."

Caroline suppressed the smile. *Yeah, she finds out what it is read each month and buys the same books.*

"If it weren't for you, I wouldn't have even talked with

her." Stephanie said to Caroline.

"Me?"

She nodded. "You suggested a few times, I join in or come in when they were there. Glad to have you back. You gonna hang onto Greystone now and come back the way Annabelle did? We miss you."

"Miss me?" Caroline arched an eyebrow. "I thought you couldn't wait for me to return to Seattle? You asked when I was leaving every time I saw you."

Stephanie folded a napkin in small squares. "You fit in with them so easily. Made me feel like an idiot. Just wanted you to go." She threw away the napkin. "You are so different from your mother. She was so insolated. Spent more time with her antiques than others."

Caroline tilted her head. Annabelle didn't socialize much after Grant had died. She spent most of her time in the basement refinishing furniture. She talked with clients and dealers. Never thought much about that. What else had she missed?

Irene asked, "You going to stay now that David wants you here?"

"David?"

"He flew out to get you and you came back."

Small town. She'd forgotten how Irene knows everything going on. Who told David flew to her? How many know he is staying at my house?

"I don't know what I'll do? I came back because of Meg."

Irene shook her head. "So sad. What chances do the doctors give her? Can we do anything?"

Caroline filled them in on what she knew.

"I almost forgot." Stephanie pulled an envelope from her bag. "This was buried in the back of a drawer in the room you stayed in. Sorry I didn't see it earlier." She handed it to Caroline. "It was stuck to the top. Your name is on it."

Caroline frowned. The brown envelope. A realtor had sent that to her the first day and she stuffed it in a drawer in the bed and breakfast. So many events happened so quickly. She'd forgotten about it.

Annabelle's handwriting. Annabelle had known she would

show up here. *She left me a note.* So many surprises from a mother she thought she knew so well.

She placed it under her arm. Fortified with coffee and sticky bun, she returned to Meg's room. Her position had changed. Either she moved or nurses had moved her. She stared down at Meg. *Come on, Meg, fight this.*

She took the envelope from her bag and sat next to the bed. "Kit, if you're reading this ,you did arrive in Lakeside and have figured out parts of your past. I hope you can forgive me."

Forgive? What did Annabelle do that she didn't know about? She read the next three pages. She folded the papers back in thirds and replaced them in the envelope. Reclining back in the chair, Caroline closed her eyes. Life certainly handed her changes in spades.

Most of Annabelle's note supported what she learned from Dr. Morgan. She apologized for returning to visit Jennifer.

Conflicting emotions swamped her thoughts. The pain Annabelle felt, the guilt she carried leaving one baby behind. Yet, Annabelle had never chosen to share any of this with her. The anger toward Annabelle when she had inherited the house had vanished as she investigated that past.

What would she have done if she were a young girl and known she were pregnant? If she had been as young as Annabelle and the baby she had carried had died, how would she have recovered? Her times were different from her mother's—either of them.

She picked up the envelope then replaced it in her bag. Later. She'd finish reading it later.

When the nurses came in to check vitals, Caroline left. Soon Readers' Haven Book Club would be in.

Tina had dinner ready when she walked in the door. Greystone never smelled like basil, thyme and garlic when she lived here. "Great enticing aromas. I'm starving."

Tina skipped and twirled in a circle. "I love this place. I had such a great day. Have lots to tell." She stopped. "Now about your quest? I did visit the cemetery. Have no news there. How were Meg and your day?" She placed forks, spoons, and knives on the counter as she talked. "I talked with artists, toured galleries. Wonderful day." She dished out lasagna and pieces of Italian bread.

Caroline ate as Tina chattered about all the sights and interests she discovered. Tension eased from Caroline's shoulders. Having Tina as a friend, so enthusiastic about life, was catching.

She pulled the envelope out of her bag. "Stephanie handed me a note—one that Annabelle wrote to me."

"Annabelle left you a note?"

She nodded. "One was waiting for me when I got here, but it was misplaced. I think I'm glad I didn't have it before." She tapped the edge of the envelope on the counter top. "It wouldn't have made much sense. I wouldn't have looked in the right places."

Tina frowned. "Did she explain why she came here so often? What made her write it? She knew you would come here." She turned her stool. "Willing to share any of it?"

She pulled the note out and read, "I felt I deserted Jennifer for a life—you were such a wonderful baby. I easily traded her for you." Caroline skipped parts and read sections. "Silly reactions. I visited her grave and told her all about you—your tiny growth steps. Your triumphs. You were a gift to our lives. I was blessed with a wonderful daughter. I always loved you from the time I held you when you were days old." She skipped to page two. "Your birth mother suffered. She didn't want to give you up, but sacrificed so you could have the life she couldn't give you. She was young, a widow with no money, no education. Her grandmother helped her."

Caroline tapped on the note with her nails. Not according to Doc Morgan. Her grandmother created a tale for both young women. "I only contacted her once to let her know you were okay and loved." She folded the note. Neither said anything at first.

"What a secret Annabelle held for all those years." Tina said. "Sounds like a painful time."

"I never doubted their love. Annabelle and I were close. I never asked beyond that." She wiggled her foot back and forth on the rung. "Until I came here and all changed." She bit her top lip. "I should have talked to her more."

"The important part … You never doubted they loved you."

"At first, I felt guilty about Annabelle. If I found my natural parents, would it change what I had with Annabelle and Grant?" She slid the brown envelope back and forth. "But I didn't find my parents—or mother. What I found were Meg, David, Larkin even Irene..."

"You're thinking of staying this time?"

"I don't know. I fit in here. I don't know if I can pull myself away. David is becoming important, critical in my life." The last words came out in a whisper.

"I'll miss you, but you are ... If this is where you want to be."

"I don't know. I've always lived in Seattle. Annabelle and Grant are there."

"No matter where you are, they will be part of you. They raised you. You were their daughter. If you change, move, nothing can change that."

Caroline placed the note in the envelope. The tug of war continued. She grew up in Seattle, but Lakeside touched her and she regretted returning to Seattle.

After Meg gets better. After we know how to deal with that. Then I can concentrate on me, my decision.

"Smells wonderful in here." David arrived, slamming the front door behind him.

"Want some?" Tina reached for a plate before getting an answer.

He filled them in on his talks with doctor. Nothing really had changed. Still a waiting game.

"Irene and Stephanie are getting along." Caroline filled him in on her stay.

He nodded finished his mouthful of food. "Irene has organized the book club to visit at lunchtime and in the evening until the night nurse comes on." He took another bite, washed it down with the water Tina placed in front of him. "Stephanie said she wants us to have quality time." He chuckled. "They were less than subtle. They are matchmakers. They want you to stay."

Tina chimed in, "You are less than popular in town. Women, I think from book club, whined about the bookstore being closed." She turned on the teakettle. "They think you let

Larkin down and apparently, that's really bad."

"Guess it's unanimous. No one wants you to go. Irene, Stephanie and book club need you. Larkin needs you." He put down his fork. "I need you."

Tina put down the tea bag. "I'm going upstairs."

"I think we both need to focus on Meg. That's as much as either of us can deal with. The rest … some answers. Hopefully, when we know what is going on with Meg, we …" She tapped her upper lip with her thumbs. "We will know what will work for both of us."

David put down his fork, leaned back in his chair and stared up at the ceiling.

She cleared the table.

CHAPTER TWENTY-FIVE

The next morning, she and Tina went to the hospital after David. They sat in semi-circle of chairs in a waiting room outside Meg's door. Nothing had changed.

"No one was in her room. What's wrong? Is she—" Jason's arrival interrupted her reverie.

Caroline greeted him with a hug. "They took her down for tests. We all kinda gathered here." She tugged on the sleeve of his shirt. "This is Tina, my friend in Seattle. This is David Montgomery." She faltered. *What can I call him?*

"I finally get to meet Mr. Hottie." He shook David's hand.

David looked over at Caroline with one eyebrow raised. "What name?"

A flush crept across her face. "Not my label. Tina called you that when I called her."

"You should hear how she described you. And your kayak trips."

He stood. "You described our kayaks trips?"

"Not all of them. Not that one. Not that detailed ..."

Jason covered his ears with his palms. "La-la-la. TMI. I don't need to hear this."

Tina's laugh filled the room. "Guess I missed that one. I need more information for sure."

Caroline ushered Jason to a seat on the other side of David. She shared a two-seater couch with him, Tina remained to Caroline's right.

"How is she?" Jason faced them. "Have things improved?"

David shook his head. "Not that we know of. Nurses are optimistic. Doctors are cautious."

"She strikes me as a fighter. That blindness didn't make her sit in a corner and mope. I'm betting on Meg."

"You here to see her and help?" Tina eyed Jason. Caroline recognized the look on her face. She had a million questions and was already deducing much about Uncle Jason.

"I'm here for my niece." He patted the top of Caroline's hand. "She is attached to that woman and from our phone conversation, very worried."

Tina stood next to him. "Hi, Uncle Jason. I like you. Glad you're here so I could meet you."

Jason peered at the people in the circle. "You are the old friend who has known her forever. Her voice of reason."

"Voice of comic relief," Caroline muttered.

Tina rolled her eyes. "I'm her old friend and her devil's advocate. We debate the voice of reason."

"You have things I need. I need to see my niece growing up, hear stories. I missed all that. Visualize her Seattle family. Learn more about Grant and Annabelle."

Tina nodded. "I can do that. Some I can show you on a computer." She edged her chair out creating more of a circle to ease conversation. "While I'm here, I'm searching for any clues to Caroline's natural mother. She's been coming here every day to see Meg. I can help."

"Good, I can only stay today. I can help you, too if you'd like."

Tina pulled in closer. "Tell me what you remember about her mother. Caroline filled me in, but I'd really like to pester you for more details."

Jason settled back in his chair. "I was ten, more interested in playing baseball than anything else. My memories are sketchy." He folded his hands in front of his face, rested his chin on his folded fingers. "The image, almost as though it were a photograph in my head, is my mother standing on the porch yelling at a young girl. She had blondish hair, a dark blonde and was pregnant. Not much to go on."

"Do know why she was there?" Tina pressed. "Anything said?"

"As the adult looking back at the details, the circumstances, you put things together. She stopped to see my parents. They were related. She pregnant with Jeffrey's baby and distraught because he died. My parents were her only link to him." He tapped his knuckles on his upper lip. "She was in pain. She clung that flag to her chest."

"What flag?" David leaned toward Jason.

"My brother died serving his country. She held his honorary flag. From the way she clutched it—it was the only thing she had left."

"Do you remember any other details?" Tina asked. "Any little thing might be a clue."

Jason shook his head. "I was a young boy. I could describe an outfielder's stance, the home game colors, but what she looked like, or any subtle details, no." He rested his hands on the arms of the chair. "I remember about the flag. My mother was furious about the flag."

"Why do you think that? Had the woman, the mother said anything to make your mother angry?"

He shook his head. "It was the flag. She wanted it. She had lost a son. I don't think she believed that woman was really married to my brother."

David twisted in his seat. "An American flag folded in a triangle. Wrapped in plastic?"

"I don't remember the plastic, but the flag was one of those they gave to family who'd lost someone to war."

David stared at the floor as though memorizing its patterns.

Jason and Tina chatted about Caroline's childhood. David remained rooted to the spot, staring and not talking.

"Hey," Caroline whispered. "Still worried abut Meg? You got awfully quiet."

He studied her as if seeing her for the first time. He moved away and leaned on the armrest. She squirmed in her chair.

Why the intense scrutiny? Had he just noticed something about her he'd missed.

"No, it's not Meg." He didn't fill in anything.

He was distant, almost angry. Was it Jason's comment? Had Tina said something about her that he saw her in a new light? Was it because she had friends waiting?

She leaned close to him. "Too many in the room? Should we leave until you get word from the doctors?"

"No." He stood. "All Meg's doctors are meeting tomorrow and will fill me in. I need to—do something. I'll catch up with you later." Without a kiss or explanation, he left.

Silence filled the room.

Finally, Tina asked, "What was that? All of a sudden, he shuts down and then leaves. Is he always that moody?"

The door remained shut. "I don't know. He isn't moody. He didn't say." Her abs tightened as though someone was tying them off with a twist tie.

She attempted to share conversations with Tina and Jason, but her effort was half-hearted. What happened that she had missed? What upset David so much?

Tina departed to continue the ancestor search.

She and Jason sat near Meg. Jason entertained her with stories about his children. She laughed, which lifted her spirits from gloom that had settled after David's departure. They stayed by Meg's side until book club arrived to take their turns near Meg. Caroline looked over her shoulder at Meg as they left. No change. At least, she wasn't alone.

Jason walked out with his arm around her. "At least I could make you smile for a time and not worry about David's frowning face."

"You noticed a difference?"

Jason scowled. "You raved about him. He withdrew from all of us, didn't say goodbye. Not even to you." He squeezed her shoulders. "I'm sure whatever is bothering him is a passing thing. He will be fine when he gets to Greystone for dinner."

She closed her car door and fastened her seatbelt. Yeah, except he didn't even say he was coming for dinner. Even Jason noticed changes. David withdrew from her as though he knew something about her. Something that hadn't bothered him before.

She prepared clams and spaghetti for dinner, which took time and required attention. She didn't want to focus on David. Jason napped in a room. He had worked, then driven to New Jersey.

She texted both David and Tina dinner would be around six. Neither had responded. After sticking the garlic bread in the oven, she wiped down every counter in the kitchen. She started on outside of the cupboards when Jason stumbled in.

"Mmm, smells great." He walked around the counter and hugged her. "Life has taken such a marvelous turn in my life. I have a niece." He sniffed the air. "Who really knows how to cook." He let go, looked around the kitchen. "I can be of some help. If you point me in the right direction, I can set the table." He opened the cupboard Caroline indicated. "Four of us?"

Caroline sighed. "I think. I haven't heard from Tina or David."

"I don't need to rush back." He placed plates on the dining room table. "We can have a glass of wine together while we wait to see who shows up." He squeezed her shoulder before reaching for the silverware. "I'm sure he will be here with some valid explanation for his behavior."

She leaned against the counter. Such unfamiliar and unnerving behavior from him.

Tina arrived, throwing the door open with her hip, an overly stuffed cloth bag slung over her shoulder, her sketchbook and pencil case in one hand and a bottle of wine in the other. "Had my cell phone off. Sorry I didn't answer. I have stuff to show you."

Jason gripped the wine and the sketchbook from her hands. He placed the sketchbook on the coffee table in the family room. "We were just sharing wine. You two go sit and I'll pour and bring it in the family room."

"There's a cheese and fruit tray in the refrigerator."

Tina stopped mid-stride. "You celebrating?"

"No, just keeping busy."

Jason handed each a glass and sat down in the chair. Tina dumped the heavy bag on the floor next to the rocker and eased into the rocker with a deep sigh. Caroline picked up an apple and a piece of cheese. She took a deep gulp of wine.

They ate snacks in silence. The cheese stuck in her throat. No word from David.

Tina placed her glass down. "Maybe David couldn't stand it. The pressure is too much. Meg is his family now."

Caroline nodded. But she thought he wanted her at his side. What had happened between the night in her Seattle house and now?

Jason rose. "I can't eat. Let's go to the hospital. Maybe he's there, has learned news and can't share it."

Caroline nodded.

The three wedged themselves in the front seat of Jason's truck. She closed her eyes and leaned back. If he had learned more about Meg's condition and couldn't bring himself to share it, that made all this so much worse. Losing David. Losing Meg. She pressed her fingertips into her temples. Her world crushed in around her.

Readers' Haven Book Club clustered in the waiting room. They moved so Tina and Caroline had seats. Jason paced. No David.

David paused in the hallway. He clutched the package next to his abdomen. This affected the women he loved the most.

His gut said this was best and he had no choice. He wavered, then took a deep breath and entered. He pulled the package from under his shirt.

Jason noticed first. "My God," slipped out.

Caroline stopped chatting with Irene as silence enveloped the room.

Jason's large fingers gripped his cheeks. An anguished look was frozen on her face.

The scene moved as though he were watching an old-fashioned newsreel. He couldn't stop the next frame, but he couldn't to move the action any faster.

"What?" Caroline was the first to break the silence. "David, where did you go?"

He handed her the flag wrapped in the old clear sweater bag.

"My God," Jason repeated. "Is it?" He reached for the flag then stopped. "Where did you get this?"

"Meg's nightstand drawer."

"Ohhh." The word stretched as though it were several syllables.

She hugged the flag close to her chest. Jason moved next to her and patted her shoulder.

The vise that had gripped his chest since he left this room released. David knelt before them and placed his hand on her knee. "When you—" He nodded to Jason. "—described the flag. It triggered a memory." He licked his lips.

The others in the room leaned forward. "When I was ten, I played in Meg's room, saw the flag in an open drawer. I picked it up." He rubbed the center of his forehead. "Meg yelled at me. Scared me. She never yelled."

"Meg. The pregnant mom." Caroline dropped the flag on her lap and ran her fingers around the edges. "My mom."

"My sister-in-law." Jason stood next to Caroline. David sat cross-legged before her.

"Meg." Caroline whispered. She opened the bag and slowly pulled out the flag. She held it to her cheek. Meg. If she had been able to pick the person she had searched for it would have been her. The connection she felt to her. Her wisdom. Their friendship.

A photograph slid out of the fold and fell to the floor. Tina picked it up, looked at it. A soft gasp escaped before she handed it to Caroline.

The picture. It was her. She knew it. She touched the edge. She remembered Grant taking it.

Tina pointed to a note on the back in Annabelle's handwriting. Caroline read aloud. "She is loved and happy. We don't ever want to give her up. She is curious, generous and loves us. When she asks, I'll explain. Please let us keep her in peace."

"Annabelle gave her a picture of you. They knew each other. She said in her note she never contacted your mother." Tina poked Caroline's knee with each word.

"Or maybe Annabelle gave the note and photo to someone to give to Meg." David said.

"But it's Meg." Caroline clutched the picture to her chest.

No one moved. Tina moved behind her friend and touched her shoulder.

"Oh." Jason grabbed the back of the nearest chair. "My dimple. The eye and hair color." He took a deep breath. "Remember when I met her? She knew I was a Kelly. She knew I was Jeffrey's brother."

No wonder Meg had been so moved and then silent. What a strange experience for her. Her husband's brother suddenly appears in her life. Yet, she never explained anything to her.

She reached for David's hand. "She knows, but doesn't want to admit. Doesn't want to recognize me as her daughter. It was so long ago."

"I don't know. Meg is usually so open. Easy to read." David stroked her hand.

"She's kept that secret a long time. No one to share it with since your mother died," Jason said softly. "Caroline said she and David's mom were close."

"Did she ever say anything? Talk about Meg?"

"I can't remember a time Meg wasn't a part of our lives. I know she left after high school, went to college and stayed away." He scowled. "Mom said something changed her. She wasn't going to come back, but—" He tapped their clasped hands on his knee. "The story was she came back because of me. That made my mother happy."

Caroline leaned her head over on David's arm. "You would be worth coming back to."

Oh my God, what word choice. She didn't come home to him. He seemed oblivious to her statement. Only Tina looked at her as though she had just admitted she didn't believe in Santa. Her thoughts all jumbled together. The puzzle pieces snapped rapidly together—the clues she had missed.

"Your mother helped deliver me. They did live in this house then." She filled in David and Jason with her conversation with Doc Morgan.

"You two have history together. Your parents were friends," said Tina.

David nodded. He told them stories of Meg and Suzanne.

Jason sat in a comfortable chair close to the group.

Tina added stories about she and Caroline.

Caroline snuggled next to the warmth and security of David's body and listened to Tina's tales. What a day. Meg. Annabelle had given Meg a photograph. She still wasn't clear if Annabelle had a long-standing relationship with Meg. Still pieces of the puzzle to find.

Caroline blinked, her head ached. David leaned over her. He was no longer beside her. The book club was gone, the room quiet. She was curled up on a small couch in the waiting room. She stood wavering.

"Come on, you fell asleep. Let's go home." David said.

They returned to a house with cheese and wine glasses still on the bar. The spaghetti still on the stove top.

"Go on, Jason and I are going to finish cleaning up." Tina pushed her toward her room.

"I can help clean up," she replied.

"You fell asleep in the middle of my stories. I could have said anything about you. You were too tired. Go to bed."

She followed David upstairs.

David sat on the end of the bed. "Hope Meg awakens soon. I have so much I want to ask. Your history is tied into mine."

Caroline paused outside the bathroom door. "If she doesn't, I—"

David cuddled her. "Meg is your mom."

David fell asleep quickly. His arms wrapped tightly around her was just what she needed. She didn't know if she wanted to cry or shout for joy. She sighed and moved closer to him. *Thank you David for being here.* She closed her eyes.

By two, she was awake. She stared at the ceiling. David's steady rhythm was reassuring, but she couldn't sleep. She slipped out from beneath his arms and walked downstairs.

She padded through the darkened halls to the library. Pulling her knees up to her chest, she rested her chin on her right knee. She'd found her natural mother. But now what? Meg might never wake up. If she doesn't want me, even as an adult, what difference does it make? She rocked back and forth.

A creak on the steps stopped her rocking. She had awakened David anyway. "Where are you?"

"In the library."

"In the dark?"

"I didn't want to wake you."

"Down here alone in the dark. Don't think you would have awakened me." He scooped her up in his arms. She rested her head in her favorite spot on David's chest.

Her mind was churning. Part of her wanted to leap and celebrate. "It's Meg!" The other part wanted to cry. Meg might not know who Caroline was or if she did, she might not want anyone else to know. Meg's regressions, her blindness and coma, might have been caused by Caroline's appearance in New Jersey. The stress of hiding her secret of thirty years had reappeared and that stress caused her relapses.

David stroked her back. "Want to share any of those thoughts?"

She wiggled out of his embrace, but kept one hand on his chest. "What if she doesn't want to be found? What if she doesn't want—" She choked on the word "me."

"You know Meg. Do you think she would not want you or not recognize you?"

"But she was young. And in so much pain over the loss of Jeffrey. Maybe I'm a reminder of that pain. I brought on her pain—her problems." She rocked.

"You might not ever know what she thinks. I think Meg would be proud of the woman you are. She'd love you." He tugged her hand off his chest and kissed her fingers. "You are easy to love."

He wrapped his arm around her shoulders. "Come on, it's a long day tomorrow. Let's go back to bed."

She followed him upstairs and easily fell asleep beside him. She was up and dressed before anyone came down stairs. She had coffee brewing and fresh pancakes made in the warmer.

David fixed his coffee. "You get some sleep?"

She nodded. "David, I need to go see Meg first thing—alone."

He paused then nodded. "Can you call me when you leave?"

"Yeah." She took her keys. "Thanks for last night—holding me."

Just as with her first visit, she hesitated outside Meg's door. My mother. The air was different. She was different. Inside that room was the person she had been searching for.

She took a deep breath and walked to Meg's side. Her head was turned to the side facing the chair. Could a person move that much when in a coma? Meg's fingertips rested on the bottom rail of the safety sides.

Caroline sat beside her. "Good morning, Meg." She rubbed the tops of her fingers. Meg was quiet and peaceful just as she had been. "I'm your daughter. I don't know if you realize that, but I think you do."

She let go of her hand and tapped her fingers on the top bar. "If you don't want to acknowledge it, that's okay." She placed both her hands on her lap. She struggled to find a comfortable spot. "I still want to be part of your life." She reached for her hand and then pulled it back. "And want you as part of my life. I … I got close to you. The person you are now. I didn't know you were my mother. I just liked you."

She tightened her grip around the rails and looked down at the quiet woman in the bed. What did she expect to happen? She was talking just to feel better. What would happen if Meg could react? "I just don't want to lose you."

Meg's hand curled around the sheet creating a scratching sound as if someone crinkled paper.

Did she do that or was that reflex? Could she move while in a coma?

Meg waved her hand in the air and reached out for Caroline.

"Oh my God." She pushed the call button.

"May I help you?" A nurse appeared

"She moved. She moved her hand. She moved." Caroline urgently repeated the words to motivate this woman to race to get the doctor.

"It could be reflex."

Meg waved at the nurse in the doorway.

"I'll page the doctor." She left momentarily and raced back in. "Doctor Summers is on his way." The nurse studied Meg and checked her vitals.

"David, he needs to be here with the doctor." She moved to the hall to call David.

Soon he ran down the hallway toward her. "She moved. The nurse and the doctor are in, another just came in. Go." She pushed him toward the door.

He walked backward as he urged her, "Come in, you're family."

She shook her head. "No. No. Doctors don't know that. Meg may not know that. Go." She waved him on.

She paced the hall from the waiting room to her door. She peeked inside, but the door was partially shut. She merely heard the doctors' low rumbles and David's voice. She couldn't hear his words, but his tone sounded excited.

Please be okay, Meg, she silently prayed as she paced.

David walked out, a wide smile lit up his face. "She squeezed the doctor's hand and opened her eyes."

She grabbed him danced in a small circle. "She's coming out of it. What did the doctors say? Is she going to be okay? Did she speak?"

He leaned against the wall and guided her into his arms. He shook his head.

"You look as though you'll fall over."

He tilted his head back. "The doctors aren't willing to predict anything. She isn't talking yet. They don't know the extent of the head injury." He wiped tears from his cheeks with the back of his hand. "We still don't know."

She rested her head against his chest. Silently, she said a prayer of thanks. "She's awake. That's an improvement."

"You going in now? Maybe she will respond to you. She was upset you went to Seattle."

"No, no, no. I may trigger another incident."

"She fell. You didn't trigger her fall."

"I ..." How could she explain her anxiety? She was afraid. Afraid of? Meg looking at her and slipping into a coma? She tugged on the collar of her T-shirt. "She could have a relapse. The shock of knowing I'm her daughter. Maybe she'll worry we told someone." She shook her head. "Wait a few days. Let her get stronger. Let the doctors assess her improvement. Then we'll know if—"

David tapped his upper lip with his forefinger. "I think you are wrong about this." He walked to her door, then back. "She's told me how much she admires you. Your leaving was a loss to her. I think she needs to know who you are."

"I think she does know. And hasn't said anything." She backed away.

For the next week, David visited Meg in short trips. Meg talked. Her vision had returned. She was still weak, but improved rapidly.

Caroline took long walks around Lakeside seeing sides of the area she had missed. She missed the interaction with people who shopped at Readers' Haven.

The following week, she and Tina spent a day at Sea Isle City Beach. Tina had already connected and frequently met with others to paint, tour galleries and even attended a pottery class at the Clay College.

Time passed slowly. At the end of the month, the doctors, a therapist, David and Meg met to decide the next steps in Meg's recovery. Caroline accompanied him for support, but remained in the waiting room.

Doctor Summers interrupted her pacing. "You're Caroline?"

Did he know? Had David told him about her relationship with Meg? Her heart banged against her chest.

"From Seattle. But you came back to see Meg?"

She nodded. She swallowed. No spit in her mouth. She ran her tongue along the roof of her mouth.

"She's asking to see you." He looked at his knees. "David has made excuses." He looked up, pinning her to her place with his dark eyes. "It's important to her. She wants to talk with you. If you came all this way." He flexed his fingers that rested on his knees. This time his gaze was softer. "I know a coma is frightening, but she is stronger. She isn't going to regress."

Easy for him to think that. He didn't know what she means to her. What do she say to Meg? It was easy talking when Meg couldn't ask questions.

"She is getting stronger. She will be released by the end of the weekend to rehab. She's asking for you. You going in?"

She smoothed the front of her skirt then stood.

"David has gone with the therapist to look at two rehab centers. He'll call you later." He nodded then walked swiftly down the hall.

CHAPTER TWENTY-SIX

She'd been looking for answers. Now she would know. She wrapped her arms around her waist to control her quaking. Her past was waiting. The door was slightly ajar.

She pushed it open. Meg was sitting up in her bed ensconced in many pillows. She studied Caroline's face with an intensity that made Caroline pause in the threshold.

"You know." Meg's words were soft as though she were whispering in a theater.

Caroline nodded. It had been easy pouring out her soul to a mute woman. Now the words stuck in the back of her throat. Her answers to the unspoken questions about her past and her newfound family were just steps away. She clung to the door frame.

"Is that why you fled so abruptly? Did you finally figure out the connection? What do you know about your adoption?"

Caroline edged forward but stopped at the end of Meg's bed. The door was still open behind her. "I came back because of you. I thought you needed ... David needed someone." A knot tightened in her stomach. "I researched, conned others and put together bits and pieces. Found Jeffrey Kelly's death certificate. Discovered he had a brother. Learned Annabelle's connection to Jennifer, about her visits to the cemetery." She picked at the ends of the blanket covering the end of the bed. "I had no connection to Margaret Whitcom Kelly until last night."

"How?" She cleared her throat. "How did you learn?"

"Jason described you. You were pregnant and clutching a flag."

Meg wound her sheet around her hand. "He remembered? He was there?"

"He observed the scene but was too young to comprehend that." Caroline stroked her upper lip. "David knew where you had a flag."

Meg curled forward. "The flag is the only thing I have of Jeffrey's. I'm so sorry. I just couldn't do it." She made no effort to hide or wipe away tears.

Caroline moved to the chair next to the bed.

"She had a baby's room set up, a crib, playpen, dresses, blankets. All ready for a baby she wouldn't bring home. She needed you, too." She gripped Caroline's fingers. "I couldn't … wasn't. Nothing to give you. No home. No place to stay. I couldn't. Without Jeffrey." The last words were whispered. Soft sobs shook her body.

Caroline knelt down beside the bed. She dropped the bed rail. "We don't have to talk about this. I didn't come here to upset you. I didn't want to cause anyone pain."

She sighed heavily, her voice filled with anguish. "I'm so sorry." She fell back against the pillows and closed her eyes. The pillows puffing around her accented her frailty and her vulnerability.

Caroline stroked the top of Meg's hand. "I've had an excellent life. Annabelle and Grant are supportive, loving parents. I love them. I miss them. I didn't know much until I inherited the house and came here." Thin ice. Should she retreat to the shore or move ahead? Should she ask the loaded question? The one that dug at her heart.

"You never mentioned you were looking for family or your connection to Annabelle." Meg turned in the bed.

"I didn't think I wanted a connection with family. I had a family—Annabelle and Grant." She took a deep breath. "When I found Jason. The search changed. I found someone. It wasn't just a name. He is a warm, generous person who wanted to be in my life. Finding Jason spurred my drive to find more family." She covered her mouth with her fingers. *Hold it together. She may not want a family connection.* "When did you know who I was?"

Meg moved her hand. She smoothed her top sheet. "As soon

as I touched your hand the day I met you. Maybe a mother's instinct."

"You never said anything to me."

"I wasn't sure Annabelle even told you that you were adopted."

"Did you talk to Annabelle? Did you meet at the cemetery?"

"We never met face to face when you were a baby. When she started visiting the house yearly, I wasn't sure if she was your mother. She never talked of her family." Meg folded her hands in front of her. "She enclosed a picture of you in a washstand I purchased from her."

Caroline gasped. The picture from the flag. Annabelle had slipped it into the antique. Tina had found the bill of sale. Pieces fit together. The answers were coming fast. Except for the one she was afraid to ask: Do you want me in your life now, Meg?

"She made it clear on the picture you were okay and I was to stay away from her and you. I was grateful for a word. As long as she kept coming here, I knew things were okay. The year she didn't, you showed up instead." She reached for Caroline's hand. Her thumb stroked the top of it. "I thought of you. Wondered." She sat up in bed "I'm relieved—glad you had a wonderful life. You are an incredible woman any mother would be proud of."

Words stuck in Caroline's throat. But are you the "any mother?" Was that a break-off line?

"I couldn't have given you the life Annabelle did." She picked at a loose thread on the white blanket. "Can you forgive me?"

"Forgive you?" The tears she had barricaded within broke loose and flowed down her cheeks. A sob escaped with her words. "Do you want me in your life?"

"Why would I not?"

"I'm a reminder of such a tough time in your life." Sobs interrupted her words. Now the hard stuff. The answers she needed. "I didn't know if you would want …"

Meg stroked the top of her hand. "How could I not want you my life."

Her head sank on top of her arms, she let the sobs rack her

body. "I want you in my life."

"Now that we've found each other, do you think either one is going to let go." Meg placed her head on top of Caroline's and wrapped her arms around her shoulders. "As adults, we can share our lives."

Caroline took a deep breath to control her sobs. She'd found her other mother. Meg handed her a tissue. "I couldn't care for you then, but I can share your life now."

"While you are finishing your rehab why don't you move back to Greystone with me. We have a lot of past to share." Caroline sat up and wiped her eyes and cheeks.

"You're staying?"

"I have no real reason to return." She leaned back in the chair. "Tina is the only tie I have to Seattle. She's busy with her art."

"You sure you want me? I won't be able to help. You will be settling in a new life and new place."

"I could use your help. Your wisdom. It's a big step for me. I'll need someone to throw out thoughts to." She moved closer. "We have years to catch up on."

"You have a house. Many who want you to stay."

"I have so much here. You're here." She shifted her position.

"Have you told David?" Meg fluffed the pillow behind her back.

"No, not yet." Caroline tilted her head. "I think I just made up my mind."

"Your heart knew long ago. It took longer for your mind to catch up."

She nodded. When did she realize? When she quit Andoer? When she came back? She had Meg, David, friends, a job … She glanced at her watch. "Meg, I need to leave. I have to get to Readers' Haven before it closes." She stood, grabbed her bag from the floor. "You okay here until Irene and the book club come in?"

"I have a lot to think about. I'll be fine." She leaned back on her pillows.

"If you talk to David, don't let on I'm staying. I have a lot to straighten out before I tell him."

"As long as you describe in detail how he took the news so

I can savor that, I patiently wait."

She gave her a quick hug. "Bye." She stopped at the door. "I'll see you tomorrow morning. We have time together." She trotted back and gave her another hug. "We found each other." She attempted to walk dignified down the hall but couldn't resist a quick Salsa move. *Meg. I found Meg and she wants me to be in her life.*

Life is a tapestry of interconnections. Meg. Annabelle. Suzanne. Strong women in her past. Add Jason, David, Tina. A simple inheritance had changed how she viewed her world and what she wanted. She jogged to Readers' Haven Bookstore. Lights were on inside. She wasn't too late.

A long white table had been set up in the middle of the floor. Larkin and Ryan sat in the middle surrounded by stacks of papers. Dylan cooed in a nearby swing while his sister shook a rattle above his head. Larkin looked as though she had run her fingers through her hair too many times. Tufts of it stuck up in odd angles.

Larkin jumped up as Caroline came in. "What a wonderful surprise. I didn't know if we would see you while you were here. How is Meg?"

She filled them in on Meg's medical progress. She sat in one of the two chairs across from both of them. The stacks were applications. Two blank ones lay on the table to her left.

"We are trying to decide on a manager for the store." Larkin pointed to three pages before her.

"Too late to fill one of these out?" She picked up an application.

"You?" Larkin clapped her hands and squeezed her husband's arm. "You're coming home? You're staying?"

She nodded. "No one knows yet. I just decided."

"And you want to work here?" Ryan jumped knocking over the chair.

"I love the work, the people. If it's not too late, I'll apply. You can talk, let me know."

Larkin ripped the three applications in half. "You're hired." She flopped into the chair. "Oh, this is so good."

"It won't pay what the job you had in Seattle." Ryan said.

"I'll be okay. I can work a second job, something on the

Internet. I'll figure it out. But I don't want to lose this one." Caroline signed the application and handed it to Larkin.

Ryan shook her hand. "Welcome back. She's been so stressed out about this." He tossed all the applications in the trash. "We are thinking of expanding, adding a research element. Both online and here. Larkin said you have experience. Interested in expanding?"

"Love it." She grinned. What a turn in her life. "I haven't told anyone yet."

Larkin arched an eyebrow. "So don't tell Irene you are taking your job back?"

Caroline laughed. "No, can we talk Monday and fill out paperwork?"

Larkin nodded. "I can open Monday. We can work together and set up schedules and duties." She glanced at her husband. "Besides I want to be here when Irene and that book group walk in."

She could work here again. Joy bubbled inside. This was the right move. The future stretched ahead in so many varied and impelling pathways.

She stood. "Thanks. See you Monday."

On the way back to the house, she danced a few silly side steps. Good thing no one saw her. They might lock her away somewhere.

At the first intersection, she stopped. Tina ambled toward her.

"I have so much to tell you. I was just coming to look for you." Tina breathed as though she had been running.

"Me, too." She licked her lips. "I'm not going back to Seattle. I'm staying."

Tina squealed and immediately engulfed her friend in a big hug. "I'm happy for you."

"That's not what I expected."

"I hate that you will be far away." She placed a hand on her hip. "But you're different here. You love it. David and Meg."

"We can talk, Skype, visit. Nothing can change the friendship."

"No. We're cemented together wherever. Besides, I'll be visiting. I have a show scheduled here next fall."

"Really? That's incredible. Two ends of the country showing your paintings!"

"I know. Been a productive trip. I have so many ideas, photos of future paintings. I'll visit you often. I love this place."

"Me too." They headed down the street toward Greystone.

"What are you going to do about Annabelle's place in Seattle?"

"You can stay there." She tapped Tina in the arm. "I wouldn't move you out. You have so much work in the basement. Eventually, I'll rent it. You can rent it if you want."

"Would you sell it?"

Caroline stopped. "Sell it?"

"I know it was your family spot and you may not want to ever sell it." Tina smoothed back her hair. "But the artist's group. The one who works with me. They come in weekly. They want a place. I was supposed to ask, but I didn't think you would give it up or move."

Caroline stumbled. Sell it. She had no intention of returning. She hadn't thought much ahead.

"They have grants, funds to start an artist's colony. You can think about it."

Caroline nodded. "Too far ahead yet. But I'll think about it."

"David and Meg must be elated. Actually, David must be to the moon."

"I haven't told him." She filled Tina in on her plans and the upcoming events.

"How are you going to tell him?"

They walked as they planned. "I want something special. Not a restaurant."

"Something that was special to just you two." Tina suggested.

"I got it." She skipped two steps. "Kayaking. We'll take a little trip. Private. Our place."

"Oh that kayak trip." Tina wiggled her eyebrows.

She blushed.

"Pack a picnic—a little wine, cheese, blankets. Enjoy."

"Great idea! I have to think of an excuse and not give it away." She'd become good at lying and half-truths. She shook her head. That has to stop. "David is working at county workshops. He will be finished Saturday afternoon."

"Do it. I leave Saturday night. If you are having … fun, I can get Uber to the airport."

"No, no, I'll be back in time. I need to say goodbye."

As soon as she returned to Greystone, she called, "David, this has been tough week for both of us. Think we could escape for a couple hours tomorrow afternoon and kayak?"

"Awesome idea. I feel like I've been stretched to the limit. I need to hear your version of your chat with Meg. She is floating on the air. So glad she found you." David said.

"It's been a… incredible, life-changing." She bit her tongue. Don't give it away. "I need to get away somewhere."

"Are we watching the stars and bringing sleeping bags?"

Her body tensed. Oh, I would love that. A night with David under the stars. His hands, lips. Stop. "Not this time. I have to go to the airport. Tina is flying to Seattle tomorrow night."

A long silence.

Come on, David, say, yes. She didn't want to blurt this out over the phone.

"You're not flying with her? This isn't a goodbye party instead of a note."

She closed her eyes. "No, I'm not going back yet." Eventually, she needed to pack up and move, but not yet. "This is just a get away together. Just the two of us."

His chuckle loosened the tightness in her shoulders. She could just picture that grin.

"Workshop doesn't end until noon. Can you meet me at my place at one?"

"Great! I'll go see Meg first."

"I want to hear about you and Meg." She heard him tapping a pencil on a counter. "I'll bounce ideas off you about therapy places. I need to see you. Awesome idea."

She hung up the phone. Bounced on her toes and did her best imitation of Rockettes line kick. Good thing no one was around.

•

The next morning, she arrived at the hospital in time to share Stephanie's sticky buns with Meg.

"Oh," Meg mumbled as she took a big bite from the roll. "She brought those over early this morning." She placed the roll on a plate, took a sip of coffee. "Oh, so good. Tell me about yesterday. What triggered your excitement?"

Caroline wiped her fingers and her mouth after devouring her our sticky bun. "I have a job. My old job. I talked with Larkin."

"Wonderful!" Meg hit her button and rolled the bed up to a sitting position. "We missed you and hated it when the shop was closed. Book club couldn't find a comfortable place to meet."

"And I'm meeting David this afternoon for a picnic on Micheal's Island."

Meg's smile lit up her face. "You are just full of good news. Makes me want to jump out of bed and click my heels."

Caroline reached for the bed railing.

"Relax. That's only in my head. I'll save that until after rehab." She put down her sticky bun. "If you still want me I talked with my doctor about staying with you, he supports it. I don't have to stay at the rehab center."

"Of course, I want you there."

"He wants you to be part of the rehab plan. He'd like you to sit in on meetings." Meg swirled the coffee in the mug. "I told him about finding you. He wasn't surprised we were related. He observed the resemblance earlier."

Caroline cut another piece of sticky bun for herself and passed one to Meg. She licked her upper lip. "David's dad, called me 'Maggie May' at David's family reunion. He had mistaken me for you. His mind was not on the present."

Meg wiped her lips. "Poor Bentley. He is such a kind man. He was so good to me."

"Tina found a yearbook picture with you and Suzanne next to each other. I can see a resemblance in that one. In the yearbook, you are listed as Maggie May as well."

Meg crumbled her napkin and dropped it beside her. "After I lost Jeffrey and then you, I just wasn't that girl. I left Lakeside, moved near an aunt in Ohio, attended college as Meg. I dropped the Whitcom from my middle name and changed my name to Meg Kelly Ottinger."

Caroline placed her coffee cup on the side table. "My middle name is Kelly."

"Kelly?" Meg sat up. "Your mom kept your connection to the family."

Caroline nodded slowly. "I never thought of it that way until you and I talked the other day. Kelly was just a girl's name. I didn't realize it was a family name."

Meg pushed herself away from the pillows and sat up straight. "What a generous thing for your family to do."

"On my original birth certificate, I was listed as Suzanne. Was I named for David's mother?"

Meg chuckled. "Oh yes. David's mother was my best friend since we were five. She helped deliver you."

"Doc Morgan said your friend helped. I'd forgotten. David's mother."

"My grandmother wouldn't acknowledge my marriage, didn't want a pregnant granddaughter to embarrass her. My parents followed my grandmother's orders. I had nowhere to go. Suzanne's parents took me in, helped me and you arrived early—in the middle of a storm."

"Doc and his wife described the night."

Meg pressed her palms together. "Suzanne would be thrilled about the love between you and David."

"Don't get ahead of yourself here. We're ..." She couldn't suppress the wide grin. Was this love? She couldn't have moved back to Seattle without him. She just wanted to kick up her heels and dance just thinking about their adventure today.

"You've progressed in that relationship. I can tell from that goofy look on your face. You like that David of mine."

"I do."

"Do you love him?"

Her heart fluttered a little faster. A warm flush overcome her body. Love? She didn't want to be away from him. His touch of his fingers, the leathery, woodsy smell that was just his and that grin that turned her emotions inside out. "I don't have a label yet for what I feel for David. I want to be with him."

"You two figure it out. I can be the ardent observer."

"I need to leave soon to go meet him." She wrapped the remaining sticky buns and placed in the corner of Meg's side table. "Jason may call you today. He checked in on you when you were in a coma."

"Oh Jason," Meg touched her eyes with her fingers. "His voice sounded just like his brother's. And the same dimple."

"He's coming again next month and bringing his wife, son and daughter. You have a niece and nephew."

"Oh I do!" She clapped. "Christmas will be so much better this year. A daughter, in-laws and niece and nephew. So much to look forward to."

She kissed Meg on the cheek. "Have a good afternoon."

"You have a good afternoon with my David. You will let me know what happens."

"Only as much as I'm willing to share."

Meg's laughter followed her down the hall.

CHAPTER TWENTY-SEVEN

Kayaks rested on the water's edge. David emerged from the shed carrying paddles and PFDs. *Mmm what a fine-looking man. Stop and just enjoy the view.* David's ass and his muscular legs. Too bad she had agreed to take Tina to the airport. A repeat of their evening of stargazing would be so good. She rubbed her hand down her left arm.

He dropped the paddles and walked toward her as she stepped from the car.

Wait for the island. Don't spoil it by leaping in his arms and screaming, "I'm staying." She looked down at her shoes. *Don't give it away.*

He gathered her in his arms. "Time together. We haven't had much time since we returned from Seattle."

She closed her eyes and inhaled the rich, earthy smell, which was just him. This was the right place to be—with David. Neither moved toward the boats.

He shifted his position first. "We should get in the kayaks." He backed up two steps. "Or go inside."

"I brought wine and snacks." She opened the trunk and dragged the cooler out.

"Guess we better get in and paddle to the island for a picnic." David carried the cooler toward the boats.

He balanced her kayak as she embarked and pushed her off. He followed. They disturbed a doe as they maneuvered around. Kayaking, she loved it and now she wouldn't have to give it up or anything else.

When they reached the island, she maneuvered on the shore. She handed him the cooler before disembarking. She barely had time to shake out the blanket before he hauled her close to him holding her snugly. He then wiggled backward until his back touched the pine trunk.

"I promise to help you with the blanket later, I just need you close."

She wound her arms inside his T-shirt. His warm body next to hers sent a shiver of desire throughout her body. His thumbs rubbed her spine. The tingle of his skin beneath her fingers, rhythmic beat of his heart against her ear thrilled her. She could forget Tina, forget her excitement over her job and just snuggle closer.

"Tell me about your meeting with Meg."

She remained in his embrace. "Both were teary and emotional. Tough to talk. So much we didn't know about the other's story."

He rubbed the small of her back.

"I felt torn. I was disloyal to Annabelle and Grant if I searched for birth parents." She pressed her forehead into his shirt, then moved back a step. "Once I connected with Jason, discovered a different family, then I needed to know."

"Meg was relieved and thrilled you know the truth. I checked up on her this morning."

"She apologized and was worried I would be angry with her for the tough decision she made." She drew erratic shapes on the front of his T-shirt with her nail.

"And you were worried she would reject you." He rubbed her cheek with his thumb.

With a deep, audible sigh, all the pent up tension left her. "I guess we were both a little silly." She studied his face as she added. "My name on my original birth certificate was Suzanne. Suzanne helped deliver me."

"My mother?"

She added the details.

David laughed aloud. "Our lives are interconnected."

"When Meg is released from the hospital, she is coming to Greystone until she can go home. I can drive her to rehab. We have much to share with each other, learn about the other."

A serious scowl replaced his smile "You're caring for Meg?"

What? Did he not want to discuss Meg? Should she have

asked him about Meg staying with her?

She nodded. "I would have talked—"

"You are not going back to Seattle this week. When do you leave?" He stepped back away from her.

"I won't go to Seattle until after Meg is better." She didn't move closer. "After she returns home, could you take a few days off and help me drive a U-Haul cross country? We could make it an adventure and stop along the way."

His arms hung limply at his sides. His head flopped back hitting the tree trunk with a decided *thunk*. He didn't flinch. He said nothing.

What did she do now? That wasn't the reaction she expected.

"I have vacation time." He moved away from the tree and stood in the middle of a small circle of trees out of her touch. He folded his arms across his chest. "You're moving antiques from Greystone? How big will the U-Haul be?"

She tilted her head. He wasn't glad? She expected … *Oh, he thinks I'm moving stuff to Seattle.* She cupped her chin and covered her lips with her fingers to hide her laughter. She inhaled deeply, then said. "I need to move a small U-Haul trailer with clothes, and a few items from Seattle to Lakeside." She enunciated each word slowly and watched his face.

It took a few seconds for the impact of her words to sink in. His yell caused the birds to scatter from the tress. He swooped her into his arms and spun around in a wide circle. "You're staying. You're moving here." He dropped her in front of him. "You are."

An unexpected joy flowed through her. Yeah, I'm moving here. "I belong here. I couldn't leave Meg or you. It just hurts too much." She placed her palm on his chest. "I couldn't live that far away. There's so much more here."

He enveloped her hand in his, brought her hand up and kissed her fingers.

"You'll help me move? We can stop places along the way."

"I'd like to spend some time in Seattle. Visit the Museum of Flight and, I know it's a tourist attraction, but I'd like to see the Space Needle."

He held her hand between his. "I investigated online.

Looked for jobs around Seattle."

She gasped. "David, you thought about leaving here?"

"Yeah." He pulled her closer so their bodies touched. "I didn't want to be so far away. Wherever you were."

"I belong here with you and Meg."

"I think so, too." He closed his eyes and rested his forehead on top of her head. "You belong here. This wasn't what I expected today. I imagined the worst case scenarios."

She leaned away so she could study his face. "You thought I was leaving today?"

"I thought you were leaving without me." Deep lines etched in his forehead lightened and were replaced by smile lines usually evident around his eyes. "Any champagne in that cooler? "

"No. We can share a bottle of wine for now."

He sat cross-legged on the blanket and steadied himself on the tree trunk. He opened the wine while she brought out fruit and cheeses. She sat beside him, her body tight against his. He draped his arm across her shoulders. He fed her a piece of cheese.

She handed him a glass of wine. "I know we can't be here long, but I wanted a private spot to tell you. I couldn't wait to fill you in on the news."

"There's more?"

"I got my job back."

"Your job? I thought you quit that day in Seattle?" He bit into a piece of cheese.

She poked his arm. "My job at Readers' Haven. I loved working there."

He chuckled. "Wait until Irene knows."

"That's what Meg said."

She rested her head in the crook of his shoulder. She closed her eyes and breathed in the aura of the moment—the strength of his arm around her, the joy of changes in her life, the smell of the pines and the sounds of the wood in their favorite spot. *Yes, David Montgomery, this is the right decision.*

"You need to take Tina to the airport tonight?"

"Yes. She has to get back."

"Tough for Tina you're not going back. You two have been

inseparable for years."

"But we can stay in touch. Her landscape paintings are in demand in Seattle. She has a show next week. Of course, she will visit here. She made friends with artists here and has two shows lined up in Lakeside."

"Good! We need Tina's adventurous side to shake things up." He stroked her arm. "As long as you aren't getting on that plane with her I won't begrudge Tina taking you away now. We do have to celebrate your move to Lakeside."

"Another moonlight kayak could be a celebration."

"Mm, yes. That was a momentous night. Maybe more shooting stars."

She snuggled closer to his body. "I already got my wish that night."

"You did?" He turned her shoulders so she faced him.

"Yes," A mischievous grin escaped. Her eyes brightened. "You fulfilled my wish and then some."

"I'll be glad to fill that wish again and again." He kissed her forehead, her nose and then captured her lips.

He positioned her on his lap. "My wish was not. Maybe in the future that wish will come true." Nestled close together, time stopped. "We have all sorts of tomorrows to celebrate, to share."

She stroked the outside of his chin with her thumb. "You did promise me a different river to kayak every weekend."

Through his shirt, the rumble of his laughter vibrated along her chest. "So I did. More kayaking and more adventures in the future are promised."

Tomorrows. Tomorrows held promise. Tomorrows in Lakeside with David and with Meg were boundless. Tomorrow with a new job, a new family and a new love.

They stayed wrapped in each other's arms until the chill of early evening awakened her sense of time. "I need to get Tina."

They packed up the picnic and paddled back. She worked side by side with David, unpacking the kayaks, placing them on racks in the shed and wiping down the equipment. He walked her to the car. She reached for him and he embraced her.

"Call me when you get back from the airport, please," he

whispered in her ear.

His breath on her skin created goose bumps down her neck. "It will be late."

"Doesn't matter. Just want to hear the sound of you."

She kissed his chest, then rose on her tiptoes and kissed him full on his lips. Her kiss was slow and thorough. She lost herself in the tenderness of it.

He moved away. "If we keep kissing, we'll end up inside."

"Or maybe on the grass right here."

She held his arm for one more minute. "See you tomorrow."

As she turned out of the drive, David still stood in the yard waving.

And many days after tomorrow.

A whole different life stretched before her—a life that included new friends and an expanded family. She loved Meg and looked forward to time together. And then there was David. She bounced in her seat.

She drove into the parking spot in front of Greystone, exited the car and leaned against the wrought-iron fence.

Home!

• • •

About the Author

Passions drive Reece Brett. According to her sister, Reece has been writing since she "could hold a crayon" and always had her "nose buried in a books." These two passions led to a writing career. She entertains herself at the mall, in a dentist's office, or at a restaurant forming imaginary life stories for those around her. These become ideas for her contemporary novels. The interactions between friends, lovers and family have always fascinated her.

Photo by Gingy'mon artwork

She shares her love of writing as a guest speaker for area colleges, local schools and writing organizations. Reece enjoys chatting with book clubs or writing groups whether it be a personal appearance or via Skype. She is a member of NJRW, RWA, WFWA and moderates Writing Community at Bogart's.

You might also enjoy:

Marlo Saunders has escaped. After testifying against her abusive criminal of an ex-husband, Marlo has taken her young son to the safety of a quiet cottage tucked away in a cove by the sea in Maine. For the first time in her life she's face to face with tranquility ... and desire. Now, the man she wants most is the one man she can least risk having at her side.

Small-town police chief Brent O'Neill knows fear and need when he sees them. But the barriers Marlo has built around her tell him the unknowns surrounding her past are far beyond what he's seen before. He'll do everything in his power to make her believe in him and the healing power of Trenton, Maine ... everything to love her.